WHITE
JENNA

Also by Jane Yolen published by Tor Books

Sister Light, Sister Dark

WHITE
JENNA

JANE YOLEN

TOR
fantasy

A TOM DOHERTY ASSOCIATES BOOK
NEW YORK

WHITE JENNA

A TOR BOOK
Published by Tom Doherty Associates, Inc.
49 West 24 Street
New York, NY 10010

First edition: September 1989

0 9 8 7 6 5 4 3 2 1

*For Beth and Tappan
and new beginnings*

SYNOPSIS

For years, the birth of a girl child in the Dales had been no cause of great rejoicing. After the first of the Garunian Wars, when the patriarchal tribes from the mainland had sailed across to slaughter the men and conquer the island country, there had been a surplus of women in the Dales. Forced into polygamous marriages or forced to expose excess girl babies on the hillsides, a woman's lot was not enviable. However, early on, a few of them had begun to reap the hillsides of the grim harvest, saving the infants and raising them in small, walled communities called Hames.

The centuries passed and the Hames were left alone. Eventually there were seventeen such separated communities filled with women, worshippers of Great Alta, the Goddess who had once been the ruling deity of all the Dales before being supplanted by the Garunian pantheon of gods. As the population regained its balance, the Hames became sanctuaries for dissident women.

The Altites, as they were called, continued to take in

the few fosterlings brought them, but to keep up their ranks often went outside the walls to breed themselves, leaving any male babies with the fathers and carrying the girl children back to the Hames. Women of the Hames also went outside as skilled warriors-for-hire, fighting in the king's army for a few years, thus honing their own skills and learning the latest in tactics and weaponry. However, the young girls were kept away from the outside as much as possible, until puberty and their mission year when they traveled to several other Hames as part of their education.

What went on behind the Hame walls was a mystery to the commonfolk of the Dales as well as to their Garunian overlords. Though the commonfolk still spoke of Alta, worshipping her as the consort of Lord Cres, who was the dark warrior god of the Garunians, and as the goddess of childbirth and the homey virtues, the only pure Alta worship belonged to the Hames. Yet as much as the commonfolk of the Dales mentioned Alta in their prayers, they could not even come close to guessing the secret She had gifted the Altite women. Trained from childhood in special breathing exercises, memorizing the words of their goddess as set down in the *Book of Light*, the Altites had learned how to call up their dark sisters, their shadow souls, when they reached puberty. Ever after, these dark sisters would appear with the moon or in candlelight or firelight, walking and talking, fighting and making love, side by side with their light counterparts.

There was persistent prophecy, rumor, and myth about one white-haired girl to be born to three mothers, all of whom would die giving her birth. This White Babe, as she was called, would become a warrior queen, a goddess, known alternately as the White One or the Anna, an old Dale word meaning "white." The prophecy, with typical gnomic misdirection, said that the child would be both white and black, both light and dark. She would conquer ox, hound, bear, and cat, signaling the end of an old era and heralding in a new.

The Garunians, who had carried a similar prophecy across the sea with them, feared such a phenomenon as a threat to their rule. So to confound the locals, they named their warlords Bull, Hound, Bear, and Cat. The Dalites told frequently quoted cante-fables about the White One's coming. And the Altite priestesses had a clear charge: nurture the White Babe and warn the other Hames when she is born.

So when a child, white-haired, dark-eyed, and seemingly preternatural in her abilities, was born to a Dale farmer's wife who died in childbirth, the story of *Sister Light, Sister Dark* was begun. The midwife, upon instructions of the farmer crazed by his bereavement, took the child to be fostered at Selden Hame, the Hame closest to their town. On the trip, the midwife herself was killed by a cat, and the cat, in turn, killed by a pair of Selden Hame light/dark sisters who were out hunting. They took the child to foster, but it was a late and first fostering for this particular pair. They grew to quarreling, a quarrel which eventually led to the light sister's exile and then the pair's death. Three mothers, and all dead, because of the strange white-haired child.

That child, Jo-an-enna, called Jenna, was mothered by the entire Selden Hame, for the priestess, Mother Alta, suspected the child was the prophecy's fulfillment, and wished to have a hand in any glory.

Young Jenna grew up beloved in her community by all except the suspicious and jealous Mother Alta. Instead of choosing to be a priestess, Jenna chose the warrior/hunter path, going through training with her special best friend Marga, called Pynt. Little, lithe dark-haired Pynt was called Jenna's shadow, and indeed the two were inseparable.

At thirteen, Jenna did not understand the priestess' enmity nor why she was sent to a different Hame for the beginning of her mission year. Resentful, angry, alone for the first time in her life, Jenna was forced to leave her friends and take a different path. She headed toward

Nill's Hame, across the Sea of Bells, a great meadow pied with lilies-of-the-valley.

But despite orders to the contrary, Pynt deserted Selinda and Alna, the other two mission-going girls, and tracked her best friend. The two were reunited halfway to Nill's Hame in the dense fog that settled almost daily over the Sea of Bells. Startled by a strange baying, fearing it to be the Fog Demon they had been warned about in tales, they stood back-to-back, swords drawn, waiting.

The strange howling chivvied a young man into their path who, it turned out, was the third son of the true king. This boy—for he was only a few years older than they—was Carum Longbow, in training as a scholar. He cried them *merci,* using the old formula. They pledged his safety and, in the fog, Jenna killed the man who had been trailing him, one of the usurper Lord Kalas' dread warlords known as the Hound.

Burying the Hound in a shallow grave, with his fearsome Hound's helm thrown on top of his body, the three made their way out of the forest to Nill's Hame. It was a strange trio: Pynt jealous of Carum's attention to Jenna and Jenna's attention to Carum; Carum falling under the spell of the tall, white-haired girl; Jenna befuddled by her own conflicting emotions.

Men were not allowed in a Hame, so Carum was disguised. As he was yet beardless and—while tall enough—was not very muscular, the disguise was accomplished with marginal success, despite his grousing. The three were led up to the room of the priestess of Nill's Hame, a strange, powerful Mother Alta who was blind, crippled, with six fingers on each hand. She recognized Jenna as the Anna of the prophecy, having once been thought to be that prodigy herself. Mother Alta showed Jenna how she had already fulfilled the beginning of the prophecy: being white-haired, with a dark companion, burying three mothers, making "the hound bow low." Jenna alone was unconvinced.

As the girls had promised to take Carum to safety to

one of the walled "Rests," sanctuaries that even Lord Kalas did not dare violate, Jenna, Pynt, and Carum started out the back way from the Hame. But they were set upon while still in reach of the walls of the Hame by Lord Kalas' men who had tracked them from the Hound's hasty grave.

Pynt was mortally wounded and carried back to the Hame by Carum. Covering their retreat, Jenna cut off the hand of one of Kalas' men. When she got back into the Hame carrying this grisly trophy with her, Carum recognized the ring on the hand as belonging to the Bull. Jenna had made the bull/ox "bow low" as well. Surely now she had to admit she was the White One. But Jenna would have none of it. She insisted she was just an ordinary girl caught up in extraordinary events.

Leaving Pynt to the ministrations of the infirmarer, and with instructions as to the location of the Rest by a water route, Jenna and Carum leaped from the third floor of the Hame straight down into the treacherous river below, linked together by a child's play rope.

Almost drowned, they managed to make it to shore and find their way to Bertram's Rest. Being a woman, Jenna could not enter the men's sanctuary, so she left Carum at the gate. He kissed her tenderly, promising everything in that one kiss, and Jenna returned to the Hame by the back route.

But it was silent at the Hame. Too silent. When Jenna came closer, she saw why. All the women had been slaughtered; many of them lying next to the men they had killed. The courtyard was filled with them, the stairs, the halls. Jenna raced desperately through the Hame to discover anyone alive, to find her wounded friend Pynt. Eventually, she came upon the place where the brave women of Nill's Hame had made their last stand: in the priestess' room. All the women of Nill's were dead and the children—including Pynt—were gone.

Sorrowing beyond measure, Jenna spent the entire day carrying the bodies of the women down to the kitchen and the Great Hall, laying them out side by side, with enough room between for their dark sisters. Then she returned to the priestess' room to bring down the great wood-framed mirror. Standing before it in the priestess' room, Jenna unknowingly recited part of the ritual of Sisterhood which called forth the dark sisters. Though a year too young and untrained in the proper rites, Jenna's great need and the intensity of her calling brought her own dark sister Skada out of the mirrored world.

Skada—as dark-haired as Jenna was light. Skada—who spoke the things that Jenna had never dared speak. Skada—who urged Jenna to deeds that Jenna never dared dream.

Jenna and Skada together tried to lift the mirror to bring it downstairs for the funeral pyre. But when they moved it, they triggered a secret door which opened under Jenna's feet, exposing a passageway where the children of Nill's Hame had been hidden from the marauding men. Pynt was there, too, bedridden and still desperately ill from her wound, but alive.

Jenna, Skada, and the young priestess-in-training Petra set the funeral pyre. Then they led the troop of children, some only babes carried by their older sisters, along the Sea of Bells and back through the woods to Selden Hame.

There the story of their adventures was told and Jenna lay claim to the title of White Goddess, not because she believed in it, but because she felt it would help the cause: *the other Hames must be warned.* Suddenly afraid of what Jenna's title might mean, the priestess denied her; but, with Petra's help (she invented prophecy in instant rhyme), Jenna convinced the rest that she was indeed the Anna of whom it was written that she *is the beginning and the end.*

Accompanied by Skada, Petra, and the twinned older warriors light Catrona and dark Katri, sworn enemies of Selden's Mother Alta, Jenna went forth on the road.

Prophecy

*And the prophet says a white babe with black
eyes shall be born unto a virgin in the winter of
the year. The ox in the field, the hound at the
hearth, the bear in the cave, the cat in the tree, all,
all shall bow before her, singing, "Holy, holy,
holiest of sisters, who is both black and white,
both dark and light, your coming is the beginning
and it is the end." Three times shall her mother
die and three times shall she be orphaned and she
shall be set apart that all shall know her.*

BOOK ONE

MESSENGERS

THE MYTH:

Then Great Alta looked down upon her messengers, those whom she had severed from her so that they might be bound more closely to her. She looked upon the white sister and the dark, the young sister and the old.

"I shall not speak to you that you may hear. I shall not show myself to you that you may see. For a child must be set free to find her own destiny, even if that destiny be the one the mother has foretold."

And then Great Alta made the straight path crooked before them and the crooked path straight. She set traps for them and pits that they might be comforted when they escaped, that they might remember her loving kindness and rejoice in it.

THE LEGEND:

It was in the town of Slipskin, now called New Moulting, soft into the core of the new year's spring, that three young women, and one of them White Jenna, rode out upon a great gray horse.

His back was as broad as a barn door, his withers could not be spanned. Each hoof struck fire from the road. Where his feet paced, there crooked paths were made smooth and mountains laid low, straight paths were pitted and gullies cut from the hills.

There are folk in New Moulting who say it was no horse at all, but a beast sent by Alta herself to carry them over the miles. There are footprints still near the old road *into Slipskin, carved right into the stone. And downriver, in the town of Selden, there are three great ribs of the thing set over the church door that all might see them and wonder.*

THE STORY:

The road was a gray ribbon in the moonlight, threading between trees. Five women stood on the road, listening to a ululating cry behind them.

Two of the women, Catrona and Katri, were clearly middle-aged, with lines like runes across their brows. They had short-cropped hair and wore their swords with a casual authority.

The youngest, Petra, stood with her shoulders squared. There was a defiance in the out-thrust of her chin, but her eyes were softer and her tongue licked her lips nervously.

Jenna was the extremely tall girl, not yet a woman for all that her hair was as white as the moonlight. Whiter, as it had no shadows. The other tall girl, but a hairbreadth smaller, and a bit thinner, and dark, was Skada.

"I will miss the sound of their voices," Jenna said.

"I will not," Skada answered. "Voices have a binding power. It is best for us to look ahead now. We are messengers, not memorizers."

"*And* we have far to go," Catrona said. "With many Hames to warn." She drew a map from her leather pocket and spread the crackling parchment upon the ground. With Katri's help she smoothed it out and pointed to a dark spot. "We are here, Selden Hame. The swiftest route would be there, down the river road into Selden itself, across the bridge. Then we go along the river with our backs to the Old Hanging Man, never losing sight of these twin peaks." She pointed to the arching lines on the map.

"Alta's Breast," said Skada.

"You learned your lessons well," said Katri.

"What Jenna knows, I know."

Catrona continued moving her finger along the route. "The road goes on and on, with no forks or false trails to this Hame." Her finger tapped the map twice and Katri's did the same.

"Calla's Ford Hame," said Jenna. "Where Selinda and Alna have begun their mission year. It will be good to see them. I have missed them . . ."

"But not much," murmured Skada.

"Is it the best place to start?" Jenna asked. "Or should we go farther out? Closer to the king's court?"

Catrona smiled. "The Hames are in a great circle. Look here." And she pointed to one after another, calling out the names of the Hames as if in a single long poem. "Selden, Calla's Ford, Wilma's Crossing, Josstown, Calamarie, Carpenter's, Krisston, West Dale, Annsville, Crimerci, Lara's Well, Sammiton, East James, John-o-the-Mill's, Carter's Tracing, North Brook, and Nill's Hame. The king's court is in the center."

"So none will complain if we visit Calla's Ford first," Katri said, her finger resting, as did Catrona's, on the last Hame. "As it is closest."

"And as our own Hame's children are there," added Catrona.

"But we must be quick," Jenna reminded them all.

Catrona and Katri stood simultaneously, Catrona folding the map along its old creases. She put it back in the leather pocket and handed it to Petra.

"Here, child, in case we should be parted from one another," Catrona said.

"But I am the least worthy," Petra said. "Should not Jenna . . ."

"Now that Jenna has seen the map once, she has it

for good. She is warrior-trained in the Eye-Mind Game and could recite the names and places for you even now. Am I right, Jenna?" Catrona asked.

Jenna hesitated for a moment, seeing again the map as it had lain under Catrona's hands. She began to recite slowly but with complete confidence, outlining as she spoke with her foot in the road's dirt, "Selden, Calla's Ford, Wilma's Crossing, Josstown . . ."

"I believe you," said Petra, holding out her hand. "I will take the map." She tied the leather pocket's strings around her belt.

They started off down the road, walking steadily, each an arm's length apart. There was little sound in their going and Catrona on the right and Jenna on the far left kept careful watch of the road's perimeter. Only young Petra, in the center, seemed in the least uneasy. Once or twice she turned to look behind them, back toward the place where the long, low cry of the Selden Hame farewell had echoed.

THE SONG:

Anna at the Turning

> Gray in the moonlight, green in the sun,
> Dark in the evening, bright in the dawn,
> Ever the meadow goes endlessly on,
>   And Anna at each turning.
>
> Sweet in the springtide, sour in fall,
> Winter casts snow, a white velvet caul.
> Passage in summer is swiftest of all,
>   And Anna at each turning.

Look to the meadows and look to the hills,
Look to the rocks where the swift river spills,
Look to the farmland the farmer still tills
For Anna is returning.

THE STORY:

They stopped only once in the woods to sleep under a blackthorn tree by a swift-flowing stream. Taking turns, they kept the night watch, leaving Petra the shortest time, and that near dawn when she would have awakened anyway. Besides, as Catrona reminded them, with the moon they watched in pairs and Petra was alone.

There was nothing to disturb their rest except the mourning of owls back and forth across the stream, and the constant murmur of the water. Once on Jenna and Skada's watch, there was a light crackle of underbrush.

"Hare," Jenna whispered to her dark sister, alert for more.

"Hare," Skada agreed. They both relaxed. Slightly.

By early eve of the next day they had passed the outlying farms of Slipskin, neatly tilled land, well cleared of rocks and roots by generations of farmers. Each acre was gently fuzzed over with green. In one field twenty horses were pastured on blue-green grass.

"There," said Catrona, "a man who sells horses. Probably supplies the king. We could *borrow* one or two and he would never know the difference."

Petra shook her head. "We had horses and flocks at my Hame. Believe me, our shepherds knew every beast by name."

Catrona snorted. "I know that, child. Just testing."

"I will *not* ride a horse again," Jenna said. "Once was enough."

"I doubt we could get three off him anyway," Catrona said. "But if we could get one, one of us could ride ahead. We need swiftness whatever the cost."

Unhappily, Jenna had to agree.

"Let me do the talking," Catrona added. "I have spent much time among men and know what to say."

"I have spent no time at all with them," admitted Petra.

Jenna said nothing, but her finger strayed to her lips and she was glad that it was still daylight and Skada not there to remind her just what she had—and had not—said to Carum when he had kissed her. Two men she had known: one she had kissed and one she had killed. She knew as little as Petra. "Yes, you speak," she said to Catrona. "We will wait behind."

"But mind you, look fetching," said Catrona.

"Fetching?" Jenna asked, genuinely puzzled.

"Men like that." Catrona threw back her head, laughing loudly.

Although they weren't sure what Catrona meant by *fetching*, both Jenna and Petra managed to smile at the farmer when he opened the dark wood door. He stared at them for a moment, as if unsure of what he was seeing, then called over his shoulder, "Martine, Martine, come quick."

"What is it?" a voice called from the room behind him.

He did not speak again until his wife, a rosy giantess, stood next to him, a full head higher than his own balding crown.

"There, the big girl, look at 'er. Look, woman."

She stared as well.

"We are Alta's own," Catrona began, stopping when she saw that they were paying no attention to her but were rather staring at Jenna. She spoke again, loudly. "My name is Catrona, from Selden Hame. My sisters and I . . ."

"By the blessing, Geo, you are right. Who else could it be," the farmer's wife said, her cheeks bright red. "Except for the hair, she's the spit of my poor dead sister."

Catrona suddenly understood. "You think Jenna a fosterling from your family? Of all houses, that we should have stopped here."

"Naaa, naaa," the farmer said, shaking his head and sounding remarkably like a penned beast. "She has eleven sisters, and all the same. Not fifty years ago the hillsides would've been full of 'em. But we got low on girls 'round here and so now girls is a commodity. You be thinking of staying, I could set you up with good husbands." He shook his head again. "Well, the niece, maybe, and the little one there. We need breeders, you know. That's why Martine's sisters, they all got spoke for early. Good stock. Not a holding this side of the Slip don't house one of 'em. *T'would be harder to miss one than find one*, as they say of blackbirds in a flock. It would be . . ."

Martine pushed her husband aside and walked past Catrona to Jenna's side. Together, their relationship was obvious. "She has the Dougal height, the Hiat eyes, remember Geo like you said when we was courtin', my eyes was *dark eyes of a spring*. And my sister Ardeen went white afore she was fifteen, and my sister Jarden afore she was twenty. Give your aunt a hug, girl."

Jenna did not move, her mind whirling.

"Her mother was bringing her to us to foster, out in the woods when a cat killed her," Catrona said. "My own sisters gave yours a decent grave and said the words you like over her. Her fosterer died, or I would tell her of you."

"Nonsense!" Martine said, turning from Jenna to speak directly to Catrona. "Her mother died at birth. Lay there bleeding like a pig stuck for market while the midwife bore the child away. If your sister fostered her, then . . ." She stopped a minute and counted on her fingers. "One for my poor dead sister, two for the midwife, and three be your sister. Oh, my Blessed be!" She dropped suddenly to her knees, her hands covering her mouth. "The White One, triple mothered. Of my own flesh and blood. Who could have guessed?"

Her husband went down more slowly, as if he had been pole-axed, and buried his face in his hands.

Jenna rolled her eyes up and sighed. She heard Petra's quick intake of breath and priestess voice behind her.

> Mothered Three,
> Blessed be.

"Stop that," she hissed back at the girl.

From her knees, Martine heard only the rhyme. She put her hands up, palms together, and cried out, "Yes, yes, that's it. Oh, White One, what can we do? What can we say?"

"As for what you can do," Catrona said quickly, "you can give us three good horses, for we are on a great mission of mercy and it would not do for the White One to walk. And as for what you can say, you can say *yes* to us and *no* to any man who asks."

"Yes, yes," Martine cried again, and when her husband did not answer fast enough, she elbowed him.

He rose, still not looking again at Jenna, and mumbled, "Yes, yes, I can give you three. And they will be good. Anyone says Geo Hosfetter gives not good horses is . . ." He sidled out of the door still talking. They could hear his footsteps going away at a run.

"I will go and help him choose," said Catrona.

"Let the White One stay a moment more," begged Martine. "She is my own flesh, my own blood. Let her tell me her own tale. I have tea. I have cakes." She gestured in toward the neat, well-lit kitchen.

Jenna opened her mouth to accept and Petra whispered by her ear, "Dark sisters will be there. Let me talk." Jenna closed her mouth and looked stern.

"The White One does not break bread with any. She

fasts on this mission and has taken a vow of silence until it is done. I am Her priestess and Her mouth."

Jenna rolled her eyes up again, but kept silent.

"Of course, of course," Martine said, wiping her hands on her apron.

"Better that you tell Her all you know so She may weigh its significance."

"Of course, of course," Martine said again. "What shall I tell? That my sister, the White One's mother, was tall and red-haired and made, we all thought, like the rest of us for easy birthing. But something was twisted up there. She died giving the child life. And then that wicked midwife stole the babe away, afore any of us got to see it. We knew the child was a girl because she told her own daughter she was taking it to one of the . . . you know . . . Homes."

"Hames," Petra corrected automatically.

"The closest one. Up the road and into the mountains, it was."

"Selden Hame," Petra prompted.

But the woman could only tell the story in her own meandering way. "Selling the babe, most likely. Some midwives be like that, you know." Suddenly afraid she might have offended them, she added quickly, "Not that you Alters buy children. Not that."

"We reap the hillsides; we do not pay the sowers," said Petra.

"I meant that. Yes, I did." Martine's hands wrangled with one another.

"And the father?"

"Died not a year later. Heart broken. Lost wife and child all to once. And crazed. Saw Alter women everywhere, he did. On the farm. At the hearth. In his bed. Two at a time. Double crazed he was." She shook her head. "Poor man."

"Poor man," Petra echoed, her voice soothingly soft.

Jenna bit her lip. *Her* mother. *Her* father. She tried to credit it and could not. Her mother had not lived under such a cozy, thatched roof, dying with her thighs covered in blood. Her mothers—and there were many of them—lived in Selden Hame. And *they* would not die in blood if she could help it. She turned abruptly and left Martine of the wrangling hands to Petra's comforting. Striding quickly across the farmyard, she headed toward the barn.

The sky above was a steely blue, and a bright pink sat on the horizon behind the barn and the fields. Once the sun slipped below the world's rim, there would be another hour before dark. And then there would be a moon. With the moon, the dark sisters Skada and Katri would reappear. Petra had been right to warn her about going into the candle-lit kitchen. Hearthlight and candlelight could also call the sisters out. No need to frighten these poor, silly strangers. *Strangers!* Jenna tried to force herself to think of them as her aunt and uncle. No, there was no blood between them. None at all. It was a mistake, that was all. But a mistake that was bringing them three horses. *Horses!* She never wanted to ride one of those broad-beamed, hard-on-the-rear, teeth-rattling beasts again.

Just as she thought of them, from behind the barn came Catrona leading three sleek mares, two reddish brown and one almost pure white. The farmer strode behind her looking, somehow, relieved. When Catrona spotted Jenna, she grinned, then quickly composed her mouth into a more respectful expression.

"Do these meet your approval, White One?" she asked Jenna.

Jenna nodded. The snow-colored mare threw her head back and whinnied.

"The white is yours, Anna," said Catrona. "The man insists on it." She held out the reins. "And he takes no coin for them."

Jenna drew in a deep breath, willing herself to like the horse. Reaching for the reins, she pulled on them gently and the horse took a few steps toward her. She patted it on the neck and the horse nuzzled her ear. Jenna smiled tentatively.

"See, White One," Geo Hosfetter said, still not looking directly at her, "the horse knows that she is yours." He bobbed his head twice. "Her name is . . ."

"Her old name does not matter," Petra said suddenly from behind Jenna. "She shall have a new one. For, as you know, it says in the prophecy:

> *The White One, the Anna,*
> *Shall ride, shall ride,*
> *And sisters with Her*
> *Side by side.*
> *The horse She sits on*
> *All astride,*
> *It will be called . . . DUTY!*"

"Oh, yes, oh yes," Martine said, hurrying up to them, "I know that. Duty, that's the name. Of course. Duty."

"Duty!" Jenna said, laughing, once they had ridden away from the farm. "What kind of a name is Duty?"

"And where did you learn that prophecy? I never heard it," Catrona said.

"It was the best I could do at the moment's spur," Petra admitted. "I apologize for that sixth line. It was a bit . . . well . . . shaky."

"You mean you *made it up?*" Catrona shook her head.

Petra, nodding vigorously, smiled.

"It is a special trick of hers," Jenna said. "She was famous for it at Nill's Hame. Prophecies and poetry on the moment. But, Petra—*Duty!*"

"Never mind," Petra answered. "They will tell their neighbors and the story will grow and grow. By the time you hear it again, you will be mounted on *Beauty* or on *Booty* and the tale will add that the White One, Blessed be, rode off, pockets ajingle with coin or followed by one hundred men all crying out with love."

"Or they will call the horse *Dirty*, which she will surely be, for we will have little time to keep her clean." Jenna pulled on her right braid. "So why did you get me a *white* horse, Catrona?"

"*He* insisted on it. 'The white one for the White One,' he said. 'And a pair of matched bays for her servants.' "

"Servants!" Petra shouted. At her voice the little bay mare startled and tried to bolt and it took a mighty sawing on the reins to control her. When the horse was steady again, Petra shrugged ruefully at her friends.

"I would not trust *that* horse in a fight," Jenna said.

"But she *should* run like the wind," Catrona pointed out. "Look at her legs. And as they say in the Dales, *The gift horse is the swifter*."

"Then let her show us her heels," said Jenna. "We have no more time for talking."

Catrona nodded.

They kicked their mounts into trots.

They were just through the town of Selden, with its neat little houses lining the cobbled lanes, and starting over the new bridge, when the partial moon rose. By its light, Skada and Katri reappeared, riding double behind their light sisters.

Jenna knew Skada was there by the familiar breath behind her; the horse knew sooner because of the added weight. It slowed its pace to accommodate the second body but did not flinch.

"Fine horse," Skada whispered in Jenna's ear.

Turning her head slightly, Jenna said, "What do you know about horses, fine or otherwise?"

"I may know little, but at least I am not set against them for no reason."

"No reason!" Jenna said. "Ask my bottom and ask

my thighs about reasons." But she said no more and focused her attention on the long bridge as they clattered across.

Once they were on the other side, Catrona signaled them to stop. They dismounted and left the horses to graze on the roadside grass.

"Why did we stop?" Petra asked. In the moonlight her face had a carved look. Her hair, which had been tightly braided and crowned, had shaken loose of its pins and the plaits now fell down along her spine. There were dark circles under her eyes, but Jenna could not tell if they were from weariness or sorrow. She put her arm around the girl's shoulder and Skada, like a parenthesis, closed her in from the other side.

"Horses, like humans, need to rest," Jenna reminded her. "It would not do to kill them on the very first day."

"Nor ourselves," Catrona said, stretching. "It has been a long time since I have ridden a horse. Those are not muscles I exercise regularly." She bent over and put her palms on the ground and Katri did the same.

"My horse is not tired," said Petra.

"He carries one. Ours will have to carry two through a night of strong moonlight," Skada said. "Unfortunately no one has ever trained horses to call up their shadows."

"Are there horses where you come from?" Petra asked.

"We have what you have," said Katri. "But we leave it behind to come here."

Catrona rubbed her horse's nose and the horse responded by nuzzling her. "We will go another few hours and then sleep." She held the horse's head between her hands and blew gently into its nostrils. "This rest is just for breathing."

"And for bottoms," Jenna and Skada said together.

Petra laughed, but Catrona and Katri stared up at the sky.

"Look," Katri said. "See how the moon sits on the Old Hanging Man's brow."

They looked. The cliffs, with their wild jut of stone, seemed crowned with the moon. A shred of cloud was just beginning to cross the moon's spotty face.

"I think it will cloud over soon," Catrona said.

"That will be for the good," added Katri.

"But then you and Skada . . ." Jenna began.

". . . will be gone," Catrona finished. "But since we are just riding, not fighting, the horses will have an easier time of it."

"As will we," Skada said.

"No sore bottoms." Jenna laughed.

"No sore . . ." Skada started to say, but just then the cloud covered the moon and she was gone.

"Mount up," called Catrona, vaulting onto her horse's back.

Jenna and Petra had slightly more trouble climbing back on theirs. Finally Jenna held the bay's reins while Petra got on. Then she caught her own horse and handed its reins to Petra.

"Steady her," Jenna said.

"Talking to your servant?" asked Petra.

"*Please*," said Jenna.

"Duty awaits," Petra joked. "So, Jenna, go to your Duty!"

"Enough," Jenna said. When she was up at last, the reins gathered back in her own hands, Jenna looked down the road. Catrona was already around the first bend, Petra halfway there. Jenna kicked her heels into Duty's white sides, and the horse started bouncing along. Gritting her teeth, Jenna kicked harder. This time the horse took off at a gallop, sending clouds of dust behind them, obscuring even the dark silhouette of the Old Hanging Man.

THE SONG:

Ballad of the Twelve Sisters

There were twelve sisters by a lake,
  Rosemary, bayberry, thistle and thorn,
A handsome sailor one did take,
  And that day a child was born.

A handsome sailor one did wed,
  Rosemary, bayberry, thistle and thorn,
The other sisters wished her dead
  On the day the child was born.

"Oh, sister, give me your right hand,"
  Rosemary, bayberry, thistle and thorn,
Eleven to the one demand
  On the day the child was born.

They laid her down upon the hill,
  Rosemary, bayberry, thistle and thorn,
And took her babe against her will
  On the day the child was born.

They left her on the cold hillside,
  Rosemary, bayberry, thistle and thorn,
Convinced that her new babe had died
  On the day the child was born.

She wept red tears, and she wept gray,
  Rosemary, bayberry, thistle and thorn,
Till she had wept her life away,
  On the day her child was born.

The sailor's heart it broke in two,
  Rosemary, bayberry, thistle and thorn,
The sisters all their act did rue
  From the day the child was born.

And from their graves grew rose and briar,
Rosemary, bayberry, thistle and thorn,
Twined till they could grow no higher,
From the day the child was born.

THE STORY:

"I am sorry," Jenna said. "I have acted foully since we left the Hame. It is as if my tongue and my mind have no connection. I cannot think what makes me act this way."

They had stopped for the night, scarcely a hundred feet off the road, in a small clearing only slightly larger than a room. There was a rug-sized meadow with great oaks overarching it, branches laced together like a cozy roof. Still, Catrona would not let them light a fire for fear of alerting any passersby.

They ate their dark traveling bread and the last of the cheese in silence. Nearby the horses grazed contentedly, hobbled by braided vines. When they had first dismounted, Catrona had shown them how to twist the green rope and secure it to the horses' front feet, tight enough to keep the horses from running off, slack enough so that they did not stumble.

Jenna decided, after much thought, that the slow, steady crunching progress the horses made was a comforting sound, not annoying. But she felt neither steady nor particularly happy about her own progress the past few days. An apology was necessary, and so she offered it.

"What is there to be sorry about?" asked Catrona. "You have slept little and seen too much this past fortnight. You have been torn from and shorn of much you know. Your young life has been turned completely upside-down."

"You speak of Petra, not of me," Jenna said, shaking her head. "And yet her mood remains sunny."

"What is it they say in the Lower Dales? That: *A crow is not a cat, nor does it bear kits.* Jenna, if you were Petra, you would be sunny despite all. It is her way. But you are Jenna of Selna's line . . ." Catrona said.

"But I am *not* of Selna's line," Jenna interrupted. "Not truly." Appalled at the whine in her voice, she buried her face in her hands, as much in shame as in sorrow.

"So. That is it." Catrona chuckled. "How can White Jenna, the Anna, the mighty warrior who killed the Hound and cut off the Bull's hand, as in the prophecies; who has ridden off to save the world of the Hames with her companions by her side; how could *she* have been born between the thighs of a woman like that." She jerked her head back to indicate the direction from which they had just come. "But, Jenna, it is bearing, not blood, that counts. You are a true daughter of the Hames. As am I."

"Do *you* know *your* mother?" Jenna asked, her voice quiet.

"Seventeen generations of them," Catrona said placidly. "As do you. I remember you reciting them, and never a hesitation."

Petra spoke for the first time. "And I can say my lines, too, Jenna, though my birth mother left me at the Hame doorstep when I was not yet weaned, with a note that said only, 'My man will not abide another such as this.'"

"I know," Jenna said, her voice a misery. "I know all the tales. I know that half the daughters of the Hames come there abandoned or betrayed. Or both. And it never bothered me until now."

"Until that silly woman and her sillier husband claimed you," Petra said, moving next to Jenna and stroking her hair. "But their claim is water, Jenna. And you are stone. Water flows over stone and moves on. But the stone remains."

"She is right, Jenna," Catrona said. "And you are wrong to worry over such nonsense. You have more mothers than you can count, and yet you count that story more than all the rest."

"I will count it no longer," Jenna said. She stood, brushed the cheese and bread crumbs from her breast, and stretched. "I shall take the first watch." She looked up at the heavy lacings of the oak and the one small patch of cloud-covered sky, then sighed and stared down at her hands. The ring on her littlest finger, the one the priestess had given her to use as identification, was a reminder of her task. She should think of that, and not of this other silliness. *At least,* she thought, *Skada is not here to bruise me about it.*

But the watch seemed longer without Skada's company, and despite her promise not to think about Martine and Geo Hosfetter—their names as silly as their manners—she could think of nothing else. If she had stayed with her true mother, her birth mother, she would surely have been as awful as they. She spent her watch braiding and unbraiding her long white hair and musing about a life she had never lived.

Morning began with a noisy fanfare of birdsong from a dozen different tiny throats, mellow and chipping, thin and full. Jenna sat up for a moment and just listened, trying to distinguish one from another.

"Warblers," Catrona whispered to her. "Can you tell them?"

"I know the one that Alna called Salli's, that one, there." She raised her hand, finger extended, at a single, melodious call.

"Good." Catrona nodded. "And what about that one, with the little *brrrrrup* at the end."

"Maybe a yellow-rump?" Jenna guessed.

"Good twice. Three times and I will admit you are my equal in the woods," Catrona said. "There—that one!" The call was thinner than the last two, and abrupt.

"Yellow throat . . . no, wait, that is a . . ." Jenna shook her head. "I guess I am not yet as good as you are."

"That was a Marget's warbler, after which Amalda named your best friend. It is good to know that I am still needed in the woods." She smiled. "Wake Petra while I see what there is to offer for hungry travelers." She disappeared behind a large oak.

Petra, who had had the middle watch, was curled up in her blanket, the waterfall of her hair obscuring her face. Jenna shook her gently.

"Up, mole, into the light. We have much traveling yet."

Petra stretched, bound up her hair quickly into two plaits, and stood. She looked around for Catrona.

"Food," Jenna said, motioning to her mouth.

As if the word itself had summoned her, Catrona appeared, but so silently, even the horses did not notice. She carried three eggs.

"One each, and there is a stream not far from here. We will water the horses and fill our flasks. If we ride quickly, we will make the Hame by midday." She gave an egg to each girl, keeping the smallest for herself.

Jenna took her throwing knife from her boot and poked a hole in the top of the egg, then handed the knife to Petra. As Petra worked the blade point into her egg, Jenna sucked out the contents of her own. It slid down easily and she was hungry enough not to mind the slippery taste.

"I will lead the horses," Catrona said. "You, Jenna, and you, Petra, pack up the rest of the gear. And do what you can to make it hard to read our signs. With horses that is difficult, I know."

She led the three horses away. Using branches as brooms, Jenna and Petra followed right after. There were no fire remains to disguise, but much evidence of the horses and their browsing which could not be totally erased. Still, the signs *could* be confused, and Jenna did what was possible. Perhaps an incompetent tracker might think a herd of deer had grazed through.

At the stream they washed quickly, less for the cleanliness and more for morale. Jenna filled their leather flasks while Petra kept a watch on the horses. Catrona went ahead to scout to make sure their return to the road would not be noted.

When Catrona came back, they pulled the reluctant horses from the water, mounted up with more facility than grace, and started off, Catrona in the lead once more.

The sun was high overhead and they had passed no one on the road. The one small town they had ridden through had been strangely deserted. Even the mill by the river had been empty of people, though the water kept the wheel turning on its own.

"How odd," had been Catrona's only comment.

Jenna's thoughts were darker than that, for the last time she had been where all motion and sound had seemed to stand still had been at Nill's Hame when she returned to find death the only occupant. Yet there were no bodies lying about the town, no blood spilling along the millrace. She breathed slowly, deliberately.

Petra's face was unreadable and Jenna said nothing, worrying more about her friend's silence than the silence in the town.

They rode on, till they came to the ford after which Calla's Ford was named. The pull-line ferry waited on the far side of the river but there was no ferryman in sight. Together Catrona and Jenna hauled on the thick line and the flat-bottomed ferry slowly moved across the water on its tether.

When it grounded, they walked their horses onto the boat in silence. Even with the weight of three horses and three women, the boat rode high in the water.

Built for more than that, Jenna thought. The silence was so oppressive, she kept the thought to herself. But she wondered, all the time that she and Catrona pulled on the water-slicked rope, whether the twenty-one horses of the king's troop could cross on such a boat. Twenty men, and the Bear. Or the Cat. Or Lord Kalas himself.

The little ark plowed across the river quickly, grounding itself with a grinding sound on the shore. The horses got off with more promptness and less urging than they had gotten on. This time both Petra and Jenna remounted with ease.

Jenna urged Duty into the lead, and the horse began an easy gallop along the well-worn road. Behind, Catrona's and Petra's bays took up the white mare's challenge. Jenna could hear their quickening hoofbeats and smiled wryly. For a moment nothing existed but the wind in her hair, the sound of the galloping horses, and the hot spring sun directly overhead.

If I could capture this moment, she thought. *If I could hold this time forever, we could all be safe.*

And then she saw what she had feared: a thin spiral of smoke scripting a warning against the sky.

"The Hame!" she cried out, the first words any of them had spoken in an hour.

The other two saw the smoke at the same time and read it with the same fear. They bent over their horses' necks, and the mares, with no further urging, raced toward the unknown fires.

As they rounded a final bend in the road, the road suddenly mounted upward. The horses labored under them, breathing heavily. Jenna could feel her own heart beating in rhythm with Duty's heaving breaths. Then they crested the rise, and saw the Hame before them, its great wooden gates shattered and the stone walls broken.

Petra reined up at the sight and gave a little cry, flinging her hand to her mouth. But Jenna, seeing movement beyond the walls, stood in the stirrups hoping to distinguish it. Perhaps it was fighting, perhaps they were not too late. Pulling her sword from its sheath and raising it overhead, she called to Petra, "Stay here. You have no weapon."

Catrona was already racing forward. Without giving further thought to the consequences, Jenna turned Duty toward the broken stones and, with a great kick, impelled the horse to leap the fallen wall.

There were three men and a woman bending over. They scattered before Duty's charge. One man, tall and ungainly, like a long-limbed water bird, turned and stared. Jenna screamed sounds at him, not words, and was about to strike when the woman ran between them and raised her hands.

"*Merci*," the woman cried, desperation lending force to her thin voice. "In Alta's name, *ich crie merci*."

The words penetrated Jenna's fury and slowly she lowered her sword, her sword arm shaking so hard, she had to reach over with the other hand to steady it. She noticed what she should have noticed before. The tall stork-man was not armed. Neither was the woman. "Hold, Catrona," Jenna called out.

Catrona's voice came back strongly, "I hold."

"Please," the woman said, "you must help, if you be Alta's own."

"We are," said Jenna. "But who are you? And what has happened here?" She looked around as she spoke, not directly at the woman. Expecting to see bodies, she saw none. Yet the gates and walls were thrown down, shattered as if by a great blast. There were weapons scattered throughout the courtyard: several bows, dozens of swords, a number of knives, three rakes, even pieces of wood that might have been makeshift cudgels.

The woman clasped and unclasped her hands. "We be from Callatown. To south. If you rode that way."

"We did," Catrona said. "And none there to greet us. Nor at the ford."

"My husband Harmon, here, be ferryman at't ford. He and I and all our neighbors been here two day, burning dead."

The tall man, her husband, put his hands on her shoulders and spoke to Jenna from behind his wife. "Grete speaks true, girl. I went out to ferry when a troop of king's horse came by. They tied me up and Grete, bless her, be down in root cellar getting it spring cleansed. She could hear their coarse mouths and kept hid, waiting till they be gone."

Grete interrupted. "It wouldna done any good to come out and fight. I knew that much."

"She does, too." Harmon had taken his hands from his wife's shoulders and swept off his brown cap, kneading it between his long fingers. "She come up later, after they be gone over the water, and cut ropes. Look, the mark be still on my wrists." He held one hand up but if there was a mark there, Jenna could not see it.

"A hundred or more they be," said a second man, coming over. "That's what Harmon said. A hundred or more."

"This be Jerem the miller and his boy," Grete said, gesturing at the two. "They was let be for they give the troop grain for horses."

"But the rest of the town, they be tied up or kilt," said Jerem. "Exceptin' the girls. Them they took. My boy sneaked out to see that night."

"Mai," said Jerem's boy. He said it quietly but his dark eyes were defiant under his thatch of yellow hair.

"Mai be his sweetheart," explained Grete, "and she be gone with the rest. And they be promised to one another."

"Why are you *here*?" It was Petra, who had dismounted upon hearing the voices. She led her horse through the maze of fallen stone. "You had your own sorrows, then. Did you come here for help?"

"For help?" Grete repeated, shaking her head.

"Bless you, girl," Jerem said, "we came *to* help. They be our mothers and our sisters and our nieces and our aunts. They came among us to give us sons."

Harmon added, "Jerem, he ground their grain and

they paid him well, in crops and in strong arms. And when I be took last year with the bloody flux, didn't a pair of 'em work all day pulling ferry for me. And four of 'em at night. And another doctored me, and two nursed me in the even."

"And takin' no payment for it. None. Not ever. It be their way, you know." Grete's thin voice rose and fell oddly.

"So we come quick as we could. When we knew what went on in town." Harmon's hands still pummeled his hat.

"But we be late," Jerem said. "We be hours too late. And they be all dead or gone."

"But where . . ." Jenna began, her hands still trembling on sword and reins.

Grete nodded toward the central building of the Hame. "We been cartin' 'em to Hall. My sons in there be helpin', though it be strange for men to work there. That be never allowed. Us women, yes, we came sometimes. To help bring in harvest, or our girls for training some. But the boys wanted to do for the sisters, settin' 'em side by side. The old lady, that Mother A, she be not quite gone when we got here, the blood all bubbling out of her like kettle to boil. She told us what to do. 'Side by side,' she said."

Jenna nodded slowly. That explained why the women's bodies were not scattered through the yard. "And . . . and the men?" she asked at last. "Surely there were some wounded, some dead."

Catrona added, "Surely they took some of them with them in such a fight."

"They drug their own wounded away. Or killed 'em on spot," said Harmon. "The men be all dead, some thirty of 'em. We burned them there." He pointed outside the broken wall, away from the road. "Foreign-looking, they be. Dark skin. Staring eyes."

"Young," Grete said. "Too young for such deaths. Too young for such killings."

"But dead all the same," said her husband, putting the hat back on his head. "And don't they say: *The swordsman dies by't sword, the hangman by't rope, and the king by't crown.*" He turned, looking over the ridge of his shoulder, and spoke to Jenna. "We be obliged for your help."

Jenna nodded, but it was Petra who spoke, her voice shaky. "We will help."

"We must be gone soon," Catrona said in an undertone to Jenna. "The others must be warned."

Jenna nodded at that, too, thinking to herself that her head must be on a string, so easily did it bob up and down. Then she whispered back, "But one hour surely will not matter. Let us find Selinda and Alna and bid them farewell."

"*An hour can spare a life,*" Catrona said. "It is something we learned many times in the army." But she gave in all the same. "For Alna and Selinda. An hour. That is all."

As Grete had promised, the sisters of Calla's Ford lay side by side in the darkening Hall. Jenna wandered up and down the many lines, kneeling occasionally to tidy a lock of hair or to close staring eyes. There were so many women, she could not count them all, but she refused to cry.

Petra, standing in the doorway, wept for them both.

"This be the last of 'em," Jerem said, pointing to an elderly woman in a long dress and apron, lying by the far door.

"Be they right?" Grete asked Catrona. "Be they in't form?"

"We will see them all right," Catrona said. "But best you leave us for now so that we may give them the proper rites."

Grete nodded, and turned to speak to the rest of the townsfolk who had gathered by the entryway, silently waiting. Her hands shooed them out like chickens toward the courtyard. She herself was the last one through the door, calling out in a whisper, "We will wait."

Jenna stared across the Hall. In the gray light the bodies of the women almost looked like carved stone. Though they had been cleansed of the blood on their hands and faces by the hard-working townsfolk, their shirts and aprons and skirts and trousers were stained with it. But the blood was black, not red, in the graying room. The bodies lay on rushes scented with verbena and dried roses, but the sharp, unmistakable smell of death overpowered the flowery bouquet.

"Shall I light the torches now?" Petra asked, her voice so quiet, Jenna had to strain to hear it. "So that their dark sisters might accompany them?" Without waiting for an answer, she went by the back hallway into the kitchen, came out with a lit candle, and proceeded to light the candles and torches that were set in the walls.

Slowly, in between the bodies, the corpses of the dark sisters took form and soon the room was crowded with them. It was as if a great carpet of death lay wall to wall.

Strangers, thought Jenna, *and yet not strangers to me at all. My sisters.*

"We must fire the Hame now," said Catrona. "And then go."

"But Alna and Selinda are not here," Jenna said. "Nor any of the younger girls. They may be hidden away like the children of Nill's Hame. We do not dare set the flames until we find them."

"They were taken," Catrona said bluntly, "you heard what Grete and her husband said. Taken. Like the girls of Callatown. Like the boy's sweetheart."

"Mai." Petra said suddenly, still lighting the torches.

"No!" Jenna shook her head violently, her voice echoing loudly. "No! We cannot be sure. Why would they want the girls? Why would they need them? We *have* to look."

Catrona put her hand out toward Jenna just as Petra

put the candle to a sconce near them in the Hall. Katri
appeared by Catrona's side and put her hand out as well.

"They *always* want women," said Katri. "Such men
do."

"They have not enough of their own." It was Skada's
voice right by Jenna's ear. "That is what Geo Hosfetter
said."

Jenna did not turn to welcome her. Instead she insisted, "We must search the Hame. We could never forgive ourselves if we did not."

It took an hour of searching to prove to Jenna that
the girls were not to be found. They even overturned the
mirror in the priestess' room, ripped down tapestries, and
knocked endlessly upon solid walls in the hope of finding
a secret passage. But there was none.

In the end even Jenna had to agree that the girls were
gone. This time she did not ask why.

"And what of the *Book*?" Petra asked, her hand atop
the great leather volume in the priestess' room. "We cannot leave it here for anyone to read."

"We do not have time to bury it," said Jenna, "so it
will have to be burned with the rest."

Petra cradled the *Book* in her arms, carrying it back
down to the Hall where she placed it between the
priestess and her dark sister. She set their stiffened hands
on top of the volume, palms up so that the blue Alta sign
showed, tying their wrists together with her hair rib-
bands. Then in a voice eerily familiar, she began to recite:

> "In the name of Alta's cave,
> The dark and lonely grave,
> Where we dwell twixt light and light . . ."

"I will not cry," Jenna promised herself. "Not for
death. Not ever for death." She shook her head violently
to keep away the tears. Skada did the same.

They did not cry.

THE LEGEND:

There were twelve sisters who dwelt in Callatown, by the ford, each one more beautiful than the last. But the loveliest of them all was the youngest, Fair Jennet.

Jennet was tall, with hair the color of the Calla's foam, and eyes the blue of a spring sky.

One day the king's own sons rode into the town, twelve handsome youths they were. But the handsomest was the youngest, Brave Colm. Colm was tall, with hair the color of dawn, and eyes as brown as bark.

Twelve and twelve. They should have been fair matched. But a king's son is like the cuckoo: he takes his pleasure where he will, then leaves to love again.

When the king's twelve sons had left, eleven sisters flung themselves into the Calla, above the ford. But the last, Fair Jennet, stayed to bury them, then she rode to the king's hall. She sang her sorrow at his table, before climbing the stairs to the highest tower. There she cast herself into the wind. As she fell, her cry was the cry of the woodcock rising to its mate.

Colm heard her and raced outside. He held her poor, broken body cradled in his arms, singing back to her the song she had caroled at his father's feast:

> "Eleven sisters side by side,
> Each one a dishonored bride,
> Married to the ebbing tide,
> And I wed to the wind."

At the song's end, Fair Jennet opened her eyes and called Colm's name. He kissed her brow before she died.

"I am the wind," whispered Colm, drawing his sword from his sheath and plunging it into his breast. Then he lay himself down by Jennet's side and died.

They say that every year, at the spring's rind, the folks of Callatown build a great bonfire. Its light keeps away the spirits of the eleven who rise like mist above the Calla waves, trying to sing every man down to his death. And they say that Colm and Jennet were buried in a single grave whose mound rises higher than the ruins of the king's tower. On that mound—and nowhere else in the Dales—grows the flower known as Colm's Sorrow. It is a flower as light as her hair, with an eye as dark as his, and it rains its petals down like tears throughout all of the long spring days.

THE STORY:

The fires burned quickly and the long, thin column of smoke wrote the sisters' epitaph against the spring sky. Catrona and Jenna stood dry-eyed, watching the curling smoke. But Petra buried her face in her hands, sobbing in soft little spurts. The townsfolk wept noisily. Only Jerem's boy was still, staring off to the west, where the sky was clear.

At last Jenna turned away, walking toward Duty who had waited so patiently by the broken wall. She patted the horse's nose with great concentration, as if the soft nostrils were the only thing that mattered in the world. She inhaled the heavy horse smell.

Catrona came over and put a hand on her shoulder. "We must go now, Jenna. And quickly."

Jenna did not look up from the horse.

"Do you go to fight?" It was Jerem's boy, who had

come up behind them. Small, wiry, he had a look of passionate intensity.

Catrona turned. "We go to warn the other Hames," she said sharply.

"And fight if we must." Jenna spoke softly, as much to the horse as the boy.

"Let me go with you," the boy begged. "I *must* go. For Mai's sake. For my own."

"Your father will need you, boy," Catrona said.

"He be having less to do now that so many be gone," he answered. "And if you do not let me go with you, I go anyway. I be your shadow. You be looking behind at every turning and at every straightaway, and I be there following."

Jenna, her hand still on Duty's nose, stared at him. The boy's dark green eyes bore into her own. "He will, too," she said softly to Catrona. "I have seen that look before."

"Where?"

"In her mirror," Petra said joining them.

"And in Pynt's eyes," Jenna added.

Catrona said nothing more but strode to her horse and mounted it with swift ease. Then she jerked on the reins and the startled mare turned toward the fallen Hame gate.

Petra's horse stood still while she climbed up, its withers trembling slightly, like ripples on a pond.

Jenna ran her hand along Duty's head and down her neck with slow deliberation. Then suddenly she grabbed hold of the saddle's horn and pulled herself up in a single, swift motion.

"Hummmph!" was Catrona's only comment, for she had turned in her saddle to watch the girls mount, but a smile played around her mouth before resolving itself in a frown.

They sat, motionless, on their horses for a long moment. Then Jenna leaned down and held out her hand to the boy. He grinned up at her and took it. Pulling hard,

Jenna lifted him onto the saddle behind her. He settled easily as if well used to riding double.

"Jareth, boy, where be you going?" Jerem ran over, grabbing onto the boy's right knee.

"He rides with us," Jenna said.

"He cannot. He must not. He be but a boy."

"A boy!" Catrona laughed. "He was promised in marriage. If he is man enough to wed, he is man enough to fight. How old do you think these girls are?" Her voice carried only to Jerem's ears. It was Petra, standing up in her stirrups, who addressed the rest of the villagers.

"We ride with the Anna, the White One, She who was thrice mothered and thrice orphaned."

The Calla's Ford folk gathered around to listen. Grete and her husband stood in the front, Jerem still by his son's knee. They were silent, staring at Jenna.

"We follow Her," Petra continued, pointing dramatically. "For She has already made both hound and ox bow down. Who would deny Her?" She paused.

Feeling that it was her turn to speak, Jenna drew her sword from its sheath and raised it above her head, wondering if she looked foolish, hoping she appeared noble. "I am the ending and I am the beginning," she cried out. "Who rides with me?"

From behind her Jareth called, "I ride with you, Anna."

"And I!" It was a dull-haired, long-legged boy.

"And I!" Standing by him, one who might have been his twin.

"And I!"

"And I!"

"And I!" The last was Harmon who, caught up in the moment, had snatched off his hat and thrown it into the air causing Petra's horse to back away nervously. The commotion gave Grete time to put her hand forcefully on her husband's shoulder, and he sank back, hatless, against her.

In the end, three boys volunteered. Jareth was given

his father's blessing and Grete and Harmon's two sons took a loan of their father's spavined gelding. Riding double, they tracked behind the mares down the darkening road toward the west.

THE MYTH:

Then Great Alta said, "You shall ride to the North and you shall ride to the South; you shall ride to the East and you shall ride to the West. And there great armies will rise up beside you. You and your blanket companions shall match sword with sword and might with might that the blood shed between you shall wash away the stain left by the careless men."

BOOK TWO

THE LONG RIDING

THE MYTH:

Then Great Alta reached into the sinkhole of night and drew up three boy babes. One was light, and two were dark, and they were weak and pulling in the sun of her face.

"And you shall grow and grow and grow," quoth she, "until you are like giants in the land. You shall ride over the world that evil may know fear."

Then Great Alta pulled them by the hair and by the bottoms of their feet until they were as large as towers, until they were giants in the land. She set them down by the fordside and sprinkled their foreheads with water and their feet with ashes that they might better endure the long riding.

THE LEGEND:

Three heroes rode out of the East. One was light as day, one as bright as noon, one as dark as eve. And their horses were caparisoned the same: one in silver as the dawn, one in gold as midday, and one in ebon as the night. They carried crown and collar and ring.

Their swords flashed as they rode and the woods rang with their battle song:

> We serve the queen of light
> We serve the queen of night
> On the long riding.

Wherever they rode, they dealt death to the enemies of the White One, the Anna. And they were known as The Three.

The tapestry in room 4/Town Hall/Calla's Cross (pictured above) is from the Great Renascence in the Weaver's Gift Period. Legend has it it was finished the week after The Three had ridden by, a patent impossibility. Such tapestries were often years in the weaving. Note especially how it pictures three knights in full armor, swords upraised, riding straight toward the viewer. One is in silver armor on a gray horse; one is in black armor on a black horse; and one is in gold armor on a horse whose skin is the color of old gold. Their visors are up and one can see their eyes. They seem to be laughing.

THE STORY:

Night came quickly and they were only scant miles down the road, but Catrona pulled them all up with a hand sign.

"You, boy!" she called to Jerem's son.

"Jareth," Jenna reminded her, even before he could speak for himself.

"Jareth, then," Catrona said. "Climb down from behind the Anna now and give her poor horse a rest. Best you ride for a while with Petra there." She pointed.

The boy pushed himself off the rear of the horse, landing as lightly as a cat, and went over to Petra's mare. Petra reached down to help him up, but he shook off her hand, went behind the horse, gave a little run-jump, and was behind her, grinning.

"I be handling a lot of horses," he explained shyly, "when the owners came to grind their grain. One told me a horse be making a giant of a small man. That's when I knew I had to ride."

Catrona nodded, but Jenna slipped her horse between them and leaned over, speaking softly. "Why have him switch now? Duty is not tiring."

Looking up at the darkening sky, Catrona whispered back. "The moon will be up soon and our dark sisters here. No need to frighten the boys or overburden Duty."

"I forgot." Jenna bit her lower lip. "Alta, how could I have forgot?"

Catrona smiled. "You are but days new to having a dark sister share your life. And even I, who have lived side by side with Katri for thirty years, sometimes forget. Not Katri, not the *fact* of her. But sometimes I forget to be prepared for her. She is ever a surprise, though she is the better part of me."

"Then we must warn the boys," Jenna said. "But what do we say?"

"We say to them what we always say—in the army or in bed—for a man hears and sees what he wants," Catrona said. "Do not worry so. In the Lower Dales they say *A man's eye is bigger than his belly and smaller than his brain*." Laughing, she turned her horse toward Petra and the gelding upon which Grete and Harmon's boys sat, legs dangling down.

"Soon we will be met by two sisters of the night," she began, in a voice of easy authority. "They are friends of ours who will travel along the way with us. But they come when they will and they leave when they will and they are not fond of the day. As long as they decide to remain with us, they will be our dearest allies, our boon companions on the road." She looked carefully at the boys. "Do you understand?"

The boys nodded, Jareth quickly and the other two with a bit more caution, as if it took them more time to sort through what Catrona meant.

"We be seeing such night sisters afore," Jareth said. "They be helping my Da once at mill and Sandor and

Marek's Da at ferry. They be there when we needed them though never when we called."

Sandor and Marek nodded.

"Good. Then you will not be frightened or confused when these two appear. Their names are Katri and Skada. Katri is the older." She smiled. "Even older than me."

"Catrona!" It was Petra who seemed shocked.

Catrona smiled mischievously. "Well, maybe only a little older."

"We be neither confused nor frightened," said Jareth solemnly, "for we be in the presence of Anna."

Sandor shook his head. And Marek, like his brother, shook his head as well. Otherwise they did not move, staring at Jenna with worshipful eyes.

"Let us dismount and feed the horses. And ourselves." Catrona climbed off her horse.

"But there be no food," Sandor said.

"None," added Marek.

Jenna laughed, a short barking sound. "We have the woods as our larder," she said. "So we can never starve."

THE SONG:

The Long Riding

Into the valley, come riding, come riding,
Into the meadow and into the dell,
Into the moonlight where shadows are gliding,
Into the forest where enemies hiding,
Riding, riding, Three come ariding
Into the mouth of hell.

Into the village come riding, come riding,
Into the hames where the sweet women dwell,
Into the rests where the men are abiding,
Into the forest where enemies hiding,

Riding, riding, Three come ariding
Into the mouth of hell.

THE STORY:

They showed the boys how to search the woods for food, and Jareth discovered a bird's nest with three eggs. The other two boys came up empty-handed, but Jenna found a ring of tasty mushrooms and Catrona a stream whose bank was dotted with cress. Petra, who had waited with the horses, came upon the greatest cache of all, a stand of nettles which stung the back of her hands. She was still complaining about them when Jenna reappeared, trailed by Jareth.

"Nettles!" Jenna said. "Then we can have nettle tea."

"But we dare not be making a fire, Anna," Jareth reminded.

"We can make a small fire in a deep tunnel," she said, "just enough to heat water to steep tea if your friends can find leaves that are dry enough."

They had cress salad sprinkled with hard-boiled egg, mushrooms, and half the tea, a feast.

"The rest of the tea I will store in my water pouch," Catrona said as they buried the tunneled fire. "Nettle tea is as good cold as hot. *And* I have a surprise." She reached into her leather pocket and pulled out a rough-weave cloth packet. Slowly she unwrapped a large piece of journeycake.

"Where . . ." Petra began.

"From the Hame kitchen," Catrona said quietly. "I knew they would have had us take it. Any old soldier knows that in battle one takes quickly and saves regrets for the morning."

They nodded, one after another, and held out their hands for a share.

The dark sisters did not come for the moon had finished its full phase and, without fire, the small light of the stars was not strong enough to call them forth. Jenna lay on her blanket staring up at the patterns in the sky, counting their names to herself in the hope that the roll call would lull her to sleep: Alta's Dipper, Hame's Horn, the Cat, the Great Hound. But she could not sleep and at last stood up and walked, barefooted, to the place where the white horse and its companion bays slept standing. When she placed her hand on Duty's soft nose, the horse blew through its nostrils lightly, a sound at once strange and comforting.

"Anna?" It was a soft voice.

Jenna turned around. Jareth was moving toward her quietly.

"Anna, be that you?"

"Yes."

He reached the horse and touched it lightly on the nose, careful to keep the horse's head between them. "I be on watch and heard you. Be there something wrong?"

"No. Yes. I could not sleep."

"You be thinking about Calla's Ford Hame?"

She hesitated, then nodded. "I am thinking about *all* the hames, Jareth. But that is not why I am restless."

"Can you tell me, Anna?"

"Do not, for Alta's blessed sake, call me that," she said, her voice edged with anger.

"Call you what?"

"Anna. That is not my name. My name is Jo-an-enna. My friends call me Jenna."

Jareth was quiet for a moment. "But I be thinking you be . . . I mean, *she* said you be . . . that be . . ."

"It seems I am," said Jenna. "Or may be. But that is only a title, something put *upon* me. It is not what I am in truth."

Jareth thought about that a minute, then whispered, "Then who *be* you? In truth?"

"Just a girl. And the daughter of many mothers."

"That be what they say of Anna. That she be thrice mothered."

"And so I was."

"And white-haired."

"And so I am."

"And the hound and ox . . ."

"So they did. But I eat like you. And I pass wind if there are beans in the pot. And when I have too much to drink, I must find a place in the woods to . . ."

"Anna," Jareth said, reaching across Duty's nose to touch her arm. "No one be saying that Anna be not human. No one be calling her a goddess without water or wind. She be . . . she be linchpin, axletree, link between old carriage and new wheel."

"But linchpins and axletrees are made by humans," Jenna said. "Not by Alta."

"Exactly," Jareth answered. "It be prophecy that be the Goddess' own."

Jenna was silent a long time, thinking about what Jareth had said. At last she sighed. "Thank you, Jareth. I think . . . I think I shall be able to sleep now."

"You be welcome," he answered, coming around to the front of the horse. "But I be afraid you get no sleep yet. It be your turn at watch." He laughed, holding out his hand, "Jenna."

She took his hand. It was as firm in her own as Catrona's. Or Skada's.

They left before morning light, going out of the forest and crossing three towns in quick succession where no lamps were yet lit and their horses' hooves the only sound. In the last town, Jenna, Petra, and Catrona waited by the edge while the boys found them food, for Jareth had cousins there.

Once they stopped to wash the trail dirt from their faces in a small, meandering stream. Five or six times they stopped to relieve themselves and let the horses graze. They slept fitfully through a night that spit intermittent rain, soaking them despite a lean-to of split saplings. Otherwise, they remained on horseback all that day and into the next.

"I smell of horse," Petra complained mildly at their waking.

"You smell no different than a horse," Jenna amended.

They laughed heartily at her words, the first such since finding the devastation at the Hame. After that their mood was somewhat lighter, even though their muscles ached and both Marek and Sandor had saddle sores.

On the eve of the second day they crested a small hill where the beginnings of a great forest spread out below them. Mile after mile of unbroken woods lay on either side of a winding road.

"That is King's Way," Catrona said, pointing to the road. "There is no other through this wilderness. Wilma's Crossing is on the other side."

"Be it not dangerous to stay . . ." Sandor began, running his fingers through his matted hair.

". . . on the King's Way?" finished his brother.

"There is less danger on it than off. This wold is known to only a few and the few are the Greenfolk. They"—Catrona spit between her second and little fingers—"they are not likely to help us. More likely to take our heads. Or our fingers. They like the small bones. Wear them dangling from their ears."

Marek and Sandor looked nervously at one another, but Jareth laughed.

"My Da be speaking often of the Greenfolk. The Grenna, he be calling them. He be saying no such thing about taking bones. They be to themselves," Jareth said. "And that be all."

Catrona smiled at him. "True, they are to themselves. They call this forest their own and do not favor intruders."

"There is no bone-taking in that," Jenna said.

"It was a joke," Catrona said.

Jenna shook her head. "And not very funny."

"Tell us more about these Greenfolk and this road,"

Petra said, adding quickly, "But no more jokes. You are frightening some of us unnecessarily."

Catrona nodded. "When the good queen Wilma built this road, long before the G'runians broke apart our land, she made a pax with the Greenfolk's council. They have no queens nor kings."

"And probably better off for it," Jenna muttered.

Ignoring Jenna, Catrona went on as her horse trembled restlessly beneath her. "The pax was this: we would leave the rest of the woods to the Greenfolk if they would leave the road alone."

Jareth leaned forward eagerly. "My Da never be telling me this. What be sealing the pax?"

"Wilma offered them iron or steel or gold but they would have none of it."

"None of it?" Marek and Sandor said together, Sandor adding, "Then what *could* seal it?"

"They sat in a great circle on the highest hill," Catrona said. "And . . ."

"Pah! There is no hill," Jenna said. "So much for stories." She swept her hand expansively from east to west. "I see no hill. Just woodland, green and rolling."

"Look at things on a slant, Jenna," Petra said. "That is what my Mother Alta taught me. On a slant."

"That is how the story goes, Jenna," Catrona said. "I tell it the only way I know. They sat on the great hill— *that Jenna cannot see*—and ate bread together, swearing that the pax was engraved on their hearts and in their mouths. They hold all their history on the tongue. They do not have writing." Catrona stood up in her stirrups and stared down at the way.

The others copied her movement, dark sisters to her light.

"It is a chancy pax at best. And never more so then now, when the last three kings of the G'runs renamed the Way and promised to build fortresses and inns along it."

"I see no buildings," Jenna said.

"Not yet. But they will come." Catrona sat back

down. "It was often spoke of when I was in the army. The men all favored it. *'Stand in the way of a cart,'* they said, *'and you will have wheel marks across your face.'*"

"It is a terrible thing," said Jenna, "to break pax with those who still hold it."

"If I be king . . ." Jareth began.

"And if horses could fly . . ." Petra said, laughing, "we would be across the wold and at Wilma's Crossing before nightfall."

"But we cannot fly." Catrona's face was stern. "And we dare not be stuck on that road with the stars our only protection. Let us find a quiet place off the road, camp the night, and be up before sunrise. It will be a long riding, whether we meet with anyone or not."

THE HISTORY:

The Greenfolk, the Good Folk, the Grenna, the Faire, are all names given to the Dalian equivalent of the Garunian brownies or little people. Though histo-archaeologists, like Magon, try desperately to prove there was an actual race of pygmy-like wood-dwellers who occupied the Old Forest above the Whilem River, frequent diggings in the area have turned up nothing. (See my monograph "Woods-Folk or Would-be Folk: An Investigation into the Whilem River Cross Dig, Passapatout Press, #19.)

Carbon dating has proven beyond a shadow of a doubt that the remains of encampments found throughout the region were at least a thousand years earlier than the dates for the Gender Wars. The few human bones lay scattered rather than buried in gravemounds, proving the hunting-gathering tribes were so primitive that they had no sense of an afterlife. What tribes there were had to have been long gone by the time of the rule of Langbrow.

Yet the persistence of stories about the "folke all greene," as the ballad goes, has caused even such worthies as Temple and Cowan to consider the possibilities. Legends of the Greenfolk's generosity toward the followers of the White Goddess are legion in the industrial towns of the Whilem River Valley. Certainly Doyle's work on the Whilem names (Green As Grass: The Unnatural Occurrence of Color Names Along the Whilem, Hanger College Press), with its suggestion that any forest communities would have a preponderance of woods/green surnames, is persuasive. Magon's rantings to the contrary, that certainly makes more sense than to say there was a small, proto-human race of faerie folk living in pre-literate splendor, supporting their candidate for queen with magicks and mysteries by the roadside and carrying away folk for rites under the nonexistent Whilem Hills.

THE STORY:

The King's Way was well pounded down, as if recent travelers had been many and recent rains few, but the forest grew right up to the edge of the road. Brambles, nettles, briars, and brush vied for space between the rangy trees. The varieties of green were numberless.

They pushed the horses unmercifully for the first few hours, but when the gelding stumbled in a hidden, dust-covered hole, nearly throwing Sandor and Marek, Catrona signaled a halt.

Dismounting, they led the horses to the road's brushy edge and Catrona picked up the gelding's left forefoot.

"I do not think he pulled anything," she said after a moment's careful examination.

"Perhaps we should rest him," Petra said. "Just in case."

"And eat," Jareth suggested. The other boys nodded. But Jenna shook her head. "No. We need to move on. We must reach Wilma's Crossing Hame before . . ." She hesitated, decided not to say what they all were thinking. "Besides, I have had the strange feeling . . ."

"That we have been watched?" Catrona asked quietly.

"Something like that," Jenna said.

"And for many miles now?"

Jenna nodded grimly.

They mounted quickly, ignoring their hollow stomachs, and urged the horses forward. As if sensing danger, the horses responded at once. The gelding raced ahead, proving itself fit. Catrona managed to overtake it, but Jenna held back to guard the rear.

When she looked over her shoulder, she saw nothing but forest and the layers of green. But then she thought she heard a low drumming sound accompanied by a high whistle. It was at least a mile farther before she realized that what she was hearing was the sound of the horses' hooves on the King's Way and the wind racing past her ears. Only that—and nothing more.

Alternately walking and galloping, they rode for several more hours, before Catrona signaled another halt. This time they moved the horses well off the road and into the cover of a grove of trembling aspen.

"I do not like this," Catrona whispered to Jenna. "We have passed no one the entire time."

"I thought that was to the good," Jenna replied.

"This is usually a well-traveled road. Carts, trains of wagons, individual travelers. Even walkers. We have come across none of them."

"We must tell the others."

Catrona put a hand on her arm. "No. Wait. Why trouble them before trouble is here?"

"I was told at Nill's Hame that *Not to know is bad, but not to wish to know is worse*," Jenna said. "These are our friends, Catrona. Our companions. We must trust our backs to them."

"They are hardly fighters," Catrona said wearily. "I trust my back to Katri and to you."

"They are all we have," Jenna pointed out.

Catrona sighed. "Yes, they are. More fools we." She put her fingers to her mouth, and whistled the others to her.

Gathered in a close circle, they listened as Catrona spelled out her fears. Jareth's forehead wrinkled in concentration, but Sandor and Marek rocked back and forth, as if the movement helped them understand what she was saying. Petra's whole body was still, and she breathed slowly, using *latani* breathing. Jenna matched her, breath for breath, but once settled into the rhythm of the expirations, she felt the familiar lightening as her real self pulled free of her body to float above it.

Catrona's voice was like a buzzing of insects as Jenna ranged over them. Her translucent fingers reached down to touch each in turn on the skull's center where the pulse beat under the fragile shield of skin and bone.

At that touch, as she had done before, Jenna felt herself being drawn down inside each of her companions in turn. Catrona was a strong fire, the hottest point in the center; Petra, a spill of cool water over a rocky race. The brothers were lukewarm, like milk fresh from the cow. But Jareth reminded her of Carum for he seemed to have pockets of fire and ice, pockets of alien heat, though she was not moved by them as she had been when centered on the young prince.

She pulled herself away, fleeing back into the air, and suddenly saw pinpricks of light in a great circle around them; dancing lights coming closer and closer. Flinging herself down into her own body she slipped into it as if into familiar clothes. "Back to mine," she cried.

On the signal, Catrona unsheathed her sword and stood back-to-back with Jenna. Jareth understood almost as quickly.

"Your knives!" he called to Marek and Sandor.

They drew their knives and stood with Petra in their center, waiting. For a long minute they could hear nothing: not a snap of twig nor rustle of grass. It was as if the forest itself had stopped breathing.

Suddenly Jenna's head went up with a jerk. "There!"

They looked around. At first there was nothing to be seen. And then—there was. A circle of some thirty mannikins surrounded them, dressed all in green, jerkins and trews, as if they had metamorphosed from the trees or brush. They were half the size of a man, with skin a greenish cast, like a translucent glaze, over fine bones. Yet they did not give the impression of fragility. It was as if the land itself had been thinned down to its essence and given human form.

Duty whickered nervously, followed by the bays. Only the gelding was silent, pawing the ground over and over with a dull thudding.

One of the green watchers moved forward, breaking the circle, and stood not three feet from Jenna. She could have leaned over and touched him on the top of the head but she did not move. He raised his hand in greeting, speaking in a strange, lilting tongue.

"*Av Anna regens; av Anna quonda e futura.*"

"Speak so we can understand," Jareth cried out, his voice cracking like a boy's.

"I can understand him," Petra said quietly. "My Mother Alta required I learn the old tongues. He says, *Hail, White Queen; hail White One now and forever.*"

Jareth grunted, but Marek spoke. "That be all right, then. Our Da be saying: *If a man call you master, trust him for a day; if he call you friend, trust him for a year; if he call you brother, trust him for all ways.*" It was the longest speech any of them had heard from him.

"But he called me none of those," said Jenna. "He called me Anna. So how would your Da say he can be trusted?"

Marek started to work out an answer, but the little man held up his hand and the boy was strangely still.

"For as long as the forest, Anna," said the little man, suddenly speaking their language, his voice only slightly accented.

"Why . . ." Jareth began, but Jenna hushed him.

"For as high as the heavens," the little man continued. "We have waited since the beginning of this time for you, cocooned in the time. Your birth has been told around many fires, your reign under many stars. First the Alta and at last the Anna, so the circle can close."

"Since the beginning of this time . . ." Jenna murmured to herself. *"And the closing of the circle . . . What does that mean?"* Out loud she said, "You have called me by a title, but I am called Jenna by my friends. Are you my friend?"

The little man grinned broadly, his even white teeth white against the green of his face. Bowing, he said, "We are your *brothers.*"

"All ways!" Marek said triumphantly.

"May be," Jareth whispered under his breath. "May be not."

The little man ignored them, speaking only to Jenna. "You may call this one Sorrel. That is not this one's true name, but your mouth would not be able to shape it nor your heart hear its sound."

"I understand," Jenna said. "I have a hidden name as well. So, Sorrel, are you king of these green folk?"

"We have neither king nor captain. We have only the circle."

"Then how is it you speak for your . . . circle?" Catrona interrupted.

"This one is first this time by the circle's leave," Sorrel said.

Nodding, Jenna sheathed her sword. "I put my weapon away *this time.* As does my sister, Catrona."

Catrona raised one eyebrow and, very slowly, replaced her own sword.

"And my men will put away their knives," Jenna added. She bit her upper lip, the only betrayal of her nervousness.

With a slight frown, Jareth slipped his knife into his boot. When Marek and Sandor hesitated, he growled at them, "Come on. Come on."

"We do this," Jenna said slowly, "because you carry no weapons against us."

There was a strange titter that ran around the circle of little men. Sorrel bowed again.

"We must tell you truly, we carry no weapons ever but these, Anna," Sorrel said. He held up his hands. His fingers were extremely long, the nails a paler green.

"And how potent are they?" Petra asked, her voice overly polite. *"Potentas manis qui?"*

He giggled, a sound like a bird's trill. *"Trez.* Very, Little Mother. Very potent indeed." He reached out suddenly and snapped off a greenwood stick, stripping it and twisting it quickly into a noose. Still smiling, he threw the noose away.

Catrona made a *tching* sound between her teeth and Jenna turned to her quickly. "These are our brothers, Catrona. *For the moment.*"

Catrona nodded slowly, her eyes never leaving Sorrel's hands.

"With our sisters, our hands are as the sweet weed, the althea, smooth and soothing," Sorrel said. "See." In one liquid movement he was at Duty's side. He stroked the horse's nose. She sighed deeply, an odd sound, and leaned into his hands.

"Why have you been trailing us for so long?" Catrona asked suddenly. Her hand rested uneasily on the pommel of her sword.

Startled, Sorrel looked up at her, then as quickly hooded his eyes.

"Oh yes," Catrona said, pleased to have surprised him. "You are not the only ones who can read the woods. We sisters of the Hames are known for it."

"We have heard that," Sorrel said. "It brings us closer. Brother to sister."

"I ask again," Catrona said emphatically. *"Sister to brother.* Why trail us as if you are our enemy if—as you claim—you are our friends."

"Not *friend. Brother!"* Sorrel said. "We must watch

and see who you are, riding through our woods. We must be sure it is the Anna. The stars tell us it is the time the circle closes. But many ride our path. We must be certain before we greet the Anna." There was a confirming murmur from the rest of the Greenfolk, as if punctuating his sentence.

Petra and the boys looked around at the sound; it came from all around them, like a noose of noise.

"Why do you surround us?" Petra asked, turning slowly, looking at each of the mannikins.

"Is the circle not the perfect form, Little Mother?" Sorrel asked. *"Perface.* In it no one is higher. No one is lower. No one is first. No one is last."

"Are you not first in this circle?" Jenna asked, casting her voice low so as not to give offense. She repeated his odd phrase: *"This one is first this time . . ."* and folded her arms across her breast. "Who else in the circle speaks but you?" She smiled.

Petra whispered in the old tongue, *"Quis voxen?"*

"The question does not suit you, Anna. Nor you, Little Mother. Such questions better fit the mouth of the Old Cat there, or her young Toms." He gestured toward Catrona and the boys.

As if on cue, Catrona spoke loudly, using the words Petra had used. *"Quis voxen?"* Her pronunciation was abominable.

"This one speaks today. Tomorrow another. The circle moves on."

Jenna stepped closer to the little man. Though she towered over him, instinctively she knew better than to kneel. To do so would demean them both. She inclined her head slightly, the only acknowledgment of his size she would allow herself. "Are we a part of your greater circle, Sorrel?"

He nodded. "As is all life."

"Yet you singled me out. You called me *Anna,* you called me queen."

"Regens," Petra whispered. "Good question, Jenna!"

"We have waited for you from the beginning," Sorrel

said. "Your coming is part of the circle. You herald the end, the close." He held his forefingers and thumbs together to make a circle sign. Jenna saw that his long, thin fingers had an extra knuckle each.

"What end?" she asked. "What end do I herald?"

"The end to what we know," Sorrel said. "This time."

"Be he meaning the end to what he and the Greenies be knowing?" asked Marek aloud, clearly puzzled.

"Or the end to what *we* be knowing?" added Sandor, looking at Marek.

"We go. You go with us," Sorrel said.

"No," Jareth said. He reached down and pulled his knife back out of his boot. "The Anna be going to rescue her sisters. And we with her. We do not go with you. *My Da told me*: who be going with the Grenna, stays with them. Years later and all the folk we know be dead and the grass be growing over their graves. You be saying it yourself; we all be hearing you. *Cocooned,* you be saying. *In time,* you be saying."

"Jareth." Jenna stretched her hand toward him. "Those are but tales."

"Nevertheless . . ." Jareth began, "we must not be forgetting the sisters." The hand holding the knife began to shake. He steadied it with his left hand on the wrist.

Jenna looked at Sorrel. "He is right, you know."

Sorrel shook his head. "You are too late to help those sisters. Any of them, Anna. The only way is the circle. You will leave stronger than you come."

"*Too late!*" Jenna's voice shook. To calm herself, to help herself think, she took three deep *latani* breaths and tried to concentrate on matching Sorrel breath to breath. She was shocked to find his expirations so slow, she became dizzy in the attempt. Closing her eyes, Jenna considered his words. *Too late to help those sisters.* She knew he spoke the bald truth. But there were fifteen more standing Hames, including her own. Fourteen that needed to be warned. She could not leave them unready. She

opened her eyes and stared at Sorrel. His woods-green
eyes stared back, the gaze unwavering.

"Too late for *any* of them, Anna," he said as if reading her mind. *"Malas propas."*

She lifted her chin. Twisting the ring on her left
hand, she remembered what Mother Alta had said to her
when she had given Jenna the ring: *The time of endings is
at hand.* In that instance she made up her mind. "We go
with the Grenna."

"But, Jenna . . ." Jareth began.

Petra touched his shoulder. "We go quietly for we
are few and they are many."

"They be many," Jareth said, "but they be small.
Smaller than I. I have a knife. I be not afraid to die for
Anna."

"I have a sword," Catrona said. "And I have never
been afraid to die for my sisters." She purposely drew the
sword from its sheath in such a way that it made a loud,
angry scraping sound.

"We go with Sorrel," Jenna said, "into his circle. I
would have none of you die for me. Sorrel called me sister
and queen. And he promises strength. We need great
strength for the coming days. I trust him."

"For how long?" Jareth whispered hoarsely. "For how
long be you trusting him, Jenna? A day? A year? Or all
ways? Or until another be speaking from out his circle?"

"I trust him until this thing is done, however long it
takes," Jenna said. "Are you with me, Jareth? If so,
speak."

He was silent, but Marek and Sandor answered as
one.

"We be with you, Anna."

"And I, *regens,*" said Petra.

After a moment Catrona added, her voice so soft
Jenna had to strain to hear it, "And I." She did not
sheathe her sword.

At last Jareth sighed heavily. "I be going only because you be asking, Jenna. You—not *them*." He gestured over his shoulder at the circle of green mannikins.

Jenna nodded and turned to her horse. Slipping the reins over Duty's head, she pulled the mare along, grateful that the beast gave her no argument. She followed the green of Sorrel's back, wondering that she did not lose it in the myriad of greens in the forest. She could hear the others following close behind, the sound of their footsteps like an echo repeating *"Too late to help. . . ."*

THE TALE:

There was once a girl named Jenny who was walking behind her sheep over the grassy lea. When the sheep stopped to graze, young Jenny braided a crown of daisies and placed it upon her head. But thinking the daisies too plain, she plucked a single wild rose and was about to twine it into the crown as well when there was a shock of lightning without there being clouds.

Jenny leaped to her feet. Before her stood a handsome young man dressed in green.

"Who be ye?" she cried.

"I be the king of the lea," he said. "I have come at your call."

"But I called you not," said she.

"You plucked the rose, and that is the sign that calls me out from the green land."

He took her by the hand, his all green and cold, and led her under the hillside. There they sang and danced until the dawn turned dark and the stars fell like snow behind them and Jenny cried out, "I must go back to my sheep."

He let her go and she made her way back, across the long lea. But her sheep were all scattered and gone.

Sadly she made her way down the hillside to her

home to report the loss. But when she got there, the village was changed beyond her knowing it. She stopped at the first house and knocked on the door.

"Who be ye?" cried the old man who answered.

"I be Jenny, daughter of Dougal and Ardeen. Be they here?" she asked.

"Alas," cried the ancient, "I be Dougal's only descendent. And as for Jenny, that poor lass be her mother's death. Ardeen died of sorrow when her Jenny never came home with her sheep. A hundred year or more it's been."

Jenny shook her head and cried:

"The King of the Lea, the King of the Lea,
A hundred years he married me.
A hundred years in but a day
I've sang and danced my life away."

Then she disappeared back over the hill and was never seen again.

This tale is from the Whilem Valley. Twenty-seven variants have been collected.

THE STORY:

They trailed the Grenna for long hours, until the sun went down and even the shadows seemed green. No one spoke. It was as if the forest drained them of words. Except for the words in Jenna's head, which kept repeating, *"Too late . . . too late for any of them."*

She wondered if he meant too late to warn them or too late to help them; if he meant too late for the older sisters who would die unmourned or for the younger sisters carried away; if he meant only all the sisters in Wilma's Crossing or all the sisters in the land. But she did not ask him. She was afraid to know the answer. *Not to know is bad, but not to wish to know is worse.* She was tired of such wisdoms invented when need was smallest. She was tired of cryptic omens and signs to be read on the slant. She wanted only the wind in her hair again and . . . and Carum's mouth on hers. She closed her eyes and stumbled along into the gathering dark hoping that she had chosen the right way.

"Jenna!"

Her name recalled her to the woods. Opening her eyes, she looked around. They had come to a great black hole that led right into a cliffside. A pair of round, oaken doors stood ajar, looking like barrel covers cut in half.

"Jenna, look at the doors!" It was Petra who had spoken.

Jenna looked.

The doors were intricately carved: river, apple, berries, flower, stone, bird, crescent moon, rainbow, tree, fish. All familiar signs. Jenna touched each one in turn.

"Eye-Mind," she whispered.

Catrona's voice echoed hers, adding, "Why here?"

The circle of the Grenna were gone through the doors, leaving only shadows behind. Duty whickered softly and the sound seemed to go past the doors and into the black, stopping abruptly, as if cut off by an ax.

Jenna and Catrona hesitated at the gaping doors and the others gathered around them.

"We could be turning back," Jareth whispered. "You and Catrona and Petra could be riding for the Hame. Marek and Sandor and I could be holding the doors shut."

The other two boys nodded.

"For how long?" Catrona asked mockingly. "For a day? A year? Or all ways, Jareth?"

He made no answer, but his mouth twisted and he glared furiously at her.

"Old Cat!" Marek whispered to Sandor, approval in his voice.

"*Malas propas,*" Petra said, her voice low. "That is

what Sorrel said: *malas propas*. It means too late. But it also means unfavorable, inauspicious, bad luck."

"We must make our own luck," Catrona said. "And three unseasoned boys have neither the luck nor strength to hold two doors against such as the Greenfolk. Besides, we do not know if there are other doors to this hole. They might be like ferrets. Close them here, they boil out there." She pointed to the right of the doors. "Or there." She pointed to the left.

Jenna slowly touched each of them in turn: Petra on the cheek, Catrona on the shoulder, Marek and Sandor on the top of the head, and Jareth on the hand. She let her fingers linger on his for a long moment. He smiled up at her.

"All we have is one another," she said. "We do not dare separate now. Are we afraid to trust? Are we afraid of the dark? Come, give me your hands. We will go down into this black hole together and gather great strength from the journey. So the Grenna have promised."

Catrona placed her hand directly on Jenna's. Petra's came next. Last Marek's and Sandor's. Jenna felt the pressure of those hands and their comfort. She took a deep breath and passed the comfort down to Jareth's hand that still lay beneath hers. Then hands together, warmed by the touch, they moved as one into the dark.

It was not a black dark but a green one; what light there was came from phosphorescent patches on the rock walls. For a long time there was no choice to the direction they were to travel. There was only one tunnel and it led inexorably down, too narrow to allow them to change their minds and turn the horses.

No one spoke; the close dark precluded conversation. Even the horses were silenced except for the dull *thud-thud* of their hooves on the rock floor. Jenna took some small comfort in the regularity of the sound; it was like a heartbeat.

All of a sudden the single narrow tunnel branched

into three wider ones. Confused, Jenna and Catrona stopped and the others behind them stopped as well. They whispered together hurriedly, their words sounding a peculiar *swee-swashing* in the echoing space, making understanding difficult.

Finally Catrona pointed to the right. "Only that one has the green patches," she said.

In silent agreement they turned, following the right-hand path as it continued in an ever-steepening descent.

Once Jenna put her hand to the tunnel wall, but it was slippery and cold. She did not like the feel of it, like the insides of something dead, a fish or a snake or an eft. She had tried to eat an eft once, on an overnight in the woods with Pynt near their Hame when they were young. It had not been a pleasant meal. Shuddering, she wiped her hand on her sleeve. But even after she could feel the damp wall as if it had impressed itself on her palm, as if it had left a mark she would have forever.

Suddenly one of the horses snorted, a sound so loud in the confines of the tunnel that they all let out little squeaks of dismay, except for Catrona who *humphed* through her nose, sounding just like her mare. For a moment the explosion of sound and the echoes nearly deafened them. Then Jenna shushed them, pointing.

Ahead the tunnel dipped down and then ascended steeply, widening at the end into a strange light green glow.

"I will go first," Catrona whispered. "Petra, hold my reins."

Before Jenna could tell her no, she advanced on silent feet, down into the dip and then up to the very edge of the green light, her sword in her hand. They saw her quite clearly silhouetted by the light, an even paler green haloing her body. She raised her sword, in challenge or in greeting, and then in an instant she was gone. Not jumped over the edge or killed by a sword or fallen—just gone.

"Catrona!" Marek and Sandor cried out together.

The walls sent her name back to them a hundredfold. They called out again but could not seem to move.

It was Jareth, shouting as he ran, who followed Catrona into the green light, one minute haloed at the edge and the next minute vanished into a million particles of light.

"Wait!" Jenna said, her voice less an authority than a plea. "Wait." She put her hand out to the rest of them. "We must think."

But one by one, Petra, Marek, and Sandor, leading the horses, moved toward the light as if drawn by it. One by one by one, as Jenna watched, they were translated into little brilliant green dust motes that were swallowed by the whole.

Jenna put her hand on Duty's nose. She blew into the mare's nostrils. "My Duty," she said. "My duty is with all of them. I cannot command you to follow when I do not know where it is I go." She turned and walked toward the light.

As she neared the edge, she heard a fine, high singing in her head. The light dazzled her. Vaguely she heard the horse's hoofsteps behind her but she could not bring herself to look away and warn the mare off. There was only the calling light, pulling her forward; it seemed to her that there was nowhere else in the world that she wanted to be. And then she reached the top of the climb. She teetered there for a moment, with her toes curling over the ledge, and was suddenly enveloped in the light. It was warm and cool at once; soft and crystalline; smelling of sweet flowers and the pungent cabbage of the swamp. She closed her eyes to savor it all, and when she opened them again, she was hovering over a bright green grassy meadow pied with lilybells and daisies and dotted around the edges with the blood-red of trillium. *Hovering*.

Then she was down in the soft grass on her hands and knees, jarred as if she had just fallen from a high place. When she turned around, Duty was beside her, grazing contentedly. There was no high ledge, no cave, no borders to be seen. Only a rolling meadow stretching to a hill on the far horizon, and broken sporadically by small stands of trees, a land of elegant, timeless peace.

From the closest copse a thin spiral of smoke threaded its way up against a blue-green sky. She stood and walked toward the trees, slowly, as if traveling through a dreamscape.

When she reached the first trees, she saw Petra and Catrona on the right, the boys on the left, all waiting to enter.

"You be going first, Anna," Marek said.

"We be going after," Sandor added.

She nodded and started in.

There were trees of every kind in that small grove, as if each had been planted singly: aspen and birch, larch, poplar, hawthorn, rowan, ash, willow, and oak. The trees stood tall, like pillars in a great hall, and Jenna was reminded of the *Song of the Trees* which she had sung so often as a child in the Hame, a song it was said Great Alta herself had composed, with its chorus:

> *Of all in green jerkin and all in green gown*
> *The trees in the forest they all bear the crown,*
> *The trees in the forest are cradle and hall,*
> *The trees in the forest are fairest of all.*

with the long alphabet of trees for the verse.

She picked out each tree as she walked, surprised to find they matched the song completely. If this was a dream, she told herself . . .

and then stopped for, from the center of the grove, where the single line of smoke had emerged, someone was singing the same song in a low, lyrical voice.

Jenna raised her hand and they all stopped. She cupped her ear, calling them to listen.

It was Catrona who spoke. "That voice . . ." then trailed off into silence.

Jenna turned and gathered them to her. "That is not the voice of a Grenna," she whispered.

One by one they nodded.

"Do you know this song?" Catrona asked Jareth.

"It be like a lullaby my mother be singing," he said. "Like—and not like." He whispered:

"Of all in green jerkin and all in green gown,
'Tis my baby Jareth who carries the crown . . .

least my mother be singing *Jareth.* Another's might be saying . . ."

"*Marek,*" said Marek. "And *Sandor,* when he be born."

Sandor nodded. "And both when we be sick with the pox together."

"What do we do?" Jenna asked Catrona.

"I know how to fight and how to live in the woods," Catrona said. "I am a fine blanket companion and a good provider. But this is beyond my knowing. It is priestess-work."

Petra shook her head. "I know that song from the Hame. And my Mother Alta taught me the meaning of each tree in the alphabet for so it is written in Alta's own *Book of Light.* Ash is for remembrance, birch for recovery, larch for the light, and the rest. But where we are and who is singing, I do not know. Perhaps only the Anna herself knows."

"The Anna herself is as puzzled as you," Jenna said, and muttered, "unless I am not the Anna."

"You be," Jareth said. "Even the Grenna be calling you so."

"Then who. . . ?" Jenna bit her lip.

"There is only one way to find out," Catrona said, raising her sword.

Jenna put her hand upon Catrona's. "Whoever she is, she sings a song known to the sisters and to them as well." She nodded at Jareth, Marek, and Sandor.

"She means to tell us she is both sister and mother to us."

"To us all," Petra added.

"And who is that but Alta herself," Jenna said.

"I said you would know." Petra smiled.

"It is a guess. And a poor one at that," Jenna said. "Let me go first and we will see."

"We be going together," Jareth said.

And they did, crashing through the underbrush, the horses trailing behind them.

As they rushed forward, the trees seemed to extend upward till they touched the sky and arched over, their branches laced together in a roof of green through which the sunlight shone in filtered rays. The trunks of the trees became mottled pillars of marble with dark green veins running from the top. The ground beneath their feet became a floor upon which the pattern of grass and petal and leaf remained.

In the very center of the hall was a great hearth with a green cradle standing before it. Rocking the cradle was a woman dressed in a light green silk gown with darker green leaves embroidered on the hem of the skirt and gold vining twined upon the bodice. Her hair was pure white and plaited in two braids. She wore a crown of sweet-briar, a wristlet of wild rose, and a collar of thistle inter-mixed with annulets of gold. Her feet were bare.

"She . . . she be your mother, Anna," whispered Marek.

"She be having your hair and your eyes," added Sandor. "And your mouth."

Jareth just stared.

But Petra had already knelt before the woman, offering up her palms which were as yet unincised with the blue priestess sign. Catrona, too, had knelt, placing her sword by the woman's bare feet.

Jenna shook her head. "No. No, you are not my mother. I was never cradled in that." She went to the green crib and tore away the veil of vines.

The cradle was empty.

"I was born in blood between the thighs of a Slipskin woman. I was borne off by the midwife and rescued by a sister of Selden Hame. That much I believe. That much I can accept. I killed a man called the Hound more by accident than design. And I cut off the hand of one named the Bull. If that fulfills prophecy, then so be it. But do not ask me to believe this . . . this counterfeit." She could feel the skin tighten across her cheekbones. She was too angry to cry.

The woman smiled slowly, reached down, and raised up both Petra and Catrona. She pulled Petra to stand by her right side and Catrona to stand by her left. Then she looked directly at Jenna.

"Good. Good. I would have been disappointed if you had accepted all this." She waved her hand around the hall which turned back at once into a simple grove. "Accepted it without question."

Jareth let out a loud breath.

"Without question? I have *hundreds* of questions," said Jenna. "But I do not know which one to ask first. Who are you? Where are we? Why are we here? Where are the Greenfolk now? And . . ."

"And what about your sisters?" the woman asked.

"That most of all," Jenna said.

"Come, sit, and I will tell you all I can," the woman said.

"But what be we calling you?" asked Jareth.

The woman smiled and held out her hand to him. "You can call me Alta," she said.

He shook his head. "No. Like the Anna, I be not believing . . ."

She smiled. "Really," she said, shrugging, "that *is* my name." She gestured to the ground and sat down herself. The others followed her lead. "I was named, of course, after the Goddess, as were many of the girls of my day."

"When *was* your day?" Jenna asked, pushing away Duty who had come to nuzzle against her ear. The mare shook her head vigorously and plodded away to stand near the open fire.

"You will have to suspend your suspicions, Jenna," Alta said.

"How do you know my name?"

"How did the Grenna?"

Jenna was silent. She plucked a blade of grass and put it into her mouth, chewing absently.

"I am that Alta who harvested the hillsides and set up the system of the Hames. I wrote the *Book of Light*. And I brought the wisdom of the breathing and the Eye-Mind and the mysteries of the dark sisters to the Hames," Alta said quietly.

"Then you are Great Alta herself," whispered Catrona.

"No, no, my Cat," Alta said. "I dance over no rainbows nor can I walk over a bridge of light. I was a woman wed to a king and unable to bear a child. So he put me aside and took another wife. And another. In grief, I began to gather the forgotten girl children left to die on the hills of the Dales. I fashioned little carts and towed them behind me, more in madness than with any goal in mind.

"The Grenna found me wandering, crazed, pulling seven carts full of mewling, stinking babes and brought us down here—to the Green World. They taught me how to care for the children: how to play at the wand, how to see in the woods. They told me what would be in the world to come. They showed me how to control my breath and call up my twin. And when they had done all that, they sent us back into the Dales. But it was not one day or one month or even one year that had passed. It was a hundred. And my disappearance from the Dales had become a story, a tale to frighten children at the hearthfire. *Be good or the Alta will get you.*

"When we returned, a new story began and unwanted women—the barren and the homely and the lonely—came to our aid. We built the first Hame near here."

"Wilma's Crossing," Petra said.

"Yes, Wilma's Crossing. And the rest came after. I wrote down what the Greenfolk had taught me, or at least what I could remember of it, intermixed—I suppose—with the wisdoms of the Dales. I called what I wrote the *Book of Light*. And then . . ." She sighed deeply.

"And then you returned here?" Jenna asked.

"That was much later," Alta said. "When my work was done; when I was ready to die. My women brought me to the doors of the cave as I instructed and left me. When they were gone, I came down into the core. And I have been here ever since."

Marek sat up. "But, Alta, that be . . ."

". . . hundreds of years," finished Sandor.

"Time moves differently here," Alta said. She reached up and took off the briar crown, setting it by her side. "And I had to wait until the Anna came."

"Be others coming afore?" Jareth asked.

"A few. And they saw the hall and the cradle. They heard the song. They ate my bread and drank my wine. And then they left to find themselves alone and pale on the hillside, their loved ones long in the grave. But they knew *me* not. They knew only their own dreams." She took off the thistle collar and set it upon the crown.

"Why me?" asked Jenna. "Why us? Why now?"

"Because what I began must now end," Alta said. "The time has come for the world to turn again. Core to rind, rind to core. The Grenna call it the world's paring. It happens every few hundred years."

"Every few hundred years!" Jenna was both astonished and outraged.

Alta laughed. "Do you think we of the Dales are all there is in the world? We are but one apple on a vast tree. One tree in a vast grove. One grove in . . ." She pointed beyond Jenna.

Remembering the other groves in the meadow that extended to the horizon, Jenna whispered hoarsely, ". . . in a vast green."

"Yes, Jenna. You want to be and not to be *The* Anna. But there are many Annas. Have been many. Will be again. Oh, they will not all be called *Anna*. Their names will be a multitude." Alta touched Jenna's mouth with her finger. Her finger was cool. "But you are *The* Anna for *this* turning. And you have many things yet to learn." Standing, she said in a voice that, while sweet, could not be denied: "Come." She stood, taking crown and collar with her.

They rose and followed her straight toward the fire, Jenna by her side and the others in a line behind. As they approached the fire, it seemed to recede before them.

"So it is with time here," Alta commented, continuing on toward the flames. At last, having reached some particular destination known only to her, she stopped and gestured around them.

Looking carefully, Jenna saw they were in a cozy kitchen just like the one in Selden Hame. Any minute she expected to see Donya, Doey, and their helpers come bustling through the door. There were metal sconces on the wall with tallow candles shedding a brilliant light, a roast on a spit turning of its own accord over a well-set fire. Yet as sharp as the central image was, the edges were soft and unfocused as are things seen out of the corner of the eye. And for all the hominess, there was a strangeness, an aloneness at the heart of the place. Jenna felt uneasy. She drew in three deep breaths.

At last she spoke. "This is not real either. No more than the cradle; no more than the hall."

"Not real?" Marek said, disappointment clear in his voice. "But it be like our Da's house."

"*Just* like," added Sandor.

"It is nothing but glamour and seeming," Jenna warned. "Look at the candles. Look at the fire. There are no shadows here."

"And no dark sisters," Catrona said.

"You are right." Alta nodded solemnly. "You are right *in a way*. And you are wrong as well. This *is* only a seeming but it is constructed out of your memories and your desires and your dreams. It is not meant to tempt or distract you. It is meant to comfort and remind you."

"It is too odd here," Jenna said, shivering. "I feel no comfort, only a strange hollowness."

"Let it come to you," Alta said. "Sit—and allow it room in your heart."

Petra sat down first, drawing up a solid-looking oaken chair with inlaid panels of wood. The chair was so large that when she sat back, her feet barely touched the floor, only enough to stir up the rushes that had been sweetened with dried roses and verbena.

Jenna breathed in the familiar scent, remembering. Just so the Great Hall at her Hame had smelled. Just so. She shook her head vigorously and remained standing.

The boys all sprawled suddenly on their bellies by the hearth, like puppies after a long run. Sandor took a stick and began poking at the fire and Marek stared dreamily into the flames. Jareth put his chin on his arms, but his eyes still moved restlessly around the room.

Sighing deeply, Catrona lowered herself into an armed chair with a deep cushion, stretching her legs toward the fire. She put her head back and stared at the ceiling, smiling.

Jenna's fingers traced the design on the back of Catrona's chair. Alta's sign was encised there: the circle with the two peaks that almost met in a cross. *It was too perfect,* she thought. She distrusted perfection. In the Dales they said *Perfection is the end of growing. In other words—death. I did not bring them all here to die in comfort.* Out loud she said, "You told us we had many things yet to learn. Teach us—and then let us go."

Alta smiled. "Much I have to teach you, you know already, Jenna. The Game of Eye-Mind that trained you for the woods. The game of wands that trained your sword arm. And you have called your sister even before your first flow. You love both women and men, and that, too, makes you ready for what is to come. But Jenna, Jo-an-enna, you are still so much a child. You fear your destiny. You fear to hold power. You fear to reach beyond your own hearth."

"I do not fear that. After all, I am here." She shifted back and forth uneasily from foot to foot.

"Annuanna," Alta said sharply.

Jenna stood perfectly still. It was her secret name, that only her foster mothers—and they long dead—and the priestess of Selden Hame knew. She felt herself trembling, not on the outside but on the inside; not with fear but with a kind of readiness, like a cat after its prey.

"When you are in the world beyond the green, you must remember how my fire always goes ahead, expanding as far as I let it, always beyond reach and yet by my hand. So must your dreams be, so must your desires be."

The trembling inside stopped, replaced by a sudden icy calm. *Riddles,* Jenna thought angrily. Then she said the word out loud: "Riddles."

"Not riddles," said Alta, shaking her head. "But like the wisdom of the Dales, which you and your companions so love to quote, merely a useful tool for understanding. For remembering. Remembering is what you must do most of all, Jenna. Remember my fire. Remember the green world." She waved her hand across the table and it was suddenly crowded with goblets, platters, and plates.

As if wakening from a deep dream, Petra, Catrona, and the boys came to the table and began to eat noisily and with gusto. There was pigeon pie, salads of cos and cress, platters of fruit. There were ewers of wine, both deep red and golden white, and the soft rosy-colored wine that Jenna fancied most of all.

"And will this faery food sustain us?" Jenna asked abruptly, reaching over and picking up a loaf of braided bread. She waved it toward Alta.

"It will," Alta said. "Just as my fire warms you. Just as my chairs give your legs rest."

Downing a second cup of the dark red wine, Catrona added, "Just as this wine strengthens my heart."

"That wine . . ." Jenna began, putting her hand on Catrona's arm, "does you no good. You know it eats away at your stomach. We cannot have you sick for days with the flux."

"This wine will not harm her," said Alta. "It will strengthen her for the coming fight."

Jareth pushed himself away from the table with such force his cup overturned, spilling wine along the grain of the wood. In the flickering candlelight, the wine picked up the color of the oak, looking then like old blood until it dripped over the table in a golden fall. "What be this fight?" he asked harshly. "You be knowing more of it than we. Tell us. Finally."

"It is the fight that began in my time and must end in yours," Alta said. Her voice was so soft, they all had to strain to hear it. "It is the fight that goes on and on in this circle. The fight to bring light and dark together. The fight to bring men and women together."

"And if we win it," Jenna asked as quietly, "will it be won for all time?"

"One apple on a vast tree, Jenna," Alta reminded her. "One tree in a vast grove."

"One grove in a vast green," Jenna said. "I remember. I remember, but it does not make me glad." She stood, and the others stood with her. "Is there more to learn?"

"Only this," Alta said. She took off the wristlet of rose, and set it alongside the collar and crown on the table. "Take the crown, young Marek."

When he held it gingerly between his palms, Alta put her hands over his. "And you shall crown the king."

Then she looked back at the objects on the table. "Sandor, take up the wristlet."

He bent over, picked up the wristlet, letting it sit in his right palm. Alta covered his right hand with hers. "And you shall guide the king's right arm."

Alta herself picked up the collar from the table. She

held it for a long moment without speaking, staring at Jareth as if weighing her words.

Jenna felt something inside go hot and then cold. She bit her lip. If Marek was to crown the king—whoever he was—and Sandor to guide his arm, then what could the collar mean? Slave to that unnamed king? Or a noose around his neck?

Not Jareth, she thought. *Not my good friend.* She put out her hand to stop Alta's words.

"No!" she cried. "Do not give it to him. If it is to be his death, give it to me instead."

Alta looked up and smiled sadly. "What you and Catrona and Petra must do is written in your hearts. You learned it from the *Book of Light* when you were children. You carry it inside. But for the men who do not understand it yet, there must be these reminders. And the collar has been waiting for the last of the heroes. I must give it to him, Jenna. I must."

"I be not minding, Anna," Jareth said, his eyes steady on hers. "And I be not afraid. I be following you, and you already bringing me to a stranger destiny than I might otherwise know, safe in the mill beside my old Da. That Anna be willing to take my death for me be enough."

Not Anna—Jenna, she wanted to say. But she saw that for such courage she had to be the Anna for him. So she kept silent.

Alta placed the collar around his neck and it turned into a band of purest green.

"You shall not speak again until the crown is in place and the king's right hand has won the war. After that, all that you speak shall be accorded great honor. But if this collar is broken before time, what you say could shatter the fellowship, lose the throne, and the circle would remain unclosed forever. For with this collar, you will have read the hearts of men and the minds of women and none likes to be reminded of what they think and feel by another."

Jareth put his hand up to his throat, turning slowly to gaze at each of his companions. His eyes grew large and small, like moons, as he stared at them. At last he looked at Jenna, until she dropped her glance, uneasy with his fierce examination.

"Oh, my poor Jareth," she whispered, putting her hand out to him.

He opened his mouth as if to speak, but no words came out, only a strangulation of sound. He did not touch her hand, pulling away to stand instead shoulder to shoulder with the other boys.

"And now," Alta said, "you must go. I will give you bread and wine for the journey, for it is a long riding between here and tomorrow. And if you speak of what you saw and heard in this green world, you will be believed no more than if you spoke with Jareth's voice. Farewell." She raised her hand and, as if they had been commanded, the horses trotted over to her. She picked up their trailing reins, holding them out.

One by one Jenna and her companions walked to their mounts. Jenna got up first. Next Catrona, her unsheathed sword in hand. Jareth got onto the bay mare, then reached down to help Petra up. Last of all, Marek and Sandor leaped onto their horse.

"Will we see you again?" Jenna asked Alta.

Alta smiled. "You will see me again at the end of your life. Come to the doors and they will open for you. You—and one other."

"One other?" Jenna whispered the question. When there was no answer to it, she turned her horse and headed in the direction Alta pointed, toward the far horizon.

The others followed.

At the beginning they rode slowly, as if reluctant to leave Alta's meadow. Then one at a time they kicked their horses into a gallop. First the sun, then the stars, fell behind them like snow, though it was neither day nor night but a kind of eternal dusk. As they rode summer followed spring, winter followed fall, and yet the road remained the same. They rode on and on toward the place where land and sky met.

Once Jenna glanced back. She saw Alta standing by her grove, in a circle of Grenna. When she looked again, Alta, the mannikins, and the grove were all gone.

THE MYTH:

And then Great Alta said, "The crown shall be for the head, for one must rule with wisdom. And the wristlet shall be for the hand's cunning. But as for the collar, which surrounds the neck, it shall be for the tongue, for without tongue we are not human. How else can we tell the story that is history; how else can we hymn or carol; how else can we curse or cry? It is the collar that is the highest gift of all."

BOOK THREE

BLANKET COMPANIONS

THE MYTH:

Then Great Alta drew apart the curtain of her hair and showed them the plains of war. On the right side were the armies of the light. On the left side were the armies of the night. Yet when the sun set and the moon rose they were the same.

"They are blanket companions," quoth Great Alta. "They are to one another sword and shield, shadow and light. I would have you learn of war so you may live in peace."

And she set them down on the bloody plain for their schooling.

THE LEGEND:

There is a barren plain in the center of the Dales, where but one kind of flower grows—the Harvest Rose. Little grass, and it quite brown; little water, and it undrinkable; only dust and gravel and the Harvest Rose.

It is said that once the plain was a forest of great trees, so tall they seemed to pierce the sky. And the cat and the coney lived in harmony there.

But one day two giants met on that plain, their heads helmeted but their bodies bare. For three days and three nights they wrestled with one another. Their mighty feet stomped the good earth into dust. Their mighty hands tore trees from the ground. They flailed at each other with the trees as though with mere cudgels or sticks. And at last, when the two of them lay dying, side by side, they

*ripped off their helmets only to discover they were so
alike, they might have been twins.*

*The blood from the battle watered the torn and
dying earth. And at each drop grew the Harvest Rose, a
blood-red blossom with a white face imprinted on the
petals, each and every face the same.*

THE STORY:

When they emerged from a final copse of trees lining
the great meadow, the moon was full overhead.

"The moon?" Jenna was puzzled. "When we left it
was not moon time."

"It has been more than one moon since you left, sister," a voice whispered in her ear. Jenna turned slightly.
Skada was sitting behind her. Her face was a good deal
thinner than Jenna remembered. And older, somehow.

"Just how many moons . . ." Jenna began, then
glanced past Skada to stare at the rest of her companions.

Catrona and Katri on the bay mare stared back.
There was a streak of white running through Catrona's
short cap of hair, a matching streak in Katri's. Jareth,
with his green collar tight across his throat, had a leaner
look and Marek a downy moustache feathering his lip.
Sandor's cheeks were sprinkled with the beginnings of a
beard. But it was Petra who had changed the most. She
was no longer a girl but a young woman, with a soft
curve of breast showing beneath her tunic.

Jenna put a hand up to her own face, as if she might
feel any change there, but her fingers held no memories.

"Look at us! Look!" Marek said, his voice booming
into the night.

"I . . ." Sandor began and then, as if surprised by the
depth of the syllable, stopped.

Opening his mouth, Jareth strained for a sound. When none came, he closed it again, shaking his head slowly at first, then faster and faster, banging his fist on his thigh in frustration.

It was Petra who spoke for them all. "The legends are true. *Cocooned in time,* the Grenna said. But they did not say how much time. How long . . ." her voice trailed off.

Jenna got off her horse, followed by Skada. Turning to her dark sister, she asked: "How many more than one moon, Skada?"

"I do not know. Many. After a time, I lost the count."

"Yet we ate not nor did we sleep," Catrona said. "We hold no memory of those passages through time. How can that be?"

"It is because of Alta," Petra said.

"And the Grenna," Catrona added.

"It be because of Anna," Marek and Sandor said together.

They all dismounted and the boys were quickly introduced to Katri and Skada. But the dark sisters' arrival was only a small, familiar mystery inside the larger one. It was the question of time that consumed them all.

"Is it one year or . . ." Catrona hesitated.

"Or hundreds?" Katri finished for her.

"Hundreds!" Marek seemed surprised at the possibility. "It be not hundreds. What about our Ma then?"

"And our Da?"

"What about our sisters?" Petra asked. "And the warnings?"

Jenna twisted the priestess ring around her little finger. She was not heedless of the sisters. But she had to know first where they were—what time and what place. Staring at Jareth, she whispered, "You have not mentioned his Mai." She did not add her own names: Pynt and A-ma and all the sisters at Selden Hame. What use was such a tally when they were so lost? She would not even *think* of Carum, would not conjure his face now. But Skada knew. She reached out and touched Jenna's hand.

They were not tired, but they thought it best to rest the night. In the daylight they might discover the path, might recognize some familiar landmark. Besides, the horses would fare better in the day without the added burden of the dark sisters. And they all needed to think.

"To focus," Catrona said, using the very word and tone Jenna remembered from their days in Selden Hame when Catrona had taught her about living in the woods.

As part of that focus, they taught the boys how to match them breath for breath around a small campfire. Catrona felt the need for light far exceeded the danger. She told the boys the story about the five beasts who quarreled before they discovered that breath was the most important part of life. Jenna recalled Mother Alta telling that tale, and how it sat heavily in the priestess' sour mouth. Catrona's telling was far more sprightly. The boys laughed when she was done, even Jareth, though his laughter was silent.

After the story, Marek and Sandor regaled them with rhymes their Da had taught them, all about pulling the ferry across the water. *Teaching rhymes,* Catrona called them.

"Every craft and every guild has them," she said. "The baker, the herdsman, the miller . . ."

Jareth interrupted by placing his hand on Catrona's. He gestured to himself.

"A miller . . . a miller," muttered Katri.

They were all embarrassed into silence until Petra began to sing a lullaby in a sweet voice that soon had them all rubbing their eyes.

"We will rise with the sun," Jenna said.

"*Before* the sun," Catrona amended.

THE SONG:

Sisters' Lullay

Hush and sleep ye,
Shush and keep ye,
Safe within the
Hame's strong walls

Naught shall harm ye.
We shall charm ye
With the song the
Night bird calls.

> *Sisters strong shall*
> *Keep the cradle*
> *Sisters long shall*
> *Watch the way*

> *Sisters all shall*
> *Guard and guide ye*
> *Till ye wake at*
> *Break of day.*

Hush and sleep ye,
Shush and keep ye,
Alta watches
From above.

We will praise ye,
We will raise ye,
Light and dark in
Alta's love.

THE STORY:

They drifted into sleep one after another until only Jenna and Skada were awake, side by side on Jenna's blanket.

"I have missed you," Skada said. "And missed this world, so bright and deafening."

"Which have you missed more?"

"In equal measure." Skada laughed. Then she whispered, "But it has been hard on you."

"It has been harder on the others," Jenna said. "And the fault . . ."

". . . is not yours, dear sister," Skada said. "This is a time when a circle closes. That you are the clasp is not a fault, merely an accident of time."

"Jareth said I was a linchpin."

"We will miss his clear voice."

Jenna thought about that. It was what she had been feeling, but had not dared to say aloud. "I . . ."

"We. Is it so difficult to accept that you are not alone, Jenna? That we all share the burden?"

Suddenly Jenna remembered Alta's words: *You want to be and not to be the Anna.* How easily Alta had said it. How hard it was to accept. She wanted to be the center, the clasp, the linchpin, but she did not want the enormous weight of it. Yet she could not have the one without the other. How much easier to share. Not *I* but *we*. She reached out and touched Skada's hand. They did not speak again, just lay there hand in hand until sleep finally claimed them.

"Jenna! Jenna!" The voice seemed far away, a dying fall of sound. Jenna awoke with a start to a day bright with birdsong. Catrona was shaking her by the shoulder. She sat up, almost reluctant to leave the comfort of sleep.

Looking around, Jenna saw the horses cropping grass by a well-worn roadside, the others still asleep.

"Catrona, I had the strangest dream," she began. "There was a vast meadow and . . ." She stopped. A wide streak of white ran through Catrona's hair and the runes across her brow were deeper than Jenna remembered.

"No dream, little Jen. The meadow, the grove, the hearth and hall. No dream. Unless two can dream the same."

Jenna stood slowly. Two might possibly dream alike but that did not explain the age creeping across Catrona's face. Or the fact that Duty, who had just lifted her face from the grass, had a dusting of white hairs on her nose. Or that Jareth, beginning to stir, wore a collar of green around his neck.

"No dream," Jenna agreed. "But if it is true, then where are we? And *when* are we?"

"As for where," Catrona said, "that I know now. This is the road to Wilma's Crossing Hame. It has not changed that much in the thirty years since I was last here."

"Thirty?" Jenna asked.

"I was a girl missioning here," Catrona said. "It was my last stop—and a dare."

"Why a dare?" Jenna asked.

"Because it was so far from my own Hame and across the famous forest of the Grenna and because it was the very first Hame. And because I had boasted too much about not being afraid to come."

"And were you afraid?"

Catrona laughed. "Of course I was afraid. I may have been a bit of a boaster, but I was no fool. I never saw any Grenna, of course. Doubted they existed. But fog and mist and men I found plenty. As for the men, well, I kicked my way out of several encounters and marched with a black eye but my maidenhead intact into Wilma's Crossing Hame." She chuckled at the memory.

"And . . ."

"And they laughed at me and gave me a hot bath and told me the facts of a woman's life, which somehow I had neglected to listen to when my Mother Alta imparted them. I got my flow that next week and had a man on the way back to my own Hame. Katri never forgave me for not waiting for her."

Jenna blushed furiously.

"Yes, this is the road to Wilma's Crossing. There the road goes back through the forest." She pointed to the long, empty path. "And there are Alta's Pins." She pointed ahead to a pair of rolling hillocks, grass-covered dunes that stretched for almost a mile. "Nothing like them in the whole of the Dales."

"Thirty years," Jenna mused. She combed through her hair with her fingers, then braided it up, twisting a dark ribband around the bottom to hold the plait in place.

"Thirty—or more," Catrona said.

"How much more?"

"I would tell you if I knew, child. I puzzled all night on it." Giving Jenna a swift, sure hug, she added, "As for that dream we both had, I recall there was food in it as well." She went to her own blanket and the saddlebags that she had used for a pillow. Opening up the flap of one, she rummaged around. "Yes, here. Quite a dream, that can supply such as this." She pulled out two loaves of a braided bread and a leather flask. "Come, girl, *First up, first fed,* we used to say in the army." She broke off the heel of the bread and handed it to Jenna. "In fact, *First up, finest fed.* As I recall, you were always partial to the ends, even as a babe."

Jenna took the bread gratefully and started chewing. At the first bite, a sharp burst of some sweet herb filled her mouth. She sighed.

Smiling at her, Catrona took a long draught from the flask, then grinned. "The red. She gave us the red. Bless her."

At that, Jenna laughed. "Only you, Catrona, would

bless someone for wine." But she reached out and took a sip herself. She was careful not to mention to Catrona that the wine was not red at all but the gentle rosy drink that she preferred. Either Catrona was losing her judgment, or there was a strange magic at work here. It was not worth mentioning either way.

The others were up soon after, finishing off both loaves of bread and the flask which, though no one remarked it greatly, supplied milk for Petra and some kind of dark liquid for each of the boys, which Jenna thought might be tea.

They saddled the horses and were away just as the sun climbed between the rolling hills Catrona had called Alta's Pins.

"As I remember it," Catrona told them, "it is but a morning's walk from here to the Hame."

"Then it will be a short ride with the horses fresh," said Jenna.

Following Catrona, they threaded their way in a single line through the Pins and across a boggy meadow that was full of spring wildflowers, white, yellow, and blue. Quite soon they saw the wreckage of several buildings jagged against the clean slate of sky.

"Too late," Jenna whispered to herself as they neared the ruined Hame. She braced herself for the inevitable bodies and the horrible smell of death. "Too late for any of them." The whisper took on Sorrel's accent and she cursed herself and her companions for spending the time they had in Alta's grove.

Dismounting at the broken gate, they wandered through the silent ruins. Vines twisted up between fallen stones. The weedy arberry had taken root in the cracks. There was a scattering of linseed along the pathways, the blue flowers bending in a passing wind. But there were no bodies; there were no bones.

"This be not happening yesterday," Marek remarked

cautiously, his fingers smoothing down his new moustache.

"Nor the day before that," Petra added. She plucked up a yellow flower and crushed it against her palm. "How long . . ." her voice trailed off.

Squatting, Catrona smoothed her hand across the gravelly ruin of a side wall. "A year. Or two. Or more. It takes a season at least for arberry and linseed, tansy and hound's tooth, to take hold in a waste. A season at least for vines to begin to twist up through the walls."

Sandor's eyes grew wide. "And see how high they go."

Jareth measured the vines and they were five times the width of his hand, from little finger to thumb. He spread his hand, counting silently. *Five.*

Sitting down heavily on a great stone, Jenna drew in a deep *latani* breath. When she finally spoke she hoped her tones were measured. "We must find out what year it is. Whether one has passed or . . ." Glancing at Jareth, whose hand still silently tallied the length of the vines, she finished her thought. "Or five. We must know how long since we rode out."

"And then find out what damage to the Hames," Petra said.

Jenna nodded. "And then . . ."

"Hush! Now!" From her squatting position, Catrona had flung herself onto the ground, ear down, listening. For a moment she was still. Then suddenly she sat up. With a sweep of her hand, she whispered, "Riders!"

"Our horses . . ." Jenna cried, but she threw herself down on the ground and felt the pounding of the earth under her cheek. The riders were close. Saying no more, she drew her sword from its sheath and lay on the ground, waiting. All of her anger, unhappiness, and fear were focused for what was sure to be a fierce battle. The ground foretold many horsemen.

Petra and the boys flung themselves down as well, the boys wriggling about to draw their knives.

Jenna could see between two of the fallen stones, as if through the narrow line of an arrow slit. At first all she could make out were the trees across the road; then a gray cloud of dust from the horses' hooves rising up against the background, obscuring the trees. Slowly, the front line of the oncoming riders resolved itself and Jenna could see that one of the lead horses was gray.

"A gray!" she called over to Catrona, not sure if her voice could be heard in the building thunder. "A company of king's horse."

Catrona nodded.

Jenna could feel a shiver run across the back of her shoulders, as if something cold had snaked its way over her neck. Then she shook her head and whatever it was she had felt was gone. Looking aside at the others, she nodded. The boys nodded back but Petra's eyes were wide and unseeing. Jenna guessed she was praying.

A prayer would not be amiss, she thought, trying to remember one. But the pounding of the hooves and the rising dust and the sun on her head and the fear that her friends might die because of her pushed all prayer from her mind except the one word: *now . . . now . . . now.*

Then Catrona leaped up, sword raised, and Jenna followed, screaming what was left of her fear into the faces of the galloping troop. She could feel heat in her face and the remains of the rosy wine threatening to leave her stomach and a throbbing of a vein over her right eye.

And then suddenly the first of the horses, a black gelding, was pulled to a rearing stop by its rider. Behind it, the gray and then the others fanned out. There were more than twenty-one. Many more.

Jenna's sword hand began to shake. She reached over with her left hand and grasped her right wrist to hold it steady. She heard a strange braying coming from Catrona's direction and could not make it out. She dared a quick glance.

Catrona was laughing and lowering her sword. *Laughing!*

The man on the black horse was laughing as well. When the noise had settled, he spoke. "Well, well, well, Catkin. Like an old copper, ye turn op in the oddest of hands." He grinned, showing a mouth gapped with uneven teeth. His beard was luxuriantly black and white; his eyes narrow and the piercing blue of a cold spring sky; his tongue strange to Jenna's ears.

Catrona sheathed her sword. "As often as not I turn up in *your* hands, Piet."

The man Piet dismounted. He was a big man, his solid flesh starting to run to fat, but he moved with a feline grace. "Ye've not been in *my* hands for so lang a time, girl."

"How long a time?" Catrona asked, almost casually. Jenna held her breath.

Piet narrowed his eyes even more and grinned. Her caution had not fooled him. "Looking for compliments at yourn age, my catkin? Or somewhat more, eh?" He laughed. Jenna had been expecting a cold sound, and calculating, but it was full and warm. "And where is that dark, daring sister of yourn?"

"She is around," Catrona said. She held out her hand to him and he took it. Instead of shaking it, he simply held it, his massive fingers wrapping hers.

Jenna was surprised that Catrona let her hand be prisoned that way.

"I've missed ye, girl. No doubt of it. Nane to drink me doon like ye can, after a good fight. And nane like ye ever for a blanket companion, eh?"

Catrona laughed lightly, gaily, a sound Jenna had never heard her make before.

Clearing her throat, Jenna moved toward Catrona. Petra came over to stand by her side. The three boys, knives still tightly in their hands, clustered together.

"The kittens are restless," Piet said, dropping her hand at last. "Introduce us to this litter of yourn."

Catrona turned and signaled them to her and they came like bidden children, though Jenna was not happy at the thought.

"The boys are from Callatown. Sandor and Marek are, as you can see, brothers. And the small one is Jareth."

Piet put out his hand to them each in turn, nodding and saying their names aloud. Sandor and Marek gave him greeting but Jareth's silence troubled the big man.

"He is mute," Catrona explained.

"From birth?" asked Piet. "Can he sign his wishes?"

"God touched," Petra said, stepping forward. "And it is new."

"Ah, the collar," said Piet, as if he understood. "And ye child, what name is yourn?"

"I am no child, but priestess-trained. My name is Petra." She lifted her head and stared into his eyes.

"Ye be a child still to me, for all ye speak daily with gods. But well come, Petra. I like children—and I like priestesses. They all speak in riddles. It makes a big man like me feel small." He grinned at her. She could not help but grin back.

"And this beauty," he said, turning toward Jenna.

"Watch your tongue," Catrona said, "or she will have it. She is the best of us. She is the reason we are here."

At her tone, his grin faded at once. "And what do ye mean, me girl."

"She is Jo-an-enna. She is the White One. The Anna."

For a long moment Piet stared at Jenna, measuring her by some internal reckoning. Then he shook his head and laughed out loud, a wilder braying than Catrona's. When the bold laughter had run its course, he stared at her again. "The *White One?* Have ye taken leave . . . Catrona? Ye've never owned such nonsense afore. *The White One!* She's nowt but a girl."

"Nonetheless . . ." Catrona began.

Just then the man on the gray dismounted and walked over to them, limping badly, his right leg swinging stiffly from an unbending knee. "Jo-an-enna, you say. Could you be called else? A pet name? Or a family name?" His face was clearly thinned down with old pain, but Jenna thought there was something terribly familiar about his cheeks and the long lashes and the hair.

"Jenna," she whispered, staring at him. "I am called Jenna by my friends." The limping man was and was not like Carum. *But how many years had it been?* He was taller and darker and she felt nothing when she looked at him but a vague tug of reminiscence. *Nothing at all.* How could that possibly be?

"Are you Carum's White Jenna, then?" he asked. Something narrowed in his face so that he had a fox's look, sly, calculating, cautious, and feral. Carum had never looked like that.

Jenna breathed out slowly. She hadn't realized she'd been holding her breath till it sighed out of her. "You are *not* Carum," she said, but it was almost a question.

He grinned, looking more wolflike than fox. "I—Carum? What a thing I shall have to tell him when I see him next. Five years goes by and the girl he loves mistakes his older brother for . . ."

"His older brother!" It was an explosion of sound and relief. "No wonder you look like him. You must be . . ." She reached back in memory and pulled out a name. "You must be Pike."

"Pike . . . I have not been called that in years."

Piet interrupted smoothly, "He is Gorum. King Gorum. Majesty-in-exile now. Best remember."

"Five years in exile then? We have much to talk about, Piet," said Catrona.

"And plenty of time afore dark to speak of it," Piet said. "And after dark—well, plenty of time for that, too, eh?"

Catrona patted his hand.

"But why do ye call *this* girl the White One?" asked Piet. "What signs brought ye to it? Ye, Catrona, of all folk?"

The forty or so men dismounted, gathering around noisily.

Looking them all over, Catrona snorted. "I will tell it once the horses are pastured and we have split a bottle and some bread." She smiled at Piet. "You do have bread? And bottles?"

"What army goes without?" asked Piet.

"Is this an army?" Catrona countered. "Ragtag, and scarcely one shield amongst three? No helms. No pikes— begging your pardon, Majesty." She made a quick almost mocking obeisance.

"It is but part of one," Piet admitted.

"And the rest?"

"On a rade. With *his* brother."

"His brother?" Jenna could feel a strange ache suddenly start up in her belly.

"Him that's called Longbow," Piet answered.

"Longbow? Carum? On a rade? It cannot possibly be. He is a scholar, not a fighter," Jenna said.

"Perhaps back then when there weren't no war, twas a scholar, gel. Perhaps he bain reading up on bow shooting in his books. He is a good shot now, though he doesna like swords yet," Piet said. He gave Jenna another searching look, then spoke to Catrona. "Come into the Hame, gel. It's nowt but shambles, but the kitchen still stands. We have bottles well hidden. And bread. And a couple of deer hanging."

"Well, well, well," Catrona mused. "When you are not on a rade, you are in a well-stocked kitchen." She patted Piet's belly. "This is not just five years' growth."

Laughing, Piet put his hand over hers. "This belly's been longer than five years growing, gel, as well ye know. And I've been slimming these last months. But ye be no great beauty yersel. There's gray in yer hair now."

"At least I have it all."

"I have enough," he said, laughing.

Jenna's mouth drew down into a thin line, her eyes narrowing. "Should there be guards?"

"We own the road," the king said, a bit petulantly.

"Not good enough," Petra whispered. "You missed *our* coming."

"What makes ye think ye were missed?" Piet asked.

"You were just not accounted a problem," said the king.

"Not good enough," Jenna seconded, "for the sisters who dwelt here first."

"That is an old, old story," Piet said, his hand still over Catrona's. "And not a pretty one. This is a new."

"Tell us," Jenna demanded. "Tell us the story. *Now!*"

"How is it ye know it not?" came a voice out of the crowd. "If ye be the Anna?"

"And where have *ye* been all these years?" asked another, a man with a scar lacing his right eye like a mask. "Under the hill or somewhat?"

Jareth's hand went suddenly to his collar, and Sandor made a small, sharp sound, like a startled daw.

"Yes," Catrona said slowly, drawing the word out as she drew her hand away from Piet's. She turned toward the questioner. "That is exactly where we have been. Under the hill."

Piet barked a laugh. "Ye have never been a good teller, my girl. And until this moment, I would have called ye the hard-headest warrior I have ever known. But now . . ." He shook his head. "Five years ye've been gone. I went seeking ye, at that Hame of yourn. Looking for fighters, we were. And nane seen the hide of ye. And now ye appear with a child's tale and asking us to believe it."

Sandor murmured, as much to the ground as the men near him: "*She* be saying you would not believe."

"And she is right," the king said. "Under the hill. Which of us can believe such a story."

"Believe it." Jenna spoke the words angrily. "Believe it. Though we still scarcely can credit it ourselves." She would say no more.

When the horses were unsaddled and hobbled to graze outside the walls, they gathered in the open kitchen, where an unbroken chimney thrust up against the sky. There they started a fire in the hearth and set stew pots to boil. It was then that Pike, the king-in-exile as the men called him, began the tale.

THE HISTORY:

The so-called Gender Wars took place over a period of no less than five years and no more than twenty, if the Book of Battles is to be believed. The disparity in numbers is due to the fact that the G'runs counted by the years in a king's reign rather than by a running tally. As they did not count in the years when the usurper K'las was on the throne, it is unclear exactly how long the battles continued. The reign of the king-in-exile (or the King in the Hills, as Doyle translates it) may be counted sequentially with K'las' reign or simultaneously. We have few notes from the Continent that refer even obliquely to the doings in the Dales at that time. It was as if a great cloak of mist had been wrapped around the island kingdom. If K'las himself ever penned any histories, they were likely burned by his enemies. History is always written by the victors.

Magon, of course, makes much of the difference in counts, citing legend and folk stories of the strange passage of time "under the hill" in Faeryland. But as such passages are common coin in the world's folklore (cf Magon's own "Telling Time in Faerie" Journal of International Folklore, Vol. 365, #7) such maunderings do little to add to our working knowledge of the awful, devastating Dale wars.

That these were wars of succession rather than a war of men against women, no matter the appellation that has carried down to modern times, is quite certain. In the Book of Battles we see lists of both sexes fighting side by side. This was not one great war but a series of small skirmishes over a number of years in which first one and then another king was placed on the precarious throne.

The seeds of this particular anarchy had been sown when the G'runs, a patriarchal society from the Continent, had conquered the learning-centered matriarchy of Alta worshippers. But over the four hundred years of conquest, the bloodlines thinned for the G'runs married only within narrow clans, hardly ever mixing with the lower, conquered classes. The once-united clans began to vie for power after a G'runian king made the mistake of taking a Dalian for his second wife, naming their son a legitimate heir. One chief of a powerful northern clan, a crafty warrior named K'las, managed to orchestrate a bloodless coup. As he was hereditary head of the clan armies (the Kingsmen) as well as a provincial governor, he had a strong power base. He ruled, as such army-backed leaders often do, with an iron fist. Or, as it says in the Book of Battles *"never his hand came out in friendship but in anger."* Of course, the book was penned by a member of the opposing party and so we must read carefully between the lines, as first Doyle and then Cowan have done. (See especially Cowan's intriguing *"The Kallas Controversy,"* Journal of the Isles, History IV, 7.)

There is a popular legend known as *"The King Under the Hill,"* found in some thirty-three variants in both the Upper and Lower Dales, in which the king is killed upon his throne and his three sons flee the province. One is slaughtered from the back, one is badly wounded, and the third, called majesty-in-exile, lives under the hill with the Greenfolk until his troops rally and call him forth into the light of day. Magon has taken great pains in trying to justify the legend with the history as we have been able to reconstruct it. But much of his verification rests heavily on his own much-disputed thesis about an historical figure he calls the White One or the Anna or the White Goddess who fights side by side with the king. Magon mixes folklore and history liberally in a soup that ends up lacking both the meat of verifiable research or the good hearty flavoring of the folk. Cowan, on the other hand, lays down a solid substrata of history, reminding us *that there is only mention of one son in the Continental books of the period, not three, and he most probably the bastard of the Dale woman, the G'run king's second wife. Also, it would be well for us to remember, three is a potent number popular in folklore.*

According to Cowan, the battles for the throne involved not only the overthrown G'runians but a good many of the Dalites as well. After four hundred years of unquestioned subservience to the invaders, the indigenous populations (the Upper Dalite sheep farmers and fisherfolk and the Lower Dalite artisans and city dwellers) had had enough. Young men called Jennisaries (named after one of the martyred leaders, Cowan hypothesizes brilliantly) roamed the countryside destroying the towns and Hames they considered of G'run manufacture. The ruins of one such incursion can still be seen today in the Wilhelm Valley. According to Cowan—and I can only agree wholeheartedly with her—it was not torn down and sown over with sturdy grass as others of its kind because it had become a shrine. The legend goes that it was here that the martyred Jen was murdered and the king crowned.

That the eager young Jennisaries pledged themselves to the new G'run king in exchange for a vow that he would marry one of theirs is something both Cowan and Magon agree upon, though they agree on little else, because it clearly states in the Book of Battles *that "So it is pledged that the dark king and the light queen shall wed, bringing day and night into the circle, that the people themselves might rule."*

However, much else in the Book of Battles *remains unclear. For example, there is little that can be said about the final evocation:*

> *See where the queen has gone,*
> *Where her footsteps flower,*
> *For they lead into the hill,*
> *They lead under the hill,*
> *Where she waits for her call,*
> *Where she waits for her king,*
> *Where she waits for her bright companions.*

Neither Doyle nor Cowan can offer any easy solu-
tion to the puzzle of that final piece. And we must utterly
reject Magon's ridiculous proposal that the poetry means
exactly what it says—that some queen (presumably the
one of Dale extraction) remains neither living nor dead
under the hill waiting to be recalled to a battle which has
yet to be fought.

THE STORY:

"My father," the king-in-exile said, "was a good
man and a kind man. But he was also a blunt man, given
to speaking his mind. That is good breeding in a farmer
but not in a king. He had little talent for the sly exercise
of politics and he did not understand compromise. He
went where his heart led." Pike's face softened with the
memory.

"His wife . . ." prompted the man with the scarred
eye.

Someone poked up the fire in the broken hearth.

"His first wife, my mother, died giving me birth. She
had had trouble birthing my older brother, Jorum, and
the doctors warned her that she dared have no more.
Jorum was so big he had torn her all up inside. But king-
doms need heirs. One is not a safe number. So I was sown
in that ruined terrain. And killed her leaving it." He
spoke dryly. It was obviously a story well rehearsed, and
the emotion had been leeched from it by so many tellings.

Jenna said in a low voice, "I killed my own mother
in just that way." Hesitating, she added, "My first
mother."

The men nearest her murmured, turning that bit of
information over and over, and one repeated out loud,
"First mother."

Gorum seemed not to hear, but continued staring silently into the fire. Then he shook himself all over and went on. "The midwife was a lovely little Dale woman, small and dark. She sang lullabies with a voice like a slightly demented turtledove. She nursed me through that first cold year when my father could not think about babies because they made him so angry."

Jenna burst out, "My second mother was a midwife. She died carrying me in her arms."

Some of the men nodded, as if acknowledging something as yet unsaid, but Gorum simply stared at Jenna for a long moment, then turned back to the fire and his tale.

"On the day I walked toward him, taking my first baby steps away from her arms, he forgave me. I called him *Papa,* which she had so carefully rehearsed with me, and he wept and called me his *Good Son.* He married her in secret at the year's turning, not so much for love but for gratitude. His real love was buried in my mother's grave. When three years later she gave birth to a healthy babe, and she herself still strong, he announced the marriage and claimed the child an heir."

"That was Carum?" Jenna asked.

Gorum smiled at her, the first generous smile she had won from him. "That was Carum. He was small like his mother so, unlike the rest of us, he learned the art of compromise."

"Here, he's not so small as that," cried out a wiry, short man from the sitting crowd. "He be a head taller than me. That's not short."

"Short may-be," said another, "but he baint called Longbow for nowt."

The men chuckled at that. Even Sandor and Marek smiled.

Jenna blushed, though she was not sure why, and Catrona sitting next to her put a hand on hers.

"Do not mind them. You will have to get used to it. Men in a mob are all randy-mouthed. It means nothing," she whispered.

"It means *less* than nothing to me," Jenna replied, "since I do not know what they mean."

"Then why have you flushed like some spring maiden at a court dance?" asked Catrona.

Jenna looked down at her hands and twisted the priestess ring around her little finger. "I do not know," she said. "I am not sure. I do not even know what a court dance is!"

The king-in-exile laughed along with his men, then took a deep draught of his wine. "The marriage was the mistake Kalas had hoped for. A mistake he could use directly against the king. It was only an excuse, of course. He would have found another in time.

"He began to spread rumors, and those rumors sparked small rebellions: knives in taverns, rocks at the king's gate. What Kalas promised was the sanctity of the clans against the mixing of blood and seed with the Dales. *Sanctity!* As if we had not been sowing babes throughout the Dales for four hundred years! There was never an uncompromised clan on this island since the first days our forefathers set foot here.

"I have bred horses, boy and man, and this I know— the lines without a wild strain thin out. Bones break, blood runs rose. The people of the Dales make the clans stronger, not weaker. My uncle, Lord Kalas, will find this out in the end."

"To the king!" two of the men shouted spontaneously, raising their cups.

"To the kingdom," countered Gorum, raising his.

"To the Dales!" Jenna said, standing. In the late afternoon sun her white hair seemed haloed in light, electric with the puzzling wind.

The rest of the men leaped to their feet, foremost among them Piet and the king-in-exile.

"To the Dales!" they shouted, the thunder of their voices bounding back oddly from the broken walls and cracked stones. "The Dales."

They raised their cups, draining the last of the wine

in the resounding silence. And into that silence there in-
sinuated another sound, a low, insistent pounding.

"Horses!" Catrona cried. She was quick to reach for
her sword, but Piet was quicker.

Placing his hand over hers, he said, "Those are our
own."

"How can you know?" Jenna asked, coming close to
him.

"Our watch would have given warning."

"Your watch!" Jenna laughed. "They gave no warning of us."

"We needed no warning of ye—two warrior girls
and a priestess all on our side and three unarmed boys."

"What if the watch were slain. That was done at one
of the Hames . . ." She hesitated, remembering the girls
slaughtered at Nill's. "Then there would be no warning."

"Ye do not understand horses, girl. A man's eye may
be fooled but never a horse's nose." He put his finger
alongside his nose. "Their horses have been fed on oats
and ours on open graze. A horse can smell the difference.
But look!" He pointed to the horses still quietly nibbling
on the sparse grass outside the walls. "They seem content."

"Oh!" Jenna could think of no other answer.

Piet smiled and clapped her on the back. "How
could ye know horses, girl, stuck away all your life in a
Hame. Now, me—I was taught by a hard man, name of
Parke. Oft I felt the weight of his hand. But he taught me
well. His teachings have kept me alive all these years." He
spoke with a blunt jollity, but having finished what he
had to say, turned and walked purposely out of the
kitchen, his hand never straying far from his sword.

As if his movement were a signal, the rest of the men
went quickly to what seemed to be appointed places,
seven standing around the king-in-exile.

Jenna spoke hurriedly to the boys. "See how the
seven guard the king. Do likewise with Petra."

"I need no such guard," Petra began.

"Do it!" Jenna said.

The boys did as they were bid, Jareth drawing his blade, and Jenna went back to Catrona's side.

"You did not tell me about Piet," Jenna whispered.

"You did not ask," Catrona said.

"I did not know the questions."

"Then you deserved no answer."

Jenna nodded. Catrona had been her teacher, her guardian, her sister, and one of her many mothers at Selden Hame. But, Jenna suddenly realized, she had known little—*she had known nothing*—about Catrona. *And* she had never asked.

"Now, why have you told me nothing about this Longbow who calls you White Jenna and has loved you for five years?" Catrona asked.

"You did not ask," said Jenna. "Besides—there is nothing to tell."

"*Yet!*" Catrona laughed. Then her voice got strangely serious. "Did Amalda ever get a chance to explain to you the way of a woman with a man? Or did Mother Alta as part of her preparation for your mission? Though . . ." She made an explosive sound that was supposed to be a laugh but was much too bitter for one. "Though I would guess *that* one knows *aught* of it, as Piet would say. She loves only herself—and her dark sister. Perhaps I should tell you . . ." She glanced at Jenna.

Jenna colored. "I know what I need to know."

Nodding, Catrona said, "Yes—I judge you do. And the rest you can learn. But remember, sweet Jen, what they say: *Experience is rarely a gentle master.*"

The dust of the approaching riders so filled the air then, Jenna was forced to raise a hand to wipe her tearing eyes. When she could see again, there were fully a hundred dark horses milling outside the walls and occasionally pushing in through the broken gates. The smell of them was overwhelming.

Jenna saw a single gray horse in the crowd. If the king had been riding one, she thought Carum might be on the other. *Carum!* She began shoving her way toward the gray.

Using her shoulder, she pushed first one horse then another aside. As often she was pushed back by a large dark shoulder or rump. *I shall be flattened for sure,* she thought. *I shall smell like a horse.* She wondered suddenly about her hair, about the clothes she had slept in for days, about the face that must have changed in the five years—*five years!*—since he had seen her. She thought about turning back, but the horses held her hostage to her first impulse.

And then the gray loomed before her. Putting a hand on its neck, she found that her hand was shaking. All around her men were dismounting and cursing pleasantly at one another. Suddenly, she did not dare look.

Only the man on the gray remained in his saddle. At last she raised her face to stare up at him. He was enormous, towering over her on the gray. Heavily bearded, with long black hair bound up in seven braids, he stared back. Each of the braids was tied off with a piece of crimson thread. A red and gold headband, smudged with dirt and blood, was pulled so tight around his forehead, the skin was taut below it. There was a deep gash over his right eye. As he looked at Jenna, his mouth twisted into a strange smile. It was then she noticed his hands were tied behind him.

Starting to turn away, Jenna heard his harsh laugh.

"So," he said, "some of Alta's fighting sluts still live."

She paused, her hands growing icy, the palms wet. Drawing in three careful *latani* breaths, she forced herself to move away from him without speaking. She would not draw sword against him. Whoever he was, he was injured. And bound. But her eyes were as wet as her palms. *With anger,* she reminded herself, *not sorrow or fear.* Blinded with the tears, she bumped into one of the men.

"I am sorry," she whispered.

"I am not."

The voice was deep, deeper than she remembered, as if time or pain had sanded it. He wore a vest without a shirt and his arms were tanned and well muscled. Around his neck, on a leather thong, was a ring with a crest. His head was helmless and his light brown hair, now almost shoulder length, was tangled from the ride. The lashes were as long as she remembered, so beautiful on the boy, even more compelling on the grown man. There was a faint scar running from his left eye that lent him a slightly wanton look. His eyes were as blue as speedwells. He was exactly as tall as she.

"Carum," she whispered, wondering that her heart had not stuttered in her breast.

"I said we would see one another again, my White Jenna."

"You said . . . a lot of things," Jenna reminded him. "Not all of them true."

"*I* have been true," he replied, "though I heard reports that you had died. Still I did not—*could not*—credit them."

"And *I* heard that you are not called Longbow for nothing." She bit her lip wishing she could recall the words.

For a moment he looked startled, then he grinned. "I shoot well, Jenna. That's all. *Stories feed the mind when the belly is not full.*"

She forgave neither of them for the exchange.

Carum reached out and touched a piece of hair that had strayed across her brow. "Do we meet to quarrel? We parted with a kiss."

"Much has happened since then," Jenna said. "I left you in safety to return to a Hame full of dead sisters."

"I know. I couldn't rest there having heard what news Pike had of the other Hames. I feared desperately for you yet I couldn't leave Pike with his wounds. But I told the others all about you. How you were the White One of prophecy, the Anna. How Ox and Hound had bowed before you. They were ready to love you for what you had become."

"And you?"

"I already loved you. For what you were."

"You knew nothing of what I was. Of what I am."

"I know everything I need to know, Jenna." He smiled shyly and she saw the boy behind the face of the man, yet she could not seem to stop picking quarrels.

"How can you know?"

"My heart knows. It knew from the first moment I saw you and cried you *merci*. I cry it again. Here. Now."

Jenna shook her head. "You have grown a fine tongue. Is that what a prince who shoots well says."

"Carum! You are safely returned." It was the king. He threw his arms around his brother. "I always worry, you know." He smiled at Jenna. "I do not forget he is my *baby* brother."

"Not only returned safely, Gorum, but having surprised and killed a company of the usurper's horse and captured the man on the gray." He turned to his own mount and untied something from the saddlebag. It was a helm. He held it out to his brother.

Jenna felt herself turn cold. She had seen a helm like that before, had held one in her hands, had thrown it into an open grave. She stared at the thing in Carum's hands. It was dark, covered with a hairy hide. There were two ears standing stiff at the top and a snout and mouth with bloody fangs.

"The Bear!" Jenna whispered.

"By Alta's Hairs!" Gorum cried. "You have captured the bloody Bear. Well done, brother." He took the helm from Carum's hands and held it above his head. "*The Bear!*" he cried. "We have the Bear!"

The name echoed around the encampment, and the men who had been waiting joined the returning riders cheering the capture.

THE BALLAD:

King Kalas and His Sons

King Kalas had four sons
And four sons had he,
And they rambled around
In the northern countrie.
And they rambled around
Without ever a care,
The Hound and the Bull
And the Cat and the Bear.

The Hound was a hunter,
The Hound was a spy,
The Hound could shoot down,
Any bird on the fly.
The Hound was out hunting
When brought down was he
Alone as he rambled
The northern countrie.

King Kalas had three sons,
And three sons had he,
And they rambled around
In the northern countrie.
And they rambled around
Without ever a care.
And they were the Bull
And the Cat and the Bear.

The Bull was a gorer,
The Bull was a knight,
And never a man who would
Run from a fight.
The Bull was out fighting

When brought down was he
Alone as he rambled
The northern countrie.

King Kalas had two sons,
And two sons had he,
And they rambled around
In the northern countrie.
And they rambled around
Without ever a care.
And the names they were called
Were the Cat and the Bear.

The Cat was a shadow,
The Cat was a snare,
Sometimes you knew not
When the Cat was right there.
The Cat was out hiding
When brought down was he
Alone as he rambled
The northern countrie.

King Kalas had one son,
And one son had he,
And he rambled around
In the northern countrie.
And he rambled around
Without ever a care,
And the name he went under
Was Kalas' Bear.

The Bear was a bully,
The Bear was a brag,
His mouth was brimmed over
With bluster and swag.
The Bear was out boasting
When brought down was he
Alone as he rambled
The northern countrie.

King Kalas had no sons,
And no sons had he
To ramble around
In the northern countrie.
Though late in the evening
The ghosts are seen there
Of the Hound and the Bull
And the Cat and the Bear.

THE STORY:

After the horses were unsaddled, brushed, and set out to graze, the men gathered for food in the Hame's roofless kitchen. Jenna heard bits and pieces of the story of the battle as she stood, tongue-tied, by Carum's side. He was so at ease with the men, trading banter and small slanders without hesitation, she wondered what had happened to the shy, scholarly boy she had known so briefly. *War had happened to him,* she thought suddenly. *And something more.* That the *something more* might be the passage of five years was a traitorous thought she pushed far away.

They had come upon the company of horse near a small town. "Karenton," Jenna had heard one man say. "Karen's Town," another. Surprise and numbers had been in their favor. The usurper's bloody men had never had a chance. Some of them had even begged to surrender, but no quarter had been given. Except for the Bear. Longbow had insisted that *he* would be delivered in chains to the feet of the king-in-exile.

When they spoke of the Bear, the men's mouths had been soiled with his name and deeds. They called him "Slaughterer of a Thousand Women," and "Butcher of Bertram's Rest," and yet even as they spoke of the horrors, Jenna could not help thinking that there was admiration as well in their voices. The details of his merciless killings seemed more like tales to frighten young children. She had walked deliberately over to the tree where he had been bound to see whether the sign of his bloodlust was imprinted upon his face.

One of his braids had unraveled into three kinked strands, but otherwise he looked as he had on his horse: big, hairy, leering, but no more a beast than others of the men milling around.

There were two guards standing by him, swords drawn.

"Best not get close," said one, wiping his nose with his sleeve.

"He's a tricker," said the other, the man with the scarred eye.

"He's bound," Jenna pointed out. "And what can he do to me with his hands and legs so prisoned?"

The Bear's head went back at that and he laughed a loud, roaring laugh. Then he turned to the first guard. "She wants to know what I can do without hands or legs? Do you want to tell her—or shall I?"

The guard slapped him hard with the back of his hand, so hard his lower lip split open and his mouth filled with blood.

"Do not speak to the White One that way," he said.

"The White One?"

"The Anna. Who made your brothers the Hound and the Bull bow low."

The Bear sucked on his lower lip until the bleeding stopped, then he stared at Jenna, grinning. His teeth were stained. "So, you are that girl, the one who lost her dolly at the Hound's grave. The one who lopped off the Bull's hand so he died a long, horrible death when the green took him. *That* girl. I will have something special for you, later."

This time the scarred-eye man slapped him. The Bear laughed again.

"I took no pleasure in the killings," said Jenna.

"Well—I do. And pleasure in other things as well."

If Jenna had hoped for forgiveness or understanding, she got none. Not from the Bear nor from the guards, who stared at her puzzled.

"Killing them two was a blessing," the man with the scarred eye pronounced.

"Death is an odd sort of blessing," Jenna said. "The old wisdom is right: *Kill once, mourn ever.*" She walked away.

The Bear's voice boomed after her. "We add, *Kill twice, mourn never!* I will have something *special* for you. Later. And you'll remember *it* ever, you will!"

She thought she heard the sound of yet another slap. And his laughter following. But she did not turn around.

Carum was standing with his brother, Piet, and Catrona, away from the knots of men recounting battles and bawdy tales. As Jenna headed toward them, Carum detached himself from his companions and met her halfway. She stopped and he stopped. Though inches apart, they did not touch.

"Jenna . . ." he began, hesitated, looked down.

"You said to me once that there are some people, I forget their names, who believe that love is the first word God memorized," Jenna whispered, conscious of the men all around them.

"The Carolians," he whispered back, still not looking at her.

"I thought about that. I tried to understand it. I *think* I understood it when you said it but I do not know what it means now."

Carum nodded and looked up. "So much time between us," he said.

"So much blood," she added.

"Is it gone?" His voice, while still strong, held a wisp of agony.

She reached out and touched a piece of hair that had strayed across his forehead, remembering his earlier touch. "You have lived the past five years, Carum Longbow. But I have not."

"What do you mean?"

"If I tell you, you will not believe me."

"Tell me. I will believe."

She spoke of the Grenna, the cave, the grove. She described Alta in her green and gold dress. She told him of the collar, the wristlet, and crown. All the while he shook his head, as if unable to credit it.

"I said you would not believe."

Reaching out, Carum took her hands in his. He twisted the priestess ring slowly around her little finger, then twined his fingers in hers. "We have a saying in my clan that *If you have no meat, eat bread.* Jenna, what you say is unbelievable. But I have no better explanation. You would not lie to me. You have been gone these five years, not a word of you but rumors and tales. You say you lived under the hill along with the Greenfolk and Alta. You say the five years were but a day and a night. Meat or bread. You offer me bread. What can I do but take it from your fingers." He held her hands against his chest and she could feel his heart beating under the leather vest.

"You are seventeen plus five years old. You have lived each year. I am thirteen plus five years, yet I feel thirteen still."

He leaned over and kissed her forehead. "*You . . .* you were never thirteen, Jenna. *You* are ageless. But I have the patience of a tree. I will wait."

"How long?"

"How long does a larch wait? How long does an oak?" He dropped her hands, but she could still feel the touch, as if his skin had fitted exactly over hers.

Side by side, they walked back to where the king, Piet, and Catrona waited.

The sun was low on the horizon, staining the sky with red. A small, cool wind puzzled around the broken walls of the compound, lifting dust and swirling it up and over their boots. From across the road, birds cried out their evening songs, decorating the deeper rumble of the men's voices.

Seeing Jenna, the boys and Petra came forward. They followed her, then stood in a circle, shoulder to shoulder while the king spoke to them in low, urgent tones.

"We have been waiting long for you—or something like you, Jenna. The men have fought hard, but we have been so alone."

"This is all there be to our army," Piet interrupted. "Good men. Brave. Loyal. None better. But they be all."

Catrona nodded her head, as if counting.

Jenna nodded, too, adding, "But what can we do? We are but six bodies more. Yet we are ready to help, if it means helping the sisters."

Piet cleared his throat as if preparing to speak, but it was the king who did the talking. "Already the men are speaking about you. The White One. The Anna. Who made the Bull and Hound bow low. They have recalled the old stories all afternoon."

"Good men they be," Piet added, "but not cautious in their beliefs."

"*You* do not believe I am the Anna," Jenna said, both relieved and a bit annoyed.

"*Belief is an old dog in a new collar,*" Piet said.

"There are the signs," Carum said, putting his hand up and counting them out on his fingers. "The three mothers, the white hair, the Bull and the Hound, the . . ."

"You do not need to convince *me,* little brother," the king said. "I know how much we need her. As does Piet. Our belief is not necessary here. But for the men . . ."

"If we had the Anna," Piet added, "think how many others would join us just to march by her side."

"But I am the ending before I am the beginning," Jenna pointed out. "Remember, that is in the story, too."

"We have already had enough endings," the king said, slapping his bad leg. "My father is dead. Murdered. My stepmother, too. My older brother killed foully in his bath, his blood mixing with the soapy water. So I am king now in truth. But that toad, Kalas, sits upon the throne, poisoning the very air he breathes with his piji breath, while we are forced to live in these ruins and make due with a rock for a throne." His voice roughened as he spoke, his eyes narrowing until they were smudges on his face.

Jenna thought once again that he looked like a wolf, or a dog let run too long in the woods.

"You have had a lot of endings, too," Carum reminded Jenna gently.

Remembering the women, their tunics and aprons stiff with blood, laid side by side in the ruined Hames, Jenna shuddered.

Gorum added, as an afterthought, "Yes, the senseless slaughter of the women in ten Hames. The rape of their daughters." He spoke the words slowly, articulating them with care, but his voice growing raspy again at the finish. "Is that ending enough for you, Anna?"

"Ten?" It was Catrona. "*Ten* Hames?" Her eyes stared unseeing.

"I do not know," Jenna whispered. "I do not know what is enough." She reached out and touched Catrona's shoulder.

Gorum smiled his wolfish smile. "It will be enough for these men. Enough so that they will gladly follow their king. And their queen. For that is in the story as well."

"No!" Carum cried, understanding before anyone else.

"There must be *some* sign," the king said slowly, as if talking to children, "some sign for the men here and now. What better sign—than a wedding. My father married a woman of the Dales. And so can I."

"Never!" Carum cried again. "You cannot think it."

"I *think* what is necessary, brother," Gorum said. "I think what is best for the kingdom. That is what a king does. That is what a king has to do. That is why you would make a terrible king and it is lucky for the Dales that I am still alive."

"Nevertheless, you shall not force her," Carum said.

"I shall do what must be done." Gorum was no longer smiling. "And so shall you. And so shall she."

For a moment they were all silent, so silent the birdsong seemed like a battle cry. Then Jenna spoke.

"Never! There is nothing here for you." She struck herself on the breast with a closed fist.

Gorum leaned toward her. "My dear child," he said softly, "the first lesson in kingship my father taught me was that *In the council of kings the heart has little to say.* There is nothing in here"—he struck himself on the chest—"for you either. I love you only through my little brother's eyes. But the people will love you, for your white hair and your history. Kingship is all symbols and signs."

"No!" Jenna said. "You cannot make me. If you do, you would be no better than the toad on the throne, for all your breath is sweeter. What good is kingship if the heart cannot speak aloud?"

"She is right," Catrona said. "And while you talked much to me this past hour, you said nothing about any marriage."

"The weddings of kings do not concern you, woman of the Hames," Gorum said, turning sharply toward her.

Before Catrona could answer, Petra had moved into the center of the circle, her voice pitched in the strange priestess tone. "As long as men speak to women thus, the ending is not yet reached, whether one Hame is gone. Or ten. Or all."

"Right!" Marek shouted.

"This is our fight as well as yours, Majesty," Catrona said. "Indeed, it was our fight first."

"First before Kalas stole the throne? Never!" exclaimed the king.

"First when Garuns be stealing our land," Sandor said, as surprised as any of them at his outburst.

Hand to his throat, Jareth strained to speak, but what warning he had to give remained unsaid.

"First or last," Carum said, his hand lightly resting

on Jenna's shoulder, "our kingship will not be bought back with such a coin."

"*My* kingdom, brother. Not yours. Do not forget it. My kingdom until I die. And my heirs thereafter."

"I will not be the king's bride," Jenna said. "Nor give him heirs. No matter what the prophecy."

Petra intruded with the same strange oracular voice. "On the slant," she intoned. "Prophecy must always be read on the slant. We read it through slotted eyes or we read it wrong."

"Still, there must be a sign," the king said, trying to snatch back the momentum along with the power. "And this sign . . ."

"I know what sign the men be taking," Piet said suddenly. "It is not weddings that claim them." He wheeled from their circle and called out to the restless men. "Come. Come witness the White One's return."

They gathered uneasily, a great crowded circle around the smaller one.

Piet went over to one man, whispering hurriedly in his ear. The man nodded once and, unsmiling, pushed through the circle.

"Tell them," Piet said softly to the king. "Tell them who she is. They'll know her soon enow."

The king held up his hand and there was an immediate silence. Jenna thought it a miracle that so many men could keep so still.

"You have heard of Her," the king began. "And spoken of Her."

Without thinking, Jenna stood straighter, shoulders back, head high.

"She is the White One."

Petra broke in, her soft voice pitched loud enough so that all could hear her: "*And the prophet says a white babe with black eyes shall be born unto a virgin in the winter of the year. The ox in the field, the hound at the hearth, the bear in the cave, the cat in the tree, all, all shall bow before her, singing . . .*"

The men who were Garunian joined her, in the same singsong manner. *". . . Holy, holy, holiest of sisters, who is both black and white, both dark and light, your coming is the beginning and it is the end."*

Petra completed the speaking of the prophecy alone. *"Three times shall her mother die and three times shall she be orphaned and she shall be set apart that all shall know her."*

"She *is* white and dark," cried out a man from the crowd.

"And I heard her talk of three mothers," another shouted.

"And . . ." the king said, "it was her sword that slew the Hound, dropping him into a lonely grave, to rescue Prince Carum."

There was a moment of silence; then suddenly the men shouted as one, "The Hound!"

"And *her* sword cut off the hand of the Bull, Kalas' great pet ox, who later died wasting of the green illness," the king continued.

This time there was no silence. "The Bull!" they shouted back at him.

Just then the man Piet had sent away pushed through the crowd leading the lumbering, bound captive by the front of his shirt.

Piet whispered hurriedly in the king's ear and the king smiled slowly. Jenna did not like that smile.

"The prophecy says the ox and the hound, the bear and the cat, shall bow before her, singing . . ." The king held his hand high.

"Down. Down. Down," the men began to chant as Piet pushed the bound Bear to his knees before the king, pulling his shirt open so that the mat of black chest hair showed.

"Sing, you bastard," shouted the king. "Sing."

The Bear looked up and spit on the king's right hand, silencing the men. Piet drew his sword. The Bear grinned at him. Piet nodded twice, then turned and handed the sword to Jenna.

"Kill him. Kill him now, girl. Then they will follow ye for e'er and ye can marry who ye will!"

Jenna hefted the sword in both hands. It was twice as heavy as her own. She walked over to the kneeling man and stared at him.

"What do you say?" she whispered into his upturned face.

"I say you are Alta's bitch," he answered. "And no better than the dogs who follow when you are in heat. Strike now for you will not have the chance again."

She raised the sword above her head, drew in three *latani* breaths and began to count the hundred-chant to steady herself. Before ten were done, she felt again the strange lightening and she pulled out of her body to stare down at the scene below. There was the kneeling prisoner, laughing up into her face, with Piet, Carum and the king at his back, and the larger crowd of the king's ragtag army and her friends before him. Beyond, smelling the rising excitement, the hobbled horses stirred restlessly.

Jenna felt herself drawn toward the three men at the Bear's back, away from the heat of the crowd. Her translucent fingers reached down to touch them one at a time on the very center of the skull. Piet was a solid white flame, the colors unchanging. The king was a cylinder of blue-white ice that burned to the touch. And Carum . . .

She hesitated before touching Carum. She remembered how he had felt the other time she had let herself be pulled into him at Nill's Hame; how she had been drawn past pockets that were restful and pockets filled with a wild, alien heat. She had fled back into the air again, grateful to be unconsumed by his passions.

But she was stronger now. She reached out, touched him, and let herself fall.

He seemed deeper than before, with more pockets. There were the restful ones, the fretful ones, and ones filled with strange, engaging objects for which she had no name. The alien heat was there still, but somehow it did not frighten her now. Down and down, as if there was no end to him, as if she could explore forever.

Forever. She did not have forever. Her arms ached. She suddenly recalled the sword she was holding. Leaping into her body again, she stared down into the Bear's leering face.

"Kill him . . . kill him . . . kill him . . ." The chant was unrelenting. Jenna felt her arms shaking. Slowly she lowered the sword. When its point rested lightly on the Bear's chest, over the heart, she frowned.

The men were suddenly silent. The Bear's eyes were wide, preparing to look directly at his death. The entire clearing hushed, as if drawing a single breath, waiting.

"I . . . I cannot kill him this way," Jenna whispered. She took a step back and let the sword point drift slowly toward the ground.

The Bear's head went back. He roared and the roar turned into a laugh. Then he stared at Jenna. "*I* would not be so foolish, little bitch. What will your hunting pack do to you now?"

"They will do what they will," Jenna said to him quietly. "But if I am no better than you, then the ending is indeed at hand. With no beginning after." She dropped the sword and walked away.

Carum followed, the men parting to let them through. Only Jareth was smiling.

They walked silently past the broken walls, across the road, and into the trees. Jenna sagged against the thick trunk of an oak and bit her lower lip. Still she said nothing. When Carum reached out to touch her shoulder, she shrugged away his touch.

"No," she whispered.

"I understand."

"How can you understand when I do not understand myself."

"Jenna, you're thirteen going on forever. How could you possibly kill an unarmed man?"

"He is no man. He is a monster."

"He is a murderer. He is a slayer of women. He is a slaughterer of children. He is beyond saving." Carum's voice was steady. "But he is a man."

"And I am but a woman?"

"No—you are the Anna. You're better than he is. Than Gorum is. Than we all are."

"No, I am just me. Jenna. Jo-an-enna. A woman of the Hames. A woman of the Dales. Do not make me more than I am. My Mother Alta once called me a tree shading the little flowers—but I am *not* such a tree."

Carum smiled slowly at her. It was the face of the boy she remembered. "To me you are no tree, no flower, no goddess. You are Jenna. I kissed you once and I know. But for all of them you are *The Anna*. And when you put on Her mantle, you are more than *just* Jenna."

"Jenna could not kill a bound man whatever the Anna might do."

"Jen, the Anna is the best you are. And better. She wouldn't have slain him that way, either."

She leaned over and kissed him quickly on the mouth. "Thank you, Carum. Your brother is wrong: you *should* be king." Then, before he could make more than a slight sound, she turned and walked back across the road.

He had to run to catch up.

The large circle of men had broken into many smaller, knotted groups, arguing loudly. The bound prisoner was nowhere to be seen. Jenna found Catrona in the middle of one of the loudest circles, her hands moving rapidly as if they were a second and third argument.

"Catrona!" Jenna called.

The men in the circle turned and, seeing her, seemed to shrink away, leaving her face-to-face with Catrona.

"One thrust, Jenna," Catrona said. "One thrust and we would have had them. I taught you that stroke with this hand." She held up her right hand. "And now all that training for naught."

"You also taught me that in the *Book of Light* it is written that: *To kill is not to cure.* Surely that means killing a bound man."

"Do not quote the *Book* to me like some petty priestess," Catrona said. "The *Book* also says: *A stroke may save a limb.* Like any maunderings of holy writ, the *Book* can say whatever you want it to say." She was shaking with anger. "Jenna, you must think. *Think.* We need these men. We need this army. We need this king. I would not have you marry him to get his followers. But Piet was right. There was another, a better, way. And the Bear will be killed eventually—by this angry crowd, as like as not. If you had done it then, coldly and with great flourish, it would have fed the tale."

"*I* am no story," Jenna cried. "*I* am no tale. I am real. I feel. I hurt. I bleed. I cannot just kill without conscience."

"A warrior has no conscience until after the war is done," Catrona said.

Jenna put her face in her hands and wept.

Catrona turned away.

The moon rose, pale and thin, over the ruined Hame, climbing until it crowned the kitchen chimney. Jenna stood alone while throughout the encampment the arguments raged.

"You were right," came a voice from behind her.

Turning slowly, she saw Skada.

"And you were wrong," Skada said.

"How can I be both?"

"You *should* not have killed him, but you *could* have done it with words that would have still made them believe."

"What words?" Jenna asked.

"You might have said: *The Bull has bowed down, he need not die by my hand.*"

Jenna nodded. "And I could have said the moon is black, but I did not."

Nodding back, Skada laughed. "No, you did not.

And now, my dear Anna, who is both dark"—she pointed to herself—"and light"—she pointed to Jenna—"you are in a fix."

"*We* are in a fix," Jenna amended.

"So now it is *we*! At last you are including me, sharing the burden, parceling out the guilt." Skada's mouth twisted with amusement.

"How can you laugh at such a time?"

"Jenna, there is always time to laugh. And part of you is laughing already, which is why I can. I am not other than you. I *am* you."

"Well, *I* do not feel like laughing," Jenna said miserably.

"Well, *I* do," said Skada. She put back her head and let out a delighted roar of laughter.

Unable to help herself, Jenna did the same.

"There," Skada said, "feel better?"

"Not really."

"Not at all?" Skada grinned.

"You are impossible," Jenna said, shaking her head.

Imitating her, Skada shook her own head. "No, I am not impossible. I am hungry. Let us find something to eat."

Arm in arm, they walked toward the kitchen.

Jareth stopped them halfway. He tried to talk with his hands, painstakingly spelling out his concerns. His frantic fingers wove complicated messages, but all Jenna could read was a warning.

"The cat . . ." Jenna said.

"The bull . . ." Skada added.

Jareth's eyes pleaded with them, his throat straining with the effort to speak.

"We will be careful," Jenna promised. "Do not worry. You have warned us well." When they were away from him, Jenna whispered, "I would cut that collar from his neck and let him speak."

"Whatever the consequences?" Skada asked.

"Whatever the consequences." Jenna's face was tight

with anger. "How can Alta's magic be good when it punishes Her followers and Her enemies equally? Ten Hames gone. Jareth silenced. We are made murderers and monsters in Her name."

"And heroes," Skada said.

Jenna turned suddenly to face Skada. "Look around, sister. Look with care. Do you see any heroes here?"

They looked together. By the kitchen's chimney stood the king, a cup in his hand. He was staring sullenly into it as if he read some unhappy future there. By his side towered two guards in dirt brown tunics and torn trews. One was polishing his blade with his sleeve. Around the fires that blossomed throughout the compound were groups of men drinking and telling stories. Near the gate, a small fire illuminated the smudged faces of Petra and the boys. She was describing something with her hands. In a far corner, where the ruins of a staircase still ascended five steps into the air, sat Piet. On one side of him was Catrona, on the other Katri. They were both whispering into his ears. Smiling, he stretched his arms out and enfolded them both in his embrace. They stood together and walked off down the road in the moonlight.

"What does a hero look like?" Skada asked quietly. "Polished helm, fresh tunic, clean hair, and a mouth full of white teeth?"

"Not . . . not like this anyway," Jenna answered.

Skada shook her head. It was as if a breeze blew across Jenna's face. "You are wrong, sister. We are all heroes here."

THE TALE:

There was once a tyrant of whom it was prophesied that he would be overthrown only when a hero who was not born of womankind, who neither rode nor walked, who bore neither pike nor sword, could conquer him.

Long reigned the tyrant and many were the men, women, and children who were swept away by the bloody winds of his wrath.

One day, in a small village, a child was born, ripped from her dead mother's womb by the midwife's knife, lifted out through the stomach, though not from the canal. She was put to suck at the teat of a she goat, raised with the goat's own kids.

As the child grew, so did the kids, one male and one female. And they played together as if they were all in the same family. They played butt-head and climb-hill and leap-o'er-me and other games beside. And the girl grew tall and beautiful despite her poor beginnings.

The years went by, and still the tyrant reigned. But he grew old and sour. He even longed for death. But the prophecy held true and there was no hero, not even the greatest swordsman, who could kill him—though many tried.

One day, the girl and her goats came into the capital city. As was her wont, she rode atop first one, then the other, her feet dragging along the ground.

The tyrant was out walking and saw the girl who, though astride, was not riding, for her feet were on the ground. He stopped her and asked, "Child, how was it you were born?"

"I was not born but taken from my dead mother."

"Ah," said the tyrant. "And how is it you ride?"

"I do not ride, for this is my brother. And this is my sister. It is but a game we play."

"Ah," said the tyrant. "You must marry me, for you are my destiny."

So they were wed and he died, smiling, on his wedding night, conquered by love. So the prophecy was true. And the sages say surely a hero is not easily known for

*who could tell that a girl astride two goats could be a
hero when many men with swords were not.*

THE STORY:

"Jenna!" Carum found them as they stood.

Jenna turned and Skada, in perfect unison, turned
with her.

Carum stared, first at one, then the other. "It is true,
then. Not twins, but sister light and sister dark. I never
dared credit it."

"It is true," they said together.

"All the time?"

"You spoke to me before alone," Jenna said.

"The moon," Skada added. "Or a good fire. And
then I will appear."

Carum's face looked troubled, but he did not speak.

"Or a candle by the bed." Skada laughed. "Do not
make your forehead like a pool rippled by a stone,
Carum. Blow out the candle, and I am gone."

"I would not have you gone, sister," Jenna said,
reaching out for Skada's hand.

"There are times when you will," Skada said in a
low voice. "And times when you will not." She spoke
softly to Carum. "I know her mind and I know her heart,
for they are mine as well. Walk into the trees, young
prince, where the branches overlace the forest floor. No
moon can pierce that canopy nor can a dark sister appear
by her light sister's side there."

"But you will still know . . ."

She shrugged. "Jenna is what she is. You loved her
before. *And* kissed her knowing."

"I did not know."

"I am what I am," Jenna said. "And you did, too, know."

He shook his head unhappily, but at last admitted, "I knew. And I did not know."

And knowing? Skada left the question unasked but he heard it anyway.

"Come into the woods, Jenna," he whispered. "That we may talk. Alone."

Jenna looked at Skada who nodded. Jenna nodded back, slowly. Then the three walked across the road, the moonlight bright overhead. When they reached the tree-line, Skada began to tremble like a leaf in a breeze though the night was warm. There was a steady *peep-peep* of frogs from a nearby pond. Skada smiled tremulously as they walked into the woods and flickered like a shadow for a moment more, then was gone.

"Skada . . ." Jenna said, turning.

Carum's hand was on her forearm. "Don't go back," he begged. "Don't bring her back. Not right now."

They moved deeper into the dark, just the two of them. But they did not touch again.

Jenna had never talked so long and so intensely with anyone before. They rehearsed their entire lives to one another. Jenna told Carum about growing up in a Hame, and he in turn spoke movingly about life in the Garunian court. She remembered stories and songs which she shared with him; he parceled out tales from the Continent which had been reshaped by four hundred years in the Dales. They spoke about everything except the future. It was as if the past had to be dealt with thoroughly, first; and all the time they had *not* known each other accounted for. In the beginning they spoke hesitantly, offering each piece of the past as a gift that might be refused. But soon the words came tumbling too quickly; they interrupted each other over and over as one past overlapped the other.

"That happened to me, too," Jenna said as a memory of Carum's triggered her own.

"It was that way with me," Carum said, prodded by one of Jenna's tales.

It was as if their lives were suddenly braided together, there in the darkling woods so far from home.

In the middle of one of Carum's stories about his father, a man who had not let kingship intrude upon his own hearth, there was a sudden great, horrible shouting from the ruins of the Hame, and the loud stampede of horses. Jenna and Carum stood as one, though they could make nothing of the words or the cries.

"Something awful . . ." Jenna began.

". . . has happened," Carum concluded, grabbing for her hand and yanking her to her feet. They ran quickly toward the sound.

Once they were on the road, the moon, almost down beyond the line of trees beyond the Hame, lent them Skada's faint presence.

"What is it?" Jenna called to her dark sister as they ran.

"I know no more than you," Skada answered, her voice a shadow.

Racing through the broken gates, they headed toward the angry boil of men centered by the hearth. Carum plowed a path through them, with Jenna and Skada in his wake.

"Is it the king?" Carum cried.

There were a number of answers, none of them clear.

"The Bear!" someone called.

"Got loose," said another.

"The bastard. He done 'er."

"Gone. Gone to tell." It was the first man.

"No, Henk's got 'em."

"B'aint true. Got his horse. Got the king, too."

"Nah."

"The king!" Carum grabbed the man's shoulder who had mentioned his brother. "Did he hurt him? Did he hurt Pike? Did he hurt the king?"

"Not he," the man said, shaking his head so fiercely long black hair covered his right eye. "Look!" He pointed.

The men moved apart and Jenna could see that the king and Petra were bending over something, but in the shadowy dark she could not tell what held them so. Then she saw it was Piet, sitting on the ground by the broken stair, cradling a body in his arms. When Jenna went over and spoke his name, he looked up. His mouth, with its uneven teeth, opened and closed like a fish; his sky-colored eyes were clouded over.

Jenna knelt on one side, Carum the other. In the darkened corner, Skada was gone. Putting her hand out to touch the body Piet held, Jenna was unable to say the name.

It was Carum who whispered it. "Catrona."

Catrona opened her eyes and tried to smile up at Jenna. There was blood on her tunic and blood trickling down her right arm. "We were so busy . . . we did not hear . . . did not see . . . I missed the thread, Jenna."

"What does she mean—*missed the thread*?" Carum asked.

"She taught me the Eye-Mind Game," Jenna whispered, remembering. "A game to train the senses. There was a thread. I saw it. She did not. It was all so long ago."

"Jenna . . . the thread . . ." Catrona struggled.

"Hush, girl, hush," Piet whispered. "Talking takes yer breath."

Jenna picked up Catrona's right hand and it lay in hers boneless and still. She remembered when Catrona had first shown her how to thrust, with a sword that was much too heavy for her because Jenna had been too stubborn to set it down. *Your hand is your strength*, Catrona had said, *but it is the heart that strikes the blow.*

"What happened," Jenna whispered.

The king explained. "The Bear—*who should have been dead by your hand*—worked himself loose. He strangled the guards. Took their swords. When he went for a horse, he came upon Piet and his blanket companion, away from the rest. He thrust Catrona from behind, nearly skewering Piet as well. Then he was gone. Others have gone after him. I doubt they'll find him in the dark." He recited the facts as if reading them, little emotion in his voice.

Jenna stared at the ground. *Should have been dead by your hand.* He was right and there was no apology strong enough. She shook her head.

"What good are you to me, White Jenna? You have caused the death of three good fighters. No one will follow you now." His voice was low so that only those bending over could hear.

Catrona struggled to sit up, away from Piet's arms. "No, she *is* the one. On the slant. Listen to the priestess. On . . . the . . . slant." She fell back, exhausted by the effort.

"Oh, Catrona, my catkin, don't ye be going," Piet cried. He began to weep soundlessly.

"I will not let her die," Jenna said.

Piet stared up at her, fighting to control his sobs. "Ye is too late, girl. She are dead already."

"Do not sew the shroud before there is a corpse," Catrona said suddenly. "Do they not say that in the Dales?" She coughed and bright red blood frothed from her mouth.

"I will take her to Alta's grove. She will not die there," Jenna said. "Alta said I could bring one back. It will be Catrona." She slipped her arms under Catrona's body, trying to wrest her from Piet's grasp.

The movement caused Catrona to gasp and another frothing of blood bubbled out of her mouth. She swallowed it down. "Let me die here, Jenna, in Piet's arms. There are no shadows in Alta's grove. No shadows. I would not live forever without Katri. That is no life." She smiled and looked up into Piet's face. "You are alright, my Piet. For a man."

"I've always loved ye alone, girl. Ever since that first

time. Your first. And mine. We were children then. I thought to find ye when the king was on the throne. To grow old with ye, my girl. To grow old . . ." He bent his back and whispered into her ear. She smiled again and closed her eyes. For a moment Piet did not move, just sat with his mouth against Catrona's ear. Then he put his cheek against hers. No one else moved.

At last he sat back up. "That's it, then. That's the end of it." His eyes were dry but there was a dark furrow across his brow.

Petra bent over Catrona's body, putting her palm on Catrona's forehead. She recited in a calm, low voice:

> "In the name of Alta's cave,
> The dark and lonely grave
> And all who swing twixt
> Light and light,
> Great Alta
> Take this woman,
> Take this warrior,
> Take this sister
> Into your sight.
> Wrap her in your hair
> And cradled there
> Let her be a babe again."

The men were silent until she finished the prayer, and then a low murmur of voices began: angry, passionate sounds. A few cursed Jenna out loud, calling her a "bloodless bitch" and "Kalas' helpmeet."

Petra turned slowly from Catrona's body and stared around at them. She raised her hands for silence and they were, unaccountably, still. "Fools," she cried. "You are all fools. Do you not see what this means. Catrona herself said it. You must read this death on the slant."

An anonymous voice called out, "What do you mean?"

"Who has died here? Catrona. A warrior of the

Hames. Also known as Cat. *Cat!* So the Cat *has* been slain, and all because the Anna chose not to slay the Bear first."

"But it be the wrong Cat!" the man with the scarred eye said, pushing his way to the front of the pack of men.

"And how do you know which Cat Alta meant?" Petra asked. "Or which Cat the Garuns' own prophecy named?"

"But I thought . . ." he began.

"You must not *think* on prophecy. When it comes, you just know." Petra's face was alive with her feelings. She raised her voice. "Catrona . . . Cat herself reminded us before she died. She said: *She is the one.* The one who made the Hound and the Bull and now the Cat bow low."

"No!" Jenna cried, slamming her fist on the ground. "Catrona's death was not written." But her protest was swallowed up in the rising swell of the men's shouts.

"The Anna! The Anna! The Anna!" The chorus was loud and Petra, hands above her head, fists clenched, was leading it. "THE ANNA! THE ANNA! THE ANNA!"

No! Jenna thought. *Not for this. Do not accept me for this.* But the shouts went on.

"Men in mobs—so unpredictable. So easily swayed," whispered the king. He grinned and put his hands under Jenna's elbows and pulled her up to stand by his side. "One minute you are a villain, the next a saint. You need not be a king's bride, now, child. You *are* the Anna. *They* have said so. The Anna for now."

The Anna for this turning. Will-less, she stood beside him as the chants continued.

"ANNA! ANNA! ANNA!"

The horizon behind them was stained with first light. The birds, unable to compete with the cries of men, had taken flight and the sky was peppered with them. Even Carum joined the shouting chorus that echoed back and forth across the ruined walls. Only Jareth, who could make no sound, and Piet, who was still holding Catrona's body against his chest, were still.

THE BALLAD:

Death of the Cat

The trees were growing high
And the wind was in the west
When a hunter aimed his arrow
Into the Cat's broad chest.
And she died, she died
Against her lover's breast
And we laid her in the earth
So long and narrow.

It was early, so early
In the graying of the morn,
When we sang of the days
Before the Cat was born.
And how from her mother
She was so swiftly torn,
As we laid her in the earth
So long and narrow.

So, come all ye young fighting men
And listen unto me,
Do not place your affections
Upon a girl so free
For she'll take the mortal wound
Another meant for thee,
And you'll lay her in the earth
So long and narrow.

THE STORY:

They buried the two guards by the broken gates, but Jenna and Petra insisted that Catrona's body had to lie in state between two great fires until they could find the Hame's burial cave. Piet agreed. When the second fire was lit, Katri's body appeared by Catrona's side and Marek, who had not wept before, suddenly broke into loud, embarrassing sobs which even his brother could not stop.

By evening the boys had found the cave, and they accompanied Jenna and Petra and Carum who carried Catrona's body up on a wooden bier. The king and Piet stayed behind, drinking toasts to the dead warriors with the rest of the men.

"Toasts to Lord Cres, the God of Fine Battles," Carum explained as they trudged up the hill with their bitter burden.

Remembering what he had once told her about those toasts, Jenna added, "May you drink his strong wines and eat his meat forever."

"And throw the bones over your shoulder for the Dogs of War," Carum ended.

Petra shivered. "What a horrible prayer."

"Is it any wonder I prefer none," Carum said.

They placed the bier before the entrance to the cave, and Jenna went ahead to light torches in the wall. The cave was cool and dry and there were many shrouded bodies lying about. She had to be careful where she stepped. When she lit the great torches, the bodies of the dark sisters in their careful wrappings appeared, crowding the cave further.

Leaving the cavern, she took a deep breath. The shrouded bones of the dead sisters had not frightened her.

She had been to burials in her own Hame and she knew that the bodies were just the cast-off homes of the women who now lived, suckled against Alta's breast. But those were just bones and what lay at her feet in its bier, wrapped tightly in a torn shirt and blanket, was Catrona: her sister, her teacher, her friend. And the victim of Jenna's conscience.

Kneeling, Jenna put her hand on the corpse's breast. "I swear to you, Cat, the Bear will know my vengeance. I swear to you, another Cat shall die as well. That may or may not be written in any prophecy, but it is written clearly on my heart."

She stood. "Petra and I alone will take her into the cave. It is a holy place and a holy time."

"We understand," Carum said.

The other boys nodded.

Jenna picked up Catrona's body and, with Petra following, went in.

When they left again, it was dark. There was no moon.

They rode out of the ruined Hame at first light, a silent army. Petra rode Catrona's horse, which left only Marek and Sandor doubled up, though they did not seem to mind.

The king, Carum, and Piet rode at the head of the troop, but Jenna refused a place at the front. Shaking her head, she guided Duty to the middle of the pack. The men smiled when she rode among them, thinking she did it for love, never guessing she did it in order to push away the memory of Catrona's lifeless hand in hers.

One thrust, Jenna. She heard Catrona's voice at every turning. *One thrust . . . and now all that training for naught.* Her face was grim with the memory. She took Catrona's death as the death of her own innocence. What did it matter that she had already killed one man, maimed another in the heat of battle? What did it matter that she had buried a hundred dead sisters? It was *this* death that gnawed and fretted her. She felt herself growing old, the years like a cold river rushing past, and she unable to stop the flow.

Jenna spoke to no one as they rode relentlessly down the road, but her mind rehearsed what had been. *One thrust . . . one thrust,* dead Catrona continued to rebuke. *One thrust.*

As they galloped, Jenna flexed her right hand as if feeling the sword again, pommel tight against her palm. Her fingers retained the weight of Piet's heavy blade. She longed to take the moment back, thrusting surely, finally, into the Bear's burly chest. What satisfaction it would bring her now, the slipping of the sharp edges through his flesh, past bone, to strike at last the bloody, pulsing heart. *One thrust.* She could feel his heart's blood spurt up the sword to her wrist, run along the blue branchings of her veins, race past the crook of elbow, across the muscles of her forearm, and snake under her right breast to lodge in her own ready heart.

Lifting her arm at the thought, she watched, fascinated, as if she could actually see the Bear's blood traveling along the route of her arm, as if she felt the jolt of it entering her heart.

She dropped her arm to her side. *One thrust.* Yet it was not in her. She was not such a killer. Even to bring Catrona back she would not kill a bound man. She *could* not. The Anna *could* not. And she *was* the Anna. There was no question of that now. It was not prophecy that told her. Nor Carum's impassioned belief. Nor Alta's soft persuasions in the Grenna's grove. Nor the king's wily importunings. Nor all the shoutings of the men. It was simply this: the blood running from hand to heart rejected the wild hatred of the Bear and his brothers. She *was* the Anna. For *this* time and *this* turning and *this* now.

Jenna urged Duty forward. The other horsemen parted to let her through and she galloped to the lead of the riders, taking her place between the king and Carum, only slightly ahead.

THE MYTH:

Then Great Alta drew up the dead warriors with the ladders of her hair, dark warrior by the golden hair, light warrior by the black. She set them to her breast, saying, "You are my own dear babes, you are my own sweet flesh, you are now my own bright companions."

BOOK FOUR

GENDER WARS

THE MYTH:

Then Great Alta struck the light sister on both cheeks, first one and then the other, for the deaths she had caused. Then she struck her on the back for the deaths she had not caused. Then she faced her toward the sun saying, "Now you must ride long and ride hard and ride well till you start again what has been ended here." She set the light sister upon a great gray horse and blew a wind at the light sister's back that she might have speed on her journey and no memory of sorrow.

THE LEGEND:

It was in Altenland, in a village called The High Crossing, that this story was found. It was told to Jenny Bardling by an old cook woman known only as Mother Comfort.

"My great aunt, that would be my mother's mother's sister, was a fighter. Fought in the army as blanket companion to the last of the great mountain warrior women, the one that was called Sister Light. She was almost six feet tall, my great aunt said, with long white braids—not gray, mind—and she wore them tied up on the top of her head. Her crown like. She kept an extra dirk there and, when quiet was needed, would strangle her foe with them braids. She fought like a Fog Demon, all silence and whirling.

"'Twas known no one could best her in battle for she carried a great leathern pack on her back and in it was

Sister Dark, a shadow who looked just like her but twice as big. Whenever Sister Light was losing—not often, mind—she would reach into that pack on her back and set the shadow fighter free. Sister Dark could move faster than the eye could see and quiet as grass growing. They used to say of her:

> *Deep as a spell*
> *Cold as a well*
> *Hard as a hate*
> *Brutal as fate.*

That was Sister Dark.

"Of course she only used that shadow when she was desperate because using it ate away at her, from the inside out. Like all such magicks. From the inside out. My great aunt never saw it proper, mind you. No one did. But everyone knew of Sister Dark. They did.

"Well, Sister Light died at last, in a big fight, a month long it was and the sun refusing to shine all that time. And where is a shadow without the sun, mind. It could only creep out of that pack with the sun bright overhead. Did I forget to tell you that?

"After the month was gone, someone found that pack, resting on the bleached bones that had been Sister Light. Long-boned she was, too, my great aunt said. That someone opened the pack, searching for treasure to be sure, and out crept the shadow. She looked around, eyes dark and nothing to be read there but hate. The land was blasted; what had been green was dust. And Sister Light nowt but bones, mind. She put back her head and howled, a sound they say still heard on that desolate plain.

"My great aunt told me—afore she died—that Sister Dark can still be seen, sometimes, when the sun beats down full over the land. Looking for her mate, maybe. Looking for someone else to carry her. Someone she can fight for, someone she can eat away at.

*"You have to be careful, up there on the high moors.
Especially in the mid of the day. That's where the saying
Never mate a shadow comes. They'll eat away at you if
they can."*

THE STORY:

The first day of long riding tired them all except for
Jenna who rode with Catrona's restless voice in her ear.
The road passed through small woods of birch and alder
alternating with large stands of old oak, across the tops
of gently rolling grassy hills, and over two streams. The
fords had deeper pools on either side that hinted at trout
stoking their fins behind dark granite boulders, but the
king did not let them stop. As there was no wind to whisk
away the dust of their riding, behind them, for a long
way, their passage could be read as a gray sentence up
against the blue of the sky. When they stopped at last for
the sake of the weary horses and to cook a quick meal
over small fires, the king sent three scouts on ahead.

"Catrona would have rested earlier," Jenna murmured to Petra and the boys.

"And be sending scouts afore time," Marek added,
shaking his head. Clearly he thought little of the king's
woodsense, his own so newly developed.

But an hour later, the three men sent out returned
with little to warn against. The road ahead, they said,
was clear of Kalas' men, the small farm holdings un-
disturbed by soldiers or rumor of war. In fact, one shep-
herd, newly returned from the great market town of New
Steading—a good day's ride to the north—reported to
them that even the usual company of king's troop had
departed before he had left there. If the Bear had gotten

back to his master, he surely had not ridden this way, or else he had not mustered them out with his story.

The king thanked them with a drink from his own leathern flask and an embrace that Jenna noticed came strictly from his arms. His eyes and mouth were not smiling. Returning to the smaller circle that consisted of Jenna, Carum, Piet, Petra, and the boys, the king pursed his lips.

"I expect Kalas will wait, choosing the Vale of Cres for a final battle," he said. "It's the gateway to the castle and there his numbers could overwhelm us on the field." He stood with his hands clasped behind him, a line furrowing his brow. "He will wait knowing that if we are to win anything, we must go to him. He will not expend himself over the whole of the Dales."

Piet nodded. He was squatting before a small cookfire, staring into the flames. He had not eaten, but simply looked into the fire as if discovering some wisdom there.

"He would be a fool to wait so long for us," Carum said, running his fingers through his hair. "And a fool to give us time to gather strength. We might be years coming to meet him."

"I agree," Jenna said. "Surely he will strike at us when he knows he has superior numbers. He has nothing to gain by letting us find more women and men for the fight. He is no fool."

"I agree he is no fool," said the king. "Still, he believes that a troop of his horse can beat any numbers of my men. My untrained Dales men."

"But you just beat the Bear with that untrained force . . ." Petra began.

"And *that*, my dear, is why we are racing so fast, stopping only to keep the men and horses from revolting—or dying. To gather as much brute strength and numbers as we can while we have our lure still fresh and enticing," said the king.

"The lure?" Sandor asked.

"The Anna, my young friend," said the king, gesturing casually at her. "The Anna!"

"Me!" Jenna said at the same time, her right fist over her heart.

"And then we be marching onto the Vale?" asked Marek, eager for the fight now.

"No!" Piet said. For the first time he stood and looked at them all.

"Piet is right," the king said smoothly. "We will go in a great circle around the Vale, recruiting more and more to the Anna's banner. And when we are large enough and strong enough, we will march on Kalas from all sides, a great bloody circle of us, like a noose, tightening around his ugly neck." He closed his fingers slowly into a fist.

"And while we bide our time, Kalas kills more women and fires the rest of the Hames." Jenna's voice was as bitter as if Catrona spoke from her mouth. "We cannot wait. We must not wait."

"By saving a few, we would lose the many," the king warned. "You are too young to understand it."

"I am near as old as you," Jenna retorted.

"Not by ten years—or a hundred," the king replied. "War means that some must die that others might live. A king is no certain age, for he is made up of all those hard judgments. The king—and not his wife or his brother or his war chief or his friend. The decision is mine alone. We ride north to New Steading to start our recruitment."

Jareth grabbed Gorum's arm, spinning him halfway around and Jenna had to hold onto Piet's arm to keep him from striking the boy. Strangled sounds came from Jareth's throat, more animallike than man. When it was clear no one understood, he tried to beat that same message on the king's sleeve with angry fingers.

"He knows something," Jenna whispered to Piet. "We must listen to him."

"He says nothing," Piet said, shrugging away from her grasp.

The king brushed Jareth away from him. "He knows nothing and says less."

"He knows we cannot let more die just for the sake of an argument." Carum's voice was deep with passion.

Smiling the sly smile Jenna had come to fear, Gorum said, "My brother, there is no argument. There is only the king's decision. You have studied too many old texts. I have studied men's hearts. We will go from town to town gathering a great army to us and word of it will reach Kalas. He will try and warn us off by his killings. They will become even more brutal. He will be sure to let us know of them. But with every ugly act, he will win us more men to the Anna's side. And when we can match him man for man . . ."

Carum stared at his brother. "Then you do not care how many more die or how horribly?"

"I welcome it. Does that shock you, brother?" Now the king looked grim. "They say in the Dales, Longbow, that *You cannot cross the river without getting your feet wet.*"

"You are no better than Kalas," Petra said. She turned away and stared at the little groups of men chatting quietly together all down the road.

"I am much better than Kalas, because I do what I do for the right. He is only for himself. I am for my people." The king's voice was very quiet. "*My* people, not his."

Carum cleared his throat. "Gorum, in those texts you so despise, there are many stories in which a small force beats a large one by cunning and guile. Do not forget cunning and guile and rely only on the gathering of brute strength. Do not forget the tale of the mouse and the cat my mother told us the day that bully Barnoo bloodied your nose."

The king smiled again. "Barnoo is dead."

"And Jenna killed him."

"And *I* am alive. *I* am the one with cunning and guile, dear brother, not you. Do not forget it. Such stories of the little overcoming the great are only wishes devised by a conquered people. Your mother was of the Dales. You are half her blood. I am wholly Garun."

"You are . . ." Carum began angrily.

"No, brother, *you* are . . . an open book. I have made *those* books my chiefest study. When I am returned to the throne, you can be my court philosopher, my teller of tales, my fool, dispensing scholarly wisdom. Then you can remind me of the stories your Dalian mother told us and the stories in your pretty books, all interlined with pictures of pussies and mice. But *now* we are soldiers. The stories we want to hear are of our great victories." He patted Carum on the shoulder as one would a scolded pet or a small child. Then he turned and called out to his men: "Mount up. Mount up. We ride to New Steading where we shall show them the Anna." He waved his right hand.

"THE ANNA! THE ANNA!" The call came back to him, continuing under the orchestration of his uplifted arm until he was satisfied. Then he nodded at them, turned and winked at Carum as if to underline his possession of the men, and dropped his arm down with a decisive chop. The men all mounted.

The last one up was Carum, his rage barely checked. Jenna pulled her horse's head around and urged it toward him with her knees.

"He is right about one thing, you know," she whispered. "Your face is a clean slate upon which all your thoughts are writ large."

"I am useless to him," Carum whispered back miserably. "And he lets everyone know it. Even you."

"No, you are right and he is turning now, even as we watch, into as much of a callous monster as the toad on the throne. But you must tell me of that story."

"What story?"

She reached out and touched his horse's neck, the skin silken under her fingers. "The one about the mouse and the cat. If a small force can indeed overcome a great one, it would comfort me to know how before I try."

He smiled at her slowly. "Before *we* try."

Stroking the horse's neck, she waited.

Carum told her the tale in a few short sentences and

when she nodded in understanding, he sent his horse forward to the front of the line with a swift, silent, energetic kick.

The next day, close to evening, they rode into New Steading from the south. It was market day and the stalls were still open, fruits and breads and silks displayed one next to the other without any discernible order. The cobbled streets, crowded with buyers, were abuzz with the chants and cries of traders. Even above the sound of the horses, Jenna could hear the strange babble of bargains: *Fresh haddock, fresh . . . bread HOT from the . . . blood root newly dug . . . buy my weave, buy my bright weavings . . .*

Never having been in such a crowd before, she turned uneasily to stare back at her friends. Petra's eyes were wide with amazement. Beside her Marek and Sandor were openly gawking and pointing. Only Jareth seemed contained, as if his own silence cocooned him.

They rode in a disciplined line through the main street. Though a few glanced sideways down the twisting narrow ways where tiers of narrow houses leaned familiarly across the alleys, not a one dared straggle. The king was pleased: pleased with the crowds, pleased with his men, pleased with the ease of his entry. His faced showed it.

At the front of the line of riders, Duty suddenly began a high prancing which Jenna could not control. It was as if the horse, faced with an appreciative audience, remembered some previous training. Jenna nearly lost her seat at the first sideward motion. She grabbed the reins, jerking hard. This pulled Duty's head in and the horse arched her neck until her chin actually touched against her burly chest. Jenna pressed inward with knees and thighs, thinking that any harder and they would go straight through the horse's sides. Instead, it turned out to be a special signal. In response, Duty raised her own knees in an even higher strut.

Jenna felt a fool, rolling from side to side on the horse's broad back before the delighted crowd. But the market-goers cheered the horse's tricks and the king grinned broadly. No one seemed to think it foolish or dangerous, except for Jenna who clung grimly to the reins, keeping her thighs so hard against Duty, they trembled with the effort.

All the way along the main street Duty danced with Jenna fighting to keep both her seat and her dignity. Behind her, the riders began their chant of her name: "THE ANNA! THE ANNA! THE ANNA!" the sound of it bouncing crazily off the stone facades of the houses. Jenna could hardly believe so much sound could come from a simple echo until she realized there were people leaning out of the windows of the houses, waving their hands and calling back to the riders.

"THE ANNA! THE ANNA! THE ANNA!"

It was not clear that they knew what they were shouting, or if indeed they were shouting any distinguishable name. But the sound of it was deafening and some of the horses were made nervous by it, shying away or houghing uneasily through their noses. Their riders sawed at the reins and one or two actually used their whips, which further agitated the mounts. Only Duty seemed to enjoy the scene, actually playing up to the crowds.

The main street ended at wide stone steps that led up to a palatial building. Duty set her front feet on the first step, stopping suddenly, nearly flinging Jenna over her head. Jenna answered by giving a last, hard, angry pull on the reins, wrenching Duty's head up. The horse whinnied loudly, reared, and kicked her front legs in the air. Jenna hung on. An admiring cheer rose from the children who had scattered along the steps to watch.

When Duty settled down again, Jenna dismounted, shaken, and handed the reins to one eager child. Her legs ached and, for a moment, she was afraid she might not be able to stand. Then she bit her lip, almost drawing blood, and forced herself to face the gathering crowd.

The king dismounted as well, and when he did there were one or two who recognized him immediately despite the worn and tattered clothes.

"It's the old king's son," someone cried out.

"The new king, then," an enormous woman said.

"Gorum!" The name was spoken first by a black-haired young man, taken up quickly two and three times by his friends.

"The king's Pike," one added.

Word of him paced the arrival of more New Steadingers, and soon the square was packed tight with townsfolk, most of whom now swore they had known the king at once.

Gorum let the tension build and build, and Jenna had to admire how he acknowledged it, nodding slowly and turning slowly so that all could get a glimpse of him. As the crowd grew, he moved up one step at a time, always careful to keep Jenna on his right hand, Carum on his left, Piet to guard the back; until at last they commanded the very top stairs before the palace, with his men ranging down the sides like an inverted letter V, the king and Jenna at the point. Jenna wondered if Gorum and his men had long planned such a maneuver, for they moved with such precision, or if kings were just born knowing how to do such things. She glanced across at Carum who just shook his head twice but said nothing.

The king raised his hands and everyone quieted; not all at once but in a kind of ripple, from the point of the V downward. When total silence had been achieved, he began to speak, with a grand enunciation, so different from his regular speech.

"You know me, my good people."

They filled the sudden silence with his title: "THE KING! THE KING!"

He let the echo fade, then smiled. "Not King Kalas. Not that usurping, murdering, piji-eating toad. Not he."

They laughed and applauded each phrase.

"I am the true-born king, Gorum, son of Ordrum and the lady Jo-el-ean."

He waited for their approving murmur before continuing. "The king thrust off a throne made vacant by the untimely deaths of my poor murdered father and his wife, your sister of the Dales."

As if this were the very first time they had heard of the murders, the people groaned. Gorum let the groan swell up, then die away, a falling drift of sound. Just before the last of it was gone, he added, "And the cowardly killing of my brother, the saintly Jorum, who was next in line to be king."

They moaned again on cue. Jenna noticed Carum shaking his head slightly, though whether it was at the king's crafty manipulations or the naming of his older brother as a saint, she could not guess.

"But I am here for you, good folk. And as you can see, I am not alone." This time when he waited there was no vocal reaction at all, but the silence was filled with anticipation. Jenna thought he looked pleased. She was not sure why.

"You see Her," he said suddenly. "You know Her. You have already named Her." He held out his right hand to Jenna.

The child holding Duty's reins cried out in a high, piercing voice that carried around the crowded square: "The White One."

Caught up in the mummery of the moment, Jenna suddenly put her hand into the king's, moving closer to him than she had done before. His palm was ice-cold, his fingers iron-strong. Realizing what she had just done, she tried to pull her hand away, but he prisoned it in his. She could not get loose without making an ugly scene, so she stood still, her face a mask.

"Yes," the king continued smoothly as if Jenna's hand in his were easily held, "she *is* the White One, good folk. The one we have awaited. She was born of three mothers and all of them dead. She killed the Hound to save my brother Carum." He pointed with his left hand at Carum, but Carum neither moved nor nodded and Jenna felt grateful for that show of quiet dignity.

"And she slew the Bull to save her own sister. We have his ring as proof." He opened his left hand as if waiting for Carum to drop the ring in. When Carum did not move, the king hesitated for only a second, then dropped Jenna's hand with a flourish and strode over to his brother. He reached for Carum's neck, fishing up the leather thong around it. At the thong's end was a heavy crested ring. Jenna suddenly recalled the severed hand that had last worn it. Dangling the ring before the crowd, the king smiled. The watching people began to cheer.

Dropping the ring against Carum's chest, the king turned. He let the cheering continue for a long moment and then, with a savage slicing motion of his hand, cut them off.

"And because of the White One, a woman named Cat was killed just two days past." He waited for the challenge he knew would come.

"'Tis the wrong Cat," the enormous woman called out. "The Cat that was meant still lives. And drinks his milk from Kalas' hand."

Slowly the king turned toward her, his manner courteous but firm. "And do *you*, my good woman, know how to read prophecy? Are you a Garunian priest? Or a priestess of Alta's Hames?"

She looked back at him, discomforted. "I know what I know," she mumbled.

"Then know this as well, woman, prophecy cannot be read straight on. It must be read *on the slant!*" He roared the last so that all could hear. Then he walked down three steps, leaving Jenna and Carum behind him, passing grim-faced Piet, so that he was in the very middle of the V, the center of all eyes.

"The prophecy says but *Cat*. Not *this* Cat nor *that* Cat. But *CAT!* And Cat was killed. That makes three."

He held up his hand, counting slowly on his fingers. "One, the Hound. Two, the Bull. Three, the Cat. All killed by the White One, as is writ in prophecy, the Anna for whom we have so long waited. And we have but one more, the Bear, to go and the prophecy will be fulfilled. For She is the one who signals the end of the false reign, the beginning of the new. The Anna." He flung his right hand back and pointed up at Jenna.

"What you call new was once old," the enormous woman whispered, but it was clear any argument she had had already met defeat. Trying one last time, speaking loudly enough so that her nearest neighbors could hear, she added, "Besides girls dressing like men, playing at war . . . taint . . . taint natural. We've all said it." But her voice was drowned out by the cheers, first of the children, then the grown men and women. And mixed in with those cheers were the names of the king, the Anna, and Carum all intertwined.

THE SONG:

The Heart and the Crown

They rode into town
On the thirteenth of Spring.
She gave him her hand
And he gave her his ring.
She gave him her heart
And he gave her his crown,
But they never, no never
Went down derry down derry down.

Her horse was pure white
And his horse was a gray.
She wanted to go
But he asked her to stay.
She gave him her heart

And he gave her his crown,
But they never, no never
Went down derry down derry down.

Her eyes were pure black
And his eyes were so blue.
She wanted him strong
And he wanted her true.
She gave him her heart
And he gave her his crown
But they never, no never
Went down derry down derry down.

Come all ye fair maidens,
And listen to me,
If you want your young man
To be strong and free,
Just give him your heart
And he'll give you his crown
Just as long as you never
Go down derry down derry down.

THE STORY:

They had supper in the open atrium of the great town hall with the members of the New Steading council. It was a tremendous banquet, more impressive, Jenna thought, because it had been put together so quickly by the townfolk.

Though she was apprehensive, Jenna discovered that no one really expected her to speak. In fact, her presence at the dinner made most of the New Steadingers uncomfortable and few sought her out. However, most tracked her movements around the tables with cautious, fascinated eyes. It was as if they planned to commit every detail of her dinner to memory, making it into ballads and stories after.

Jenna commented wryly to Petra, "And will they sing about *The Day the Anna Ate Apples* or rather *How the White One Washed Her Fingers?*"

Laughing, Petra made up an instant rhyme.

> *"When Jenna ate apples,*
> *Her teeth crunched the pips,*
> *She stuck bits of bread*
> *Into melted cheese dips,*
> *She ate stalks of celery,*
> *Drank cups of tea*
> *And after went looking*
> *For somewhere to . . ."*

"Enough," Jenna whispered. "Enough." She put her hand over her mouth to keep from laughing aloud. But when she sat down at the head of the table, beside the king, she found she had no appetite. The near-unseating by Duty's clever prancing, the lingering feel of Gorum's cold hand, the memory of Catrona's burial, the staring of the New Steading strangers, all conspired to kill what hunger she had had. Even though they put a plate before her, she ate nothing, simply pushing the bits of vegetable and browned meats around with her knife.

The watching councillors saw that she did not eat and a few even wondered aloud at it.

The king said, as if under his breath but loud enough for those closest to hear, "The gods rarely eat of our food."

His words passed from breath to breath around the table, as he knew they would. Some even believed them.

Petra heard, but did not pass on the king's message. She could hardly keep from laughing and mouthed at Jenna: *"and after went looking . . ."*

Jenna lowered her eyes to the table and did not notice Petra tucking a piece of chicken breast, a large slice of cornmeal bread, and a spring leek into her napkin. But Jareth sitting beside her did, and he added several white mushrooms and a twist of brown bread to Petra's hoard.

After the dinner, the king spoke again, urging the councillors to conscript men for his army. "To fight the toad," he said.

They needed little urging, especially sitting as they did under the eye of the Anna and with seven or eight hearty toasts of the dark red wine behind them. They even signed a paper promising him two hundred young men and their weapons. He kissed them each on the right cheek for such largesse and promised that they and New Steading would be remembered.

Jenna waited until the writing was done. But during the congratulations, she stood. The moment she was up, all other movement ceased. Even the serving girls, weighted down with platters, stopped in mid-stride. Jenna wondered what she might say to them. The king had such ease with words, and she had none. She suddenly envied him. Opening her mouth to give at least some thanks, she found she had nothing to say, so she closed her mouth abruptly so she might not sound stupid in the attempt.

At the other end of the long table, Carum leaped to his feet. "We have had a long riding," he said. "And another to come in the morning. Even an avatar of the Goddess must rest. Human flesh, though it be just the clothing of a great spirit, tires." He walked to Jenna's end of the table and took her hand in his. Slowly he raised it to his mouth and set his lips formally on her knuckles. *His* hand and mouth were warm.

Jenna smiled. Then slowly, gracefully, she withdrew her hand. He let it slip easily through his fingers.

"Thank you," she said simply to the New Steadingers. "For everything." Then she nodded at the king, at Piet, and Petra with the boys, and turned. Carum followed her to the door.

"Don't worry," he whispered. "I'm right behind you."

*   *   *

They fumbled the first turn in the dark hall and had to backtrack.

"This is worse than the Hame," Carum grumbled.

Remembering which Hame and what she had found there on her return, Jenna said nothing. None of the doors off the hall looked familiar. *Any one of them would do,* she thought. All she wanted was to be away from the oppression of so many staring eyes.

"That one!" she said, suddenly pointing.

They went through the door and found themselves in a large room. A little light filtered in through corbeled windows that looked out onto the great stone stairs. Jenna realized they were in some sort of council room for there was a wooden table set about by heavy wooden chairs. Along the sides of the room were more chairs and several couches. She sat down on the nearest couch, drew in a deep breath, and sighed.

"What would I do without you, Carum?"

"I hope you never have to," he answered quickly.

"Do not play at word games with me. I am not one of your Garunian followers nor a peddler from New Steading."

"I don't play games with you, Jenna."

"All you Garunians play games. Your brother worst of all."

"And you don't?" His usually gentle voice was sharp.

"No. Never."

"Then can you tell me what game it was you were *not* playing when you went to my brother this evening?"

She looked up. He was only a dark shadow in the room looming over her. She could not see his face. "I did not go to him," she protested, feeling again that cold hand under hers, the iron grip of his fingers.

"I saw you."

"He pulled me. He would not let me go."

"You slipped your hand out of mine easily enough just now in the dining room."

"*You* let me go. *You* did not force me."

"I would *never* force you."

"Then what are we arguing about?" She was truly puzzled. Recalling something he had said the weeks, the months—the years—ago when they had met, she suddenly understood. "You are jealous. That is what it is. Jealous." She expected him to deny it.

He sat down beside her on the couch. "I am. I admit it. Horribly jealous." His voice was once again soft.

"And what about that oak?" She laughed. "What about that larch? Are waiting trees jealous?"

He laughed back. "Of every passing wind. Of every flying bird. Of every squirrel on a branch and every fox in its bole. Of anything capable of moving toward you."

She put her hand out blindly in the dark and found his face. She could feel, even without seeing it, that his brow was ridged; he was wearing that furrowed look he got when he was thinking. She smoothed the furrows with two fingers.

"What are you thinking of?" she asked.

"Of how I love you despite the deaths that lie between us."

"Hush," she whispered. "Do not soil your mouth with those deaths. Do not think of the Hound. Do not think of the Bull. Do not remember Catrona or the women of the Hames. We must not let their blood come between us." She realized that she had said nothing of the other word, *love,* and wondered if he realized it, too.

"I saw more of those deaths than even you have, Jo-an-enna. I cannot help think of them. I cannot help think of my part in them." But then he did hush, giving himself over to her ministrations.

For a long moment, her fingers on his forehead were the only contact between them. Then he put his hands up and found her waiting face in the dark. Slowly he ran his fingers down her braids, and began to unplait them. She did not move until he had shaken her hair free of its bindings, tumbling it over her shoulders, where it lay smelling of wind and riding.

She had all she could do to remember to breathe and then, somehow, she was right next to him and his mouth was on hers. They were lying on the sofa, covered in the canopy of her hair. She felt she had to give him something, some great gift, but she could not speak the word *love*.

"My true name," she whispered at last, "is Annuanna. Annuanna. No one knows it now but my Mother Alta, my dark sister, and you."

"Annuanna," he whispered into her mouth, his breath sweet with it.

Then mouth on mouth, tongue to tongue, without ever saying the word *love*, they learned more than she had ever been told or he had ever discovered in his books about it, and they learned it together, far, far into the night.

THE HISTORY:

The sexual taboos of the ancient Garunians and Dalites differed so greatly that one would be hard put to find any commonalities. The Garunians had a sophisticated society and had borrowed eagerly from their Continental neighbors for both their hetero- and their homosexual tastes. By the time they had conquered the island kingdom of the Dales, they had been through many baroque periods of alternating orgiastic and celibate marriage modes. We have much evidence of this from Continental sources. (See Doyle's earliest work, her doctoral thesis: "Amatory Practices, Obligatory Vows" which was later turned into the popular book I Do, We Do: Or What the Garunians Did.)

But of the Garunians after the conquest of the Dales we know little, and must make do with educated guesses. Doyle, sensibly, assumes they carried the group marriage concept, then so popular on the Continent, across the Bay of All Souls with them. Again, with eminent sensibleness, she hypothesizes that polygamy allowed the Garunian nobles to marry within the Garun hierarchy and the Dalian upper classes; a king might have wives from both without violating the strict Dale code of sexual ethics.

As the Dalites were matriarchal at that time (see Cowan's brilliant "Mother and Son: How Titles Passed Through the Dalian Line," Demographics Annual, Pasden University Press, #58.) all monies, land, and titles passed maternally so the conquest by the patriarchal Garuns must have meant quite a change. There is even evidence that the Dalites did not understand the man's role in the creation of children, believing in some odd form of female cloning, the "mirror twins" which Magon is so fond of exploring. (Diana Burrow-Jones uncovers this attitude in her chapter "The Papa Perplex" in Encyclopedia of the Dales.) However difficult the change may have been on the Dale psyches, things evidently went relatively smoothly for four hundred years. The Garun kings took wives from the Dales, staying carefully abstinent with them but nonetheless binding the Dale tribes to them in this way. The Dale wives were given the title of priestess and made honorary mothers, or Mother Altas according to Sigel and Salmon, though their evidence is still rather fragmentary.

Magon, of course, in his typical inane leaps, tries to prove that many of the later kings (especially Oran, father of Langbrow, and Langbrow himself) actually bedded their Dale wives, producing offspring. He cites as evidence a few old and rather coarse rhymes, including the infamous

> When Langbrow put his awl in
> To carve a wooden babe
> That of a larch and of an oak
> Was so securely made . . .

as well as the tender dedicatory note writ in hand (and by whose hand we do not know) on the one extant copy we *have of Langbrow's* Book of Battles: This littl booke is for thee Annuanna, my luv, my lighte. *Leaving aside the fact that Langbrow's Garunian wife was named Jo-el-ean (the infamous Jo-el-ean who refused to sit by her husband's side and thus brought down his reign in ruin and infamy) the name* Annuanna, *despite its feminine ending has long been considered a man's name, being the shortened form of* Annuannatan. *If in fact the dedication is in Langbrow's hand, it makes more sense that he would sign the* Book of Battles *to a male friend;* Annuannatan *can only be his homosexual lover, his blanket companion from the army. If Dr. Magon had done this kind of root work, he would not now be making a fool of himself in scholarly circles.*

THE STORY:

It was two days before they left New Steading, for it took that long to round up and equip two hundred young men. In fact, there were two hundred and thirty-seven by actual count, including the mayor's oldest son. And there was new clothing for the men already following the king, as well as dozens of pikes and swords loaned by the town fathers. Carum looked splendid in a wine-colored jerkin and trews and a showy white shirt pipped with gold. The king was all in gold weave. Even Piet looked resplendent, though he had chosen green and brown "to blend in with the woods," he had muttered, adding, "Gold is fine for ceremony, my lord, but war is another matter altogether."

Gorum had laughed at that. "Wherever a king is, there *is* ceremony."

"Wherever a king is, there *is* war," Carum had put in, but they ignored him.

Jenna had refused her new clothes since all they offered her were women's skirts and bodices dressed with
fancy beading. She knew the skirts would make riding
difficult, guessed the beads would catch in any brush and
leave an easy trail to follow. Instead she brushed out her
old skins, borrowing a needle and thread to mend the few
tears. She did not need to be fancy. In war one needed the
proper equipment. And as Catrona had reminded her in
training: *In a fight anything is a sword.*

She did accept their offer of a bath, however, and
spent over an hour soaking. Her only regret, as she sank
into the warm water, was that the smell of Carum's flesh
on hers disappeared in the first soaping, though when she
closed her eyes, she could recall its deep, tangy odor. She
thought she would know him anywhere, just from that
smell. Still, as the water enveloped her, she gave herself
over to its ministry. Such long ridings offered only cold
country streams and though she was used to the chilly
lavings, having had long practice out in the woods, and
washed herself dutifully every day they found so much as
a catchpool, she had, after all, been brought up in a
Hame with a famous deep-heated bath. It was the only
bit of civilization she really missed.

When had she taken her last hot bath? It felt like
forever since she and Petra had soaked in the Hame together. But in the Dales they said: *Forever is no distance
at all.*

Jenna knew that the distance was there. Something
had certainly changed Petra—or changed Jenna. She and
Carum had emerged from the council room holding
hands but once they had found the main door, had
moved apart swiftly, walking down into the town square
so removed from one another, they could not have
touched even by stretching.

They had found Petra leaning against a wall, nibbling on a piece of chicken, eyes closed.

"Petra!" Jenna whispered.

Petra's eyes opened slowly, almost reluctantly.

"And where did you two get to?"

Carum turned and left abruptly, without even trying to offer an excuse. Jenna refused to watch him go.

"I saw you did not eat," Petra continued, as if Carum had never been there at all, had not been included in her initial accusation. "So I saved a whole napkin full of food for you for later. Such theft does not come easily to me. I am trained to be a Mother Alta. And then you were nowhere to be found."

"I was . . ." Jenna began, then realized that she could say nothing to Petra. *Nothing.* Petra was still a girl, after all, and Jenna was a girl no longer. Change *had* happened, slowly, yet suddenly. And Petra had not shared it. Jenna wondered that the change did not show easily—on her cheeks, in her eyes, on her mouth, still soft from all those kisses. Reaching out, she picked off a bit of the chicken in Petra's hand.

"Thanks," she said. "I *am* starved."

"No wonder," Petra said. "If the gods do not eat of our food, they are bound to get hungry."

"*Rarely* eat," Jenna corrected her. "He said *rarely!*"

Petra handed her the leek bulb, but Jenna shook her head, so Petra chewed it herself.

"They want me to stay here," Petra said.

"Who does?"

"Everyone. The mayor . . ." She hesitated.

"Perhaps you should," Jenna said slowly, horrified at the thought.

"They said women should not be at war. That we are not strong as men. The townsfolk said that."

"And what about me? What about the Anna?"

"You are a goddess. That is different."

"Alta's women should be where they will. We are trained to war as well as to peace."

"I *knew* you would say that." Petra grinned. "And that is what I told them. That and that Alta's priestess must ride at the Anna's side. After all, many women have already died that you might ride on and I ride with you."

"That is not why they died."

"You know what I mean."

"Stick to your rhyme. You are clearer that way." Jenna bit her lip. *How could she have said such a cruel thing?*

But Petra laughed, missing the cruelty entirely, or dismissing it. "You are right, of course. If I am to be your priestess, I had better be very clear—or very obscure. But correct either way!" She gave Jenna a hug.

"Whew!" Jenna said. "If you insist on eating spring leeks, your breath will be as strong as *five* men's even if your arm is not."

They both laughed then, friends again, and walked into the town hall.

The ride out of New Steading toward the east had been accompanied by the cheering of the townsfolk. Jenna kept Duty from prancing, having been instructed by one of the men in how to keep the horse under control. She rode next to Carum, but that was as close as they had gotten since he had walked away from Petra's questions. After that they had both been too busy, always surrounded by men.

Over the thudding of the horse's hooves, the fading shouts behind them, Jenna called, "Do you . . . still . . ." She hesitated. How could she scream *that* word where others might hear it?

His mouth twisted wryly, the scar under his left eye crinkling up, as if winking wantonly at her. "Of course I still *remember,* if that is the word you want. I remember every move. Every . . . thing." He gave her a big grin. "An oak remembers. And you?"

She smiled back. "Jo-an-enna means lover of white birches."

"What?" The hoofbeats had obscured her answer.

She repeated it, calling: "If you are a tree, I am a tree."

"I am a man," he said. "Not a tree."

"I know," she whispered. "That I *truly* know."

Then their horses, forced by the ones following, broke into a canter which stopped all talk as they galloped on down the winding road.

They paused at two smaller towns on the way, adding a dozen men to their force, the king showing off Jenna as if she were some sort of exotic animal imported from the Continent. Carum grumbled about it loudly, but even he had to admit the show seemed to be working.

Piet was not so pleased. "Twelve men when we need twelve hundred," he said. "When twelve thousand would not be amiss."

"Then what about women?" Jenna asked. They were stopped at the next rest, the new boys being well introduced while the horses made quick work of the grass by the roadside. "Surely we are near some Hame." She paused, adding quietly, "There must be *some* Hame still unharmed close by. You said ten gone, but there were . . ." her voice cracked, "seventeen."

Piet grunted; what answer he meant to give was unclear. But the king shook his head. "These are not regular army men used to blanket companions. These are boys right off the farms or right out of their fathers' shops. The girls they know cook and sew. If we are to keep their minds on their new swords . . ."

"The women of the Hame know how to wield their swords. And they have a reason to . . ."

"There is *one* Hame nearby," Carum interrupted suddenly. He reached into his saddlebag and drew out a map. Spreading it across his horse's flank, he ran a finger along a wavering black line. "We are somewhere here . . ."

"Here!" Piet said, jabbing at the map with his forefinger.

Carum nodded. "And there—" His finger pointed to a strange hatching of marks. "That is M'dorah Hame."

"M'dorah?" Jenna thought back to the list that

Catrona had reeled off when their fateful journey had started. *Selden, Calla's Ford, Wilma's Crossing, Josstown, Calamarie, Carpenter's, Krisston, West Dale, Annsville, Crimerci, Lara's Well, Sammiton, East James, John-o-the-Mill's, Carter's Tracing, North Brook, Nill's* . . . remembering Nill's she set her jaw. *But there had been no mention of a M'dorah.* Aloud, she said, "I have never heard of it."

Looking up, Carum said, almost absently, "It's an odd place, Jenna. Not exactly a regular Hame, at least that's what the books say. They broke away from the first Alta and built their Hame atop an inaccessible cliff. The only way up is by rope ladder. They will have nothing to do with men. They have never sent fighters to the army. And they have never sent . . ."

"M'dorah," Petra mused. "They never send missioners out. My Mother Alta always threatened that if we did not behave, she would send *us* to M'dorah on our mission: *High-towered Hame where eagles dare not nest.* I thought it but a story."

"Perhaps that's all it is," Carum said. "But it is supposed to be nearby."

"Let us go," Jenna said suddenly. "If it exists at all, we will bring back many women fighters to swell your ranks. And they will be women who want nothing to do with your men, so the boys will not be troubled by them."

The king laughed. "Then you do not understand boys! They can make a woman out of flowers, out of trees, out of dreams. Their bodies smell of springtide all year long."

Jenna blushed furiously.

"There is nothing there. No one," Piet growled. "It means taking time out for a mere tale."

"Perhaps not," Carum put in. "Stories have to start somewhere."

"This one started as a joke after too much wine," Piet groused. "And too few women."

"From the map," Jenna said, "it looks to be less than a day's ride from here. And you *did* say you needed more fighters. *And* you wanted to buy yourself time. Let me go. I will persuade them."

"Persuade *eagles*!" Piet said.

"You are too precious to let go." The king's face was thoughtful.

"I will go with her," Carum said. "We will return."

Looking at the map carefully, the king traced the road from the hatched site of M'dorah. Finally he turned to Jenna. "We will camp there for the night," he said, pointing to the place where the road to M'dorah turned off. "You will have until morning. No sleep, but then as they say on the Continent: *Surely a dream is worth a little sleep!*" He laughed silently. "Piet will go with you. Carum, you will remain here."

He knows, Jenna thought. *He knows about Carum and me.* The thought embarrassed her, then made her mad, as if Gorum had sullied them by knowing.

Carum began to protest, but Jenna nodded abruptly, cutting off his argument. "Piet," she agreed. "And Petra. I will need my priestess with me if I am to convince them to join us."

"Piet for protection and the girl for conviction. An unlikely pair." He smiled.

"I am my own protection," Jenna said. "And Piet is for *your* convictions."

Gorum nodded solemnly. He put his hand out. "Your hand on your return."

"You have my word on it," she said. "Besides, you have here those I most care for in the world." She gestured to Jareth, Marek, Sandor. That her circling hand did not include Carum was proof to herself that she was not being entirely truthful to the king. After all, she had not mentioned Pynt or A-ma or the other women of Selden Hame either. Surely *they* were the ones she *most* cared for.

If the king noticed her omission, he did not mention

it, holding his hand steadily toward her. She was forced to take it, feeling again its lack of warmth as palm to palm they made their pledge.

The road to M'dorah was hardly a road at all, just an overgrown path where the trees suddenly widened. It was Piet who recognized it as a roadway, though when challenged afterward by Marek, he could not explain how he had known.

The king called a halt and the large company encircled the meadow, setting up camp. Scouts were sent to locate water and to track ahead down the main road. But Piet, Petra, and Jenna turned along the scant path.

Jenna looked back only once, hoping to see Carum watching. But he was nowhere in sight. She entered the trees thinking about the perfidy of men; how love, like memory, *could* be false; and conscious of Duty's broad back beneath her.

The trees were tall and full, a busy forest of much variety. Jenna identified beech, oak, whitethorn, and larch with ease, but there were many trees she had never seen before, some with spotty barks, some with needle leaves, and some with roots that twisted over and around one another above the earth like a badly plaited braid of hair. Ahead of them bright birds piped warnings from the branches, then flew away in noisy confusion. If there was sign of larger animals, Jenna did not notice for Piet kept up a quick pace, threading them through the trees on the ever-ascending path as if he knew where he was going.

After a couple of hours, the path suddenly narrowed and they had to dismount, leading the horses for another hundred yards until the path disappeared entirely. They were forced to leave the horses tied loosely, and set off on foot. The way Piet chose wound upward at an even steeper angle, and soon they were all three breathing hard. Jenna felt a small pain under her breastbone but she would not admit it out loud.

It was clear Piet understood the deep woods. He

knew how to check before stepping. But Petra, in the full skirts she had been given by the New Steadingers, was having a great deal of trouble in the pathless ascent. Her clothes caught frequently on the thorny bushes and they lost precious time freeing her. Jenna clicked her tongue against the roof of her mouth in annoyance, glad that she, at least, had kept her skins for the trip.

At last the ascending woods thinned out and they could see a clear space ahead. When they reached it, they found themselves at the start of a high, treeless plain. The plain was covered with what seemed to be a forest of gigantic, towering rocks, some slim needle points, others wider sword blades, still others enormous leaning towers of stone, all hundreds of feet high. They had to crane their necks to see to the tops.

"It is true, then," Petra said when she had caught her breath.

"The cliffs at least are true," Piet said. "As to the Hame . . ."

"Look!" Jenna pointed. Atop one of the broadest of the stones, far across the plain toward the north, was some kind of building. As they moved closer, over the rock-strewn plain, they could make it out. It had wooden galleries scaffolded into space and a roof like a series of giant mushrooms. Jenna could see no continuous path cut into the rock's side. "There *must* be steps on the other side," she whispered to herself, but the others heard.

"We'll look," Piet said.

It took them another two hours, into the fading light of evening, to circle the stone, but they found nothing.

"Then how does anyone get up?" Petra asked.

"Perhaps they fly like eagles," Piet suggested.

"Perhaps they burrow like moles," Jenna added.

They were still offering suggestions, when not twenty feet from them first a sound and then a cascading of something down the stone face brought them to the spot. It was a hinged ladder of rope and wood.

"Someone is up there," Petra said, staring beyond the ladder, her hand shading her eyes.

"Someone who knows we are down here," Piet said. He began to draw his sword.

Jenna put her hand on his arm. "Hold," she said. "It is a woman. A sister."

Piet looked up. Someone *was* descending the rope ladder. He slipped the sword back in its sheath, but his hand did not stray from the hilt.

In the swiftly darkening night, it was hard to make out the figure climbing down. The shadow was stocky, heavier on top than on the bottom, somehow badly misshapen. Jenna wondered if only disfigured women—or the deranged—would remove themselves to such a place. Then she remembered Mother Alta of Nill's Hame: blind, twisted, with six fingers on each hand. She had not needed a sanctuary apart from the others. *We women take care of our own,* she thought. *There is another reason for this forbidding Hame.*

The shadow unwound itself from the ladder and stood before them. It was a woman, of that there was no doubt by the closeweave bodice she wore. But her strange humped back was . . .

"A babe!" Petra said.

At that very moment, the child bound to the woman's back gave a cry of delight, waving its one free hand.

"I be Iluna. Who be ye?" the woman asked abruptly.

"I am Piet, first lieutenant to . . ."

Pointedly ignoring him, Iluna stepped up to Petra and Jenna, putting her back to Piet's face. The babe, seeing his heavy beard, stopped laughing and pulled in her little arm tight against her chest.

"Who be ye?" Iluna asked again.

"I be . . . I am Petra," Petra began, "of the ruined Nill's Hame, in training to be priestess to my own."

"And ye?"

"I am Jo-an-enna of . . ."

"She is the White One, the Anna, the anointed of the Great Alta," Petra said. "She is the one of whom prophecy sings."

"Nonsense!" Iluna shifted the baby slightly.

"What?" Clearly Petra was startled, but Jenna decided in that instant that she liked Iluna.

"I said *nonsense*. She is a woman. Like you. Like me. Even in the shadows I can see that. But she is a woman with a message."

"You know . . ." Petra began.

"Else she would not be here. Nor ye. No one comes to M'dorah, lest they be terribly lost, without a message or a quest." She turned back to the stone and put her hand upon the ladder. "Come. After I am half up, put thy hand to steady the rung, then mount. The bearded one stays here."

"I go with them," Piet protested.

Iluna turned, her face unreadable in the almost-dark. "If ye mount the ladder, it will be cut when ye near the top and ye shall fall the hundred feet and we will leave thy bones below. No man enters M'dorah and lives. Be ye starving at the foot of our tower, we will throw down food. Be ye wounded, we will send a healer to ye. But mount the ladder, and we will cast ye down without another thought. Believe it."

"We believe it," Petra said quickly.

"I will return, Piet. On Catrona's grave, I swear it. I will go back with you," Jenna promised.

When Iluna was halfway up, Petra began to climb, holding onto the shaking ladder with sweaty hands. By Jenna's turn, it was pitch-black, the sky overhead sprinkled with stars that gave no light. She grasped the ladder and found rung after rung by feel alone. A slight breeze brushed loose hair over her eyes. Drawing in the spider breaths meant for difficult climbs, she felt her arms and legs begin to move fluidly, the rock face a blankness before her eyes. One slow breath after another, she drew herself up the ladder. When the ladder stopped its strange tremblings, she guessed that Petra had reached the top. Twenty more rungs, and she heard voices above her, calling encouragement. The last rungs held steady as they were wood set right into the stone itself with iron bands.

"Welcome, sister," a woman called.

Jenna looked up into a lantern the woman held. It illuminated the ladder with a strong light.

"Or should I say welcome, sisters!"

"Thank you," a voice said suddenly by Jenna's side, "though in the dark I made little of the climb."

"Skada!" Jenna turned slightly, surprised to see her dark sister clinging to a shadow ladder on the rock face next to her.

"Well, Jen, and what have you been up to these past few days, eh?" In the lantern's glow, her mocking smile was unmistakable.

Unaccountably, Jenna blushed.

"You need not get red-faced on *my* account, sister," Skada whispered. "He *does* smell sweet."

"Sssssskada!" Jenna hissed. Then she laughed uneasily. Of course Skada would know everything.

As if reading her mind, Skada laughed back, "Not *everything*, sister. After all, it was very dark in that room and you lit no candles. I have only your memories . . ."

"I will light no candles. Ever! Carum would not allow it!"

"Hmmmmm," Skada said, "and have you asked him?" But then she was forced to laugh at Jenna's discomfort and Jenna, in turn, laughed with her.

"Come, sisters," the woman called down to them, "ladders are no easy places for conversation. Join us at our meal. It is a simple feast, but there is enough for three more."

"Feast?" Skada said. "And I starving!"

They scrambled up the last few rungs and the woman led them toward the building. Hung now with soft lights that bobbed in each twist of wind, the Hame was of both wood and stone, built to accommodate the various surfaces of the rock tower. Yet unlike a dirt foundation that might be smoothed for the easy placement of a house, the stone had resisted the makers who had to erect according to the cuts and crevices nature offered them. It made for a strange building, Jenna thought, with rooms on many levels and odd risers within a single room.

The dining room was on three different levels, all dictated by the rock. A great table sat on the highest level with over twenty chairs around it. On the next level there were a half dozen smaller tables with between four and eight chairs. The lowest level held serving tables, loaded down with food. When they got close, Jenna saw that the tables and chairs were not of solid make but pieced together.

The meal held many familiar foods: eggs boiled in the shell, forest greens, mushrooms, crisped and browned hare, roasted birds. But there were also strange berries Jenna did not know, and several pies whose fruits were a strange color. There was no wine, only water and a bluish watery milk.

"What of Piet below?" Jenna asked.

"Men can graze like cattle," a woman answered.

"If he were starving, we would throw food down," said another. "But Iluna says he does not have the look of a starving man." She put her hand out before her belly in gross imitation, and laughed.

The others laughed, too, as they brought their heaping plates up to the great table. Jenna, Skada, and Petra were ushered before them. When they were all seated, they introduced themselves one after another, the names coming so quickly, even Jenna could not sort them out.

"And ye three," asked Fellina, the woman who had held the lantern, and one of the few names Jenna had caught. "What message do ye bear?"

Petra began, "I am . . ." but Jenna and Skada stopped her with a hand on her forearm.

"We are sisters from different Hames but with the same message," Jenna said. "And it is a message of war." She slipped the ring from her little finger. "This was given me by the Mother of Nill's Hame."

"*My* Hame," Petra said in a quiet voice.

"Before she and all the women there were cruelly slaughtered," Skada added. "By men."

"Kalas' men," Jenna amended. The women were so quiet, she went on. "Mother Alta said that I must go from Hame to Hame to warn them that: *The time of endings is at hand.* She said the Hame Mothers would know what to do. But you are . . ." Her voice cracked, and she looked down at her plate, suddenly overwhelmed by her memories.

"We are what . . . go on, child," Fellina said gently.

Oddly comforted by being called a child again, Jenna looked up at the women around the table. The faces were different, yet they were somehow as familiar as those at Selden Hame in their concern. She drew in a deep *latani* breath and counted silently to ten. At last she spoke. "Yours is the only Hame I have found so far beside my own that has not been destroyed."

"How many have you actually been to?"

"Two. But . . ."

"But we have had reports of ten destroyed utterly," Petra said.

"Ten of how many?"

"Of seventeen," Jenna answered.

"Eighteen, if you count M'dorah," Skada added.

"No one ever counts M'dorah," Iluna said, unstrapping the baby from her back with the help of her dark sister. She began rocking the child slowly in her arms.

"I had never even heard of M'dorah till yesterday," Jenna admitted.

"I had—but I thought it only a tale," Petra added.

"Ten. Gone utterly. Ten." The number seemed to make its way around the table, drifting down even to the women sitting on the lower level. Slowly they mounted the four steps to stand by their sisters.

Jenna and Skada looked around, waiting until everyone was silent. Then Jenna spoke, articulating the way the king had on the great steps at New Steading, consciously letting her voice carry. These were *her* people. She *had* to speak now.

"I have been called the White One, the Anna, though I have not really claimed it. Whether or not you believe that is who I am, believe this: I come with a message. There is war. Men against women; men against men where women still suffer greatly. Something is ending, so prophecy warns. I do not know if it is the world that is ending, but surely the world of the Hames is being destroyed."

"Destroyed utterly," Petra muttered. "Go on, Jenna."

"We cannot let that world go without fighting to retain something of what it means. Something must remain of Great Alta's teachings. Some of us must be sure there is a place in the new for sisters side by side."

"Side by side," Iluna echoed, spinning the phrase around the table.

"What would ye have us do?" the woman next to Iluna asked.

"Come down from this hidden Hame, from this secret safety and join us. Fight with me, side by side as the old rhymes say. Do not let only men fight for us. For when men fight alone, the victory is also theirs alone."

"Ye would have us leave this *secret safety* to die among strangers? Among men?" Several voices called out, then answered themselves, "No!"

"No!"

"No!" The word spun crazily around the table.

Jenna could not tell which of them had spoken.

"Speak for us, Maltia," someone cried.

A woman and her dark sister stood at the opposite end of the table from Jenna. They were both tall, with jet-black hair ending in graying braids, as if the crown of their heads were younger than the ends. They stared down the long table at Jenna.

"I be True Speaker of this Hame," one of them said at last. "And this be my sister Tessia."

Jenna nodded her acknowledgment, as did Skada.

"We have no Mother Alta as ye have," Maltia continued. "We have no one ruler. I be the True Speaker but I do not otherwise lead. In this way we broke long ago from the false Alta's teachings, coming to this place of eagles and bright air, worshipping only the true Alta. She who waits in the green hall where it be said *Every end is a beginning* and it is also said *No one stands highest when all stand together.*"

"Jenna," Petra whispered to her, "that is what the Grenna teach."

Jenna pursed her lips and stood herself, Skada by her side. She addressed Maltia directly. "We understand more than you think, True Speaker. We have *been* in Alta's grove with the Greenfolk. We have stood in their circle. We have seen both cradle and hall."

"Ahhhh!" The sound came from all around the table.

"But . . ." Jenna said, hesitating for effect, "we were not women alone there. We were women *and* men. Petra and I and . . ." This time it was not for effect.

"And thy dark sister?" asked Tessia, her face full of a cunning Maltia's did not hold.

"There are no shadows in the grove," Jenna said quietly, "though you would have me stumble on my memories and say it was so."

"Ahhhh!"

"What men be there with ye?" Iluna asked suddenly.

"*Iluna!*" Tessia's voice was sharp. "*Ye* be not True Speaker."

Iluna seemed to draw back into herself, holding the baby against her breast as if it were a shield.

"Who *be* those men?" Maltia asked as if there had been no interruption. "Was the bearded one with the belly below one of them?"

For a moment Jenna considered lying, considered

saying that Piet had been with them, for such an admission might help him, help their cause. But then she set aside the idea as unworthy—unworthy of the audience and unworthy of Piet himself. She was, after all, talking to their True Speaker. She must be a true speaker herself. To do otherwise, was to be like the king.

"No," she said, still looking straight at Maltia, "they were not three grown men at all, but boys. One Alta gifted with a crown, one with a wristlet, and one with . . ." She put her hand to her throat, for a moment unable to speak.

"And one She gave the collar?" asked Maltia.

"Yes!" Jenna croaked. "And because of it he cannot speak."

"Ye would not have him speak his terrible truths," Tessia said. "They would bring doom on all. True Speaking be as much truth as any human can bear to hear, though it be but a shadow of the Herald's words."

"You know . . ." Skada began.

"They be The Three," said Maltia. "The Young Heralds. The Harbingers. We know. But how any followers of the false Alta could know of this, be too much of a puzzle for me. It be writ nowhere but in the *Second Book of Light*."

"The *second* Book?" interrupted Petra. "There *is* no second Book."

"It be the Book of M'dorah," said Maltia, "written by the true Alta herself when She left the grove and came to this place of high rocks to build a sanctuary, an aerie where even eagles dare not rest."

"*Where even eagles dare not rest* . . ." Petra whispered, "Jenna, Alta said others had come to the grove."

Maltia and Tessia sat down heavily in their chairs. "We must think on this."

"You have no time to think!" Skada roared, pounding her fist on the table. "You only have time to act. We must be back down and to our army before the sun's light."

"Skada!" Jenna cautioned, though Skada had spoken only what she, herself, had been afraid to say.

But Maltia and Tessia were lost to them, hands over eyes, deep into *latani* breathing and thought.

Standing suddenly, the baby still clutched against her and her own dark sister by her side, Iluna cried, "I will go, though no one else goes with me."

"And I!" Two long-faced young women stood.

"And I!" A middle-aged woman with deep carved lines from nose to mouth rose slowly. By her side rose another woman, the lines on her face more shadow than, real.

Maltia looked up. "Wait!" she cried. "We may not be part of *this* ending, nor part of this beginning either. Do not rush into it. Remember: *If ye rise too early, the dew will soak thy skin.* Do not drown M'dorah in this."

"What of the other signs?" Tessia added. "We have but one, and that may be compounded of our own longing."

"Ye have spoken truly," the middle-aged woman said. "As befits the dark sister of the True Speaker. But the White One knows of the Three Heralds. Surely that be sign enough."

"*One is not a multitude.* It says clearly in the *Book.*" Maltia's voice was low.

"What other signs?" Skada asked. "Tell them to us."

Tessia laughed. "If ye need ask, ye know them not."

"What signs, True Speaker?" Petra was standing. "We have seen many, but how are we to know which are yours without a hint. We will give you all, but you must give us some." Her voice was stronger than Jenna had ever heard, stronger even than when she had spoken at Selden Hame.

"Who anointed her to the task?" Maltia whispered.

Tessia roared out the same question. "Who anointed the White One to the task?"

Petra closed her eyes for a moment and Jenna could almost see memories crowding across her brow. Then she opened her eyes and stared past Maltia, to the window beyond. "My Mother anointed her. My Mother who had six fingers on each hand. Who saw without eyes. Who stood without . . ."

". . . without feet." Maltia's voice trembled. "Who spoke without voice. Who . . ."

"*Who spoke without voice?*" Jenna whispered to Skada. "What by the Great Goddess does that mean?"

"*On the slant,* Jenna," Skada whispered back. "Hush. We have them."

All of the women were on their feet now, reciting along with Maltia their litany of the impossible. As their voices rose to the finish, Jenna could feel the excitement. The air was electric with it.

". . . born without a father. She shall anoint the One." Maltia held out her hand toward Jenna. Tessia did the same. "Ye *be* the One. Forgive us that we did not know ye."

Jenna nodded. If there was more relief than forgiveness in that nod, she did not let them see it.

"We be ready," Maltia said. "M'dorah ends this night, as the *Book* prophesied. And what begins, we will all write together."

It took the rest of the short night for them to pack what they would need: swords, wooden shields, knives, packets of food. There were but three babes, harvested they said from farms as far away as Market, wherever that was, and these were bound to their mothers' backs.

"What place be this army?" asked Maltia as she packed a woven basket.

"At the place where the road to M'dorah and the road from New Steading meet," Jenna said. When no one seemed to understand, she knelt and sketched a map on the floor with her finger.

"Ah, New Steading," said Iluna. "That be what we call Market." She looked up. "Only the youngest of us go there, to get those things we cannot ourselves supply."

"What can you supply, here on this aerie?" Petra asked.

"We hunt. We raise birds. We have gardens," Maltia said.

"Where? We saw none," Jenna asked.

"They be well hid from prying eyes." Tessia smiled.

"And New Steading—Market—is where you take the babes?" Petra asked.

"We take only the ones left out, the ones neglected, the ones ill-treated, the ones thrown away," Iluna said.

Like me, mused Jenna to herself.

"Like my Scillia," said Iluna. "Who has but one arm."

I was whole, Jenna thought, *and still I was given away.*

"They know we will take what they do not want," Tessia said. "So next to the babes, they leave money or gifts of seed. If they leave wine, we do not take it. The *Book* says plainly: *The grape brings slow death.*"

"And they never speak of M'dorah," explained Maltia. "For we take away their shame. They say we do not exist. M'dorah be but a story to them. Women alone are not natural."

"They deny us but still they leave us the gleanings of their poor crops," Tessia added.

Skada laughed. "So it is with the other Hames. What is so different, sisters, that you shut yourselves away up here?"

"Our Alta denied us all men until the coming of the Three. Your Alta went among men and had commerce with them. Our Alta sat in the circle. Your Alta sits on a throne. Our Alta . . ." Maltia said.

"Alta has many faces," Petra interrupted smoothly, "yet in the end we are all babes again at her breast. Is that not so?"

"In the end, and in the beginning, yes," said Maltia. "And by thy coming, we know it be the end. That is why we go from M'dorah, this high and holy place." Her face was bereft of all happiness.

Jenna looked around. All the women, intent on their final duties, wore the same mask of sorrow. *They are in mourning,* she thought, *not for any one death but for the death of M'dorah.*

They set fire to the Hame, each with a torch so that everyone shared equally in the ending. It was accompanied by a plainsong chant:

> *Came we out of fire*
> *Came we out of grove*
> *Came we from desire*
> *To the rocks above.*
> *Now return to fire*
> *Now remake the grove*
> *Now the heart's desire*
> *Goes to ground with love.*

Then, driven by the fierce heat of the conflagration, they dropped a dozen ladders over the side of the rock and began their descent.

Once over the edge, with the fire unable to cast shadows, Skada and the other dark sisters disappeared, cutting the numbers of women in half. Jenna felt more alone than she had in days.

At the bottom of the ropes Piet was waiting, arms crossed. He looked as though he had been waiting in that position all night long.

"What is the fire?" he asked when Jenna reached the ground. "It set the sky ablaze. When I saw it, I would have climbed up to get girl. But there were no ladders and no footholds that I could find."

"It is the end of M'dorah," Jenna explained. "More I will not say. Now we have a hundred warriors to add to Pike's army."

"I count but half that," Piet said.

"When the moon rises . . ." Jenna began.

"It is days until the moon."

"Then the force will double."

He nodded. "But now?"

"Now we have all that move by day. There is no one left in that eagle's nest."

He nodded again and started to turn toward them. Jenna put a hand on his arm.

"Hold, Piet. They will take no direction but my own."

"The king be not pleased at that," Piet murmured.

"The king will have to live with it," Jenna answered. She turned and waved her hand and the women followed her, threading carefully down the pathless hillside. They were more silent than any army Piet had ever heard. Even the three babes, swaddled and strapped against their mothers' backs, were absolutely still.

When they got to the place where the horses were tied, Piet mounted up but Jenna and Petra remained on foot.

"Ride on, Piet, and tell King Gorum we come with a dozen dozen women behind."

"I was not to leave ye," Piet said.

"If you do not leave now, he will not know in time." Piet nodded.

"And faithful Piet," Jenna said, moving by him and putting her hand on his leg. "I have a special message for you alone, not the king."

Piet bent over, steadying the horse with the reins in his right hand.

Jenna whispered, "These women came not because they believe in me but because of some strange holding of theirs about three heralds, three messengers of their own Alta. Those messengers carry crown, wristlet, and collar."

"The boys . . ." He stopped himself, nodded again.

"Tell them. Tell the boys. Warn them."

"They will be warned."

"And something else." She hesitated. "Tell Carum I . . ."

"He knows, girl," said Piet.

"Knows?"

"And I know. We all know. We have eyes. Cat knew even afore thee."

"No one knew before me."

Piet grinned. "The first, that's the hardest. And the dearest. And the best." There was some sort of forgiveness in his eyes. As quickly, it was gone. He nodded again, sat up straight, jerked the horse's head with the reins, and plunged them both into the undergrowth.

She could hear the sound of his passage for a long time after.

With that many women, it took them several more hours to reach the deep woods. Jenna could read Piet's passage before them and hoped that he was already with the king for the sun was peeking through the interlacing of the trees. When she turned to look at the women behind her, she saw what a great swath they had left.

"An army cannot move easily in the woods," she murmured to Petra.

Petra agreed. "We do not leave a trail but a highway."

"What does it matter what we leave behind?" Iluna asked. "It is what lies ahead that matters." Her eyes were bright with excitement.

"What lies ahead," Jenna pointed out, "is war. And that means some of us will die." Without thinking, she flexed the fingers of her sword hand, suddenly remembering the feel of the sword sliding through a man's flesh. She shuddered. "Many of us will die."

Petra put her hand around Jenna's, folding her fingers tightly under. "But some of us will live, Jenna. You must remember that after the ending is the beginning. So it is prophesied."

"On the slant, Petra. We must read prophecy *on the slant,* or so I have been told often enough," Jenna said.

They walked on.

*   *   *

They were nearly halfway through the woods, following Piet's easy trail, when Jenna held up her hand. The women stopped at once as she strained to listen.

"Do you hear that?" she asked at last.

Petra shook her head. "Hear what? I hear some birds. The wind through trees. And"—she smiled—"and a baby chuckling."

Iluna put her finger over her shoulder and the baby took it into her mouth.

"No more baby," Petra said. "And the birds have quieted as well."

"No. Another sound. Deeper. Unnatural."

"I hear something." Iluna moved closer to Jenna. "But it is not one sound. It is several. Some are high, some low. Not the sound of the woods, though. I have been here often on the hunt and that I know."

Maltia and several other women moved closer to Jenna, silently over the fallen leaves and low branches. Only one twig was snapped, and it shockingly loud in the stillness. They formed a tight circle around Jenna, Petra, Iluna, and the horses, and stood in an attitude of listening.

After a long moment, Jenna said, "There. Do you hear it?"

"We hear," Maltia said. The others nodded.

Jenna drew in a deep breath. "Do you know what it means? I *fear* I do. It is the sound of sword on sword and the cries of men. I have heard that sound in my dreams. There is a battle raging—and I am not with them. I must ride." She put her hand on Duty's back.

"I will go with you, Jenna," Petra said.

"No, Petra, you have no skill with a sword, and these women need you."

"Not to show them the way, Jenna. They know these woods better than I."

"You know the world, Petra. That is the way you must show them. Come as soon as you can. And take this." She stripped the priestess ring from her finger, placing it gently in Petra's hand. "You have the map of the Hames and now the ring. If anything happens, you must carry on the warning and the women of M'dorah with you."

"Nothing will happen," Petra whispered. "You are the Anna."

"I am Jo-an-enna first and anything can happen to *her*." She mounted her horse.

"You cannot go alone into battle," Petra said.

"I will not be alone. The men are already fighting and you will come right after. Besides we have only two horses and who but you can ride." She gathered Duty's reins.

"I can!" Iluna cried. "At least I have been on a horse before. *Once* before." She turned to Petra. "Give me the lines."

"The lines?"

"She means the reins," Jenna said. She pulled back on her own reins and Duty reared suddenly, nearly throwing her. "And take the child from her back."

"I will not be parted from my Scillia. Is it not so with the sisters of thy Hame?"

Jenna nodded her head and quieted Duty while Iluna was hoisted onto the horse by Maltia and Petra and two other women. Mounting was not something Iluna had acquired in her brief riding lesson. But once atop the horse, she sat with the kind of stillness necessary, though whether from fear or from skill, Jenna could not have said. She pulled roughly on the reins once again and, as Duty spun to the right, called out to them all:

"Follow as swifly as you can. Your swords will surely be welcome. The king thought to pit force against force, but he has too small an army yet. This battle is an unwelcome surprise. His brother and I had hoped to convince him to use cunning, the mouse's wits against the cat's claw. Let us hope that there are some mice left."

Maltia put her hand on Duty's neck. "But if they all be men, how will we know which to draw against?"

The simple question stunned Jenna. What answer indeed? To these women *all* men were the enemy. In battle how could one be distinguished from the other?

Petra smiled. "If a man draws against you, True Speaker, he is your foe. Our men will be the ones who welcome your help."

Jenna nodded, though some part of her still resisted that easy answer, hearing again in her mind the woman at New Steading protesting: *Girls dressing like men, playing at war, taint natural. We've all said it.* Aloud, she spoke only soothing words. "Petra is right. The men who welcome you are the men you should aid." Then she kicked Duty hard with her heels and the horse took off down the faint path.

Behind her Iluna's horse began to trot, with Iluna hanging on grimly to the reins. Jouncing merrily, the baby at her back waved her hand at the women who followed.

It did not take them long to bull their way through the rest of the forest, the sounds of the battle drawing them on. Jenna cursed herself for the meal at M'dorah, the necessary arguments, the slow walk through the woods, all conspiring to keep her from the start of the battle. She knew that she was but one more sword, but if that sword could keep Jareth or Marek or Sandor alive . . . She did not let herself think about Carum. In her mind she called him Longbow, just another warrior in the king's troops. She urged Duty ahead with a hard kick of her heels.

Then they burst out of the woods and the battle sounds exploded around them. Jenna pulled up short when she saw the once-pleasant field. Beside her Iluna, too, reined in her horse.

To the left across the meadow, under a stand of overhanging trees, three men were setting upon one. He was hewing with his great sword, keeping them at bay. Ahead a knot of nearly thirty men were tangled together, their swords gone, wrestling and kicking, and hitting with their fists and knees. Over to the right, where a few horses grazed disconsolately, was a ring of a dozen men, swords drawn, standing shoulder to shoulder. Their swords pointed outward, and inside the circle lay several fallen comrades. One, half upraised on his elbow, was being tended by a great bear of a man. The rest of the field was littered with bodies, some in uniform, some in fine cloth. Jenna scanned nervously for one in wine-colored weave. She thought there were several, but she was too far away to be sure.

Dropping Duty's reins, she whispered, "Too late. Again too late. Just as the Grenna said." Her hands fell helpless to her sides and she was overcome by a sudden strange lethargy.

But Iluna, raising her sword, dug her heels into her horse and headed toward the stand of trees where the one man fought against the three. She screamed "M'dorah!" as she rode.

The three men scattered before her charge. Dropping the reins, she slid off the horse's back and turned to say something to the big man she had just rescued. As Jenna watched from afar, the man lifted his sword and struck Iluna in the middle of the breast with his blade. She fell, twisting at the last onto her side in order to save the child at her back. The man straddled her body and threw his head back, roaring. Jenna could hear it all the way across the field.

Suddenly the warmth of the lethargy gave way to a surge of ice-cold power. Screaming Iluna's name like a battle cry, Jenna dug her heels again and again in Duty's side and they galloped toward the stand of trees.

The man waited for her, grinning. She knew who it was even before she was halfway to him. What had been icy cold running through her body turned into a red heat in her head. She recalled Alta's words in the grove: *Remembering is what you must do most of all.* She remembered the fire on top of the towering stone, and it became a river of fire in her veins. She could feel the sweat on her forehead and under her arms.

Just before reaching the trees, she leaped from Duty's back. The horse veered right, Jenna rolled to the left, then stood, sword upraised. She wondered the man was not seared by her heat.

"So, little Alta's bitch, do you think you have the blood to do now what you could not do before? And with my hands free this time?" He lifted the sword over his head with both hands, swinging it around. It cut the air, making a horrible whirring. The sword was much heavier than hers, its blade still slick with Iluna's blood, but if its weight tired him, Jenna could not tell. She had no hope blade against blade to defeat him. She would have to cool her fire and use cunning, the cunning of the mouse.

Something sounded in the broken grass behind her but she knew better than to turn. It had to be the three who had scattered before Iluna's horse. Whoever they were, if they had been fighting the Bear, they were on her side.

"Name yourselves," she cried out to them, her eyes on the Bear.

"Anna, it be Marek."

"And Sandor."

The strangled sound coming from the third proclaimed it as Jareth. Alive—all three!

"Blessed be," she whispered, then said aloud, "Good boys!"

"Boys they be right enough," the Bear said. "Pups! And even three full-grown hounds are not strong enough to pull me down. Not even three grown hounds *and* their bitch mother." He laughed.

Jenna heard one of the boys gasp and start forward.

"No!" she cried. "Let him waste his breath in boasts. Do not crowd him. His sword has a long reach."

"A very long reach," the Bear agreed. "And after I

dispose of the pups, I will teach the bitch a lesson. A lesson you will long remember. At least as long as you live." He laughed again. "Which will not be that long after all."

"Anna . . ." It was Sandor.

"No. After this is over I will tell you a story that Ca—that Longbow told me. About a cat and a mouse. For now, I would have you remember the Grenna and how they rule."

"What be your meaning—oh!" Someone had obviously elbowed Sandor in the side. Probably Jareth. Jareth would have understood first.

The boys fanned out in a wide circle, none higher or lower, none nearer or farther, under Jareth's silent tutelage. Just like the Grenna's circle.

Then another sound reached Jenna, though she never took her eyes from the Bear. She suspected from the sound and the slight widening of his eyes that the tangle of men in the center of the field had at last unknotted itself. Or the circle of swords had dispatched several warriors. She could tell that the number of men around the Bear had doubled and guessed that none of them had arrows left, or he would have been dead by now.

"Follow Jareth's lead," she cautioned to them. "Do not get within the Bear's sword range."

"Come, little puppies; come, little snuffling hounds," the Bear taunted. "One of you must make the first move. One of you must be brave enough to show the others how to die." He kept turning, keeping them off guard, bringing his sword from left to right. "Which shall it be? You, with the pretty green band round your throat? Or you, with the long stalks for legs? Or shall it be Alta's slut, whose white braid I shall cut off and hang upon my helm?" He continued turning, addressing them all, but Jenna's warning kept them far enough away so that even when he thrust forward, they were out of his reach.

"Let him tire," Jenna said. "Do not let his sword take more of us."

"I do not tire," he said. "I will outlast you all."

If she hoped to tempt him into making a false move, he was too smart an old warrior for that. He continued circling Iluna's body, never losing his footing, never stumbling over her corpse, occasionally kicking at it as if to underscore his ability to kill them all, one at a time.

Jenna began to feel his rhythm. Catrona had taught her that: how to watch for an animal's particular rhythm in the woods. *What the pace?* Catrona had cautioned them. *What the pattern?* It had been a constant lesson in the woods, the only way to be sure a hunt would end successfully. *And this was just another hunt,* Jenna thought. *Hunting the Bear.*

What was the Bear's pattern then? He moved feint, feint, feint, thrust; feint, feint, thrust. But always, right before the thrust, there was the slightest of movements, a hitching of his right arm that signaled the forward cut of the sword. She watched another few minutes to be sure, all the while cautioning the men to wait. The waiting was clearly wearing on them, but it would wear on the Bear as well.

When his back was momentarily turned to her, she bent swiftly and removed the knife from her boot. Across the circle, several men watched her. One man's eyebrows went up. It signaled the Bear, but he did not quite know what it meant. As he turned toward Jenna, more alert than he had been before, he saw the knife and smiled, guessing what she meant to do. He hitched his shoulder. But fooling him, she flung her sword point first, as they used to do in the game of wands at the Hame.

The Bear startled for a moment and beat the sword away with his and was back at attention in seconds. But at the same moment, Jareth, alert to Jenna's every move, flung his sword as well. He had never played at wands and did not understand the balance of a sword, how to compensate for the heavy braided hilt. Instead of going point first, the sword flipped and struck the Bear in the chest with the grip. He grabbed it with his left hand, laughing.

But at the same moment Jenna flung herself through the air. Before he could bring either sword up, she was on top of him, sinking the knife point between his eyes. He fell backward with Jenna on top. When she twisted the knife a half turn to the right, she felt the grinding against the bone. His right hand still clenching the sword came up behind her, as much a reflex as a stroke. One of the boys at her back gasped loudly and she hoped he had not been caught on the blade.

Then she stared down into the Bear's face, watching as the eyes below her glazed over. There was something horribly, hauntingly familiar about the feel of the knife in the bone and the man's dying eyes staring up at her. She could not recall where she had seen such a thing before.

"For Catrona!" she whispered into his slackening mouth. "For Iluna. For all the women you have killed." She could feel his body under hers tremble slightly, stiffen, then relax. He made no answer except to exhale a sour sigh through his rigid lips.

Jenna stood slowly, her hands bloody. Even more slowly she wiped them on her vest. When she turned away, she was shaking uncontrollably, as if she had caught a sudden fever. Jareth put his arms around her, trying to hold her still, but she could not stop shivering.

And then she heard a strange, thin cry that built up to a high, unrelenting pitch.

"Scillia!" Jenna whispered, turning back, all her trembling ended by the demands of that cry. "You poor little babe. You are mine, now."

She unstrapped the child from Iluna's back and held her tightly, but the babe would not be comforted. Her cranky crying—that strange, tearless sobbing—continued.

"Let her cry," Jenna said. "She has lost both mother and home in one short day. If she cannot cry for that, she will cry for nothing all the rest of her life."

"She be just hungry," Sandor said sensibly.

"Or wet," someone else commented.

Jenna ignored them, bouncing the swaddled infant in

her left arm and leading them all across the field, past the dying and the dead.

As she walked, she made careful note of their faces. It was the New Steading boys, mostly, who had died upon that lea in their bright clothes and with their untried swords, still sheathed. There were few familiar faces among the dead. But somehow that made her all the sadder, that these boys had died strangers to her, without a word of comfort. She had promised herself not to cry for death, but she could not help it, though she wept silently that no one should hear, tears streaming from her eyes. Seeing Jenna's tears, the baby stopped her own crying and, fascinated, reached out her hand to touch a tear and trace its path. Jenna kissed that tiny hand.

None of the dead men on the field was Carum. Jenna made quite sure of that before heading toward the ring of swordsmen, now relaxed and waiting. As she approached, one came out to speak with her. She recognized him at once, Gileas with the scarred eye.

He put a hand to his forehead, a sketchy kind of salute.

"Anna, you must come quickly. It is the king. He's dying."

"And his brother?" she asked quietly, suddenly aware of the other bodies within the circle of men. "Carum Longbow. What of him?"

"Took!" Gileas answered. "Took like a good many of 'em. They blew a victory on their bloody horns, took what they could, and were fast away, leaving whatever of their men was dead and whichever was still fighting behind. Took!"

Took! Her mind could not quite hold it. She repeated it to herself over and over and still did not grasp it. *Took!*

He guided her to Gorum who lay against Piet's knees. There was a smudge of old blood around his mouth. He was not smiling. How Jenna longed to see that wolfish smile now.

"Pike," she whispered, realizing how easy forgiveness could come. She knelt by his side. The babe in her arms cooed and reached for the king.

Still unsmiling, Gorum lifted his hand and touched the child's outstretched fingers.

"Jenna," he said, his voice a shadow. "You must find him. Find Carum. Bring him to me. I must tell him. He will soon be king."

Jenna looked up, startled. "No one has told him?"

Piet shook his head.

"Told me what?" The old fire returned to his voice, then trailed off.

"That Carum . . ."

Piet put a finger to his lips.

"That Carum . . . is still fighting. Bravely. Well. Not just with the bow, but the sword, too."

"I was wrong, then. He will make a fine king." He closed his eyes for a moment, then opened them again.

"*You* are the king," Jenna whispered, "as long as you are alive. And you are not dead yet. You will live long. I know."

"You are a prophecy, girl, not a prophet. I am dead already. A king . . ." He coughed and fresh blood frothed at his mouth. He swallowed it down painfully. "A king knows even more than a girl. That is why *I* am the king." This time he managed to smile. "You will make a fine queen, Jenna. I was right about that though wrong about the other."

"Wrong?"

"Hush, dinna waste breath," Piet cautioned.

"It doesn't matter, and don't you go being a silly nursemaid now," the king said. "I need to tell her." He tried to sit a little straighter, slumped back into Piet's arms. "I was wrong. We had not the might to go against Kalas. Not yet. Not ever. Remember the story of the mouse and the cat that mother . . . did he tell you? I don't think I have the breath for it now."

"He told me."

His voice was barely audible. "Remember . . ."

"I will remember."

"You really are the end," he whispered. "At least, you are mine." His eyes closed.

"I killed the Bear," Jenna whispered, sure she was talking to a dead man.

"Of course," the king said, eyes still closed. "It was written." He did not move again.

They sat for many minutes, Piet cradling the king in his arms. No one spoke, though every now and then a cough shattered the stillness. The baby slept with a bubbling stillness and Jenna carefully set the sleeping child by Gorum's side.

Piet looked up. "Gone," he admitted at last.

Gone. The word reverberated in Jenna's head. *The king was gone. Carum was gone. One dead, the other missing. Both gone.* She was about to speak when Sandor shouted.

"Hold! An army. Through the trees."

"Hold, indeed," Jenna said. "Those are women. The sisters of M'dorah. Do you not see Petra in the lead?"

"Women, bah!" a boy's voice called out. Others echoed him.

"Shut that silly trap of yourn," Piet said. "Have ye never seen a girl fight? I have. Side by side, I have. And they are the best of us. Certainly better than thee, boy. And the Anna here, is the best of all. Hasn't she just done the Bear? What has thee to squawk about now?"

"Nowt." The boy looked down. The ones who cheered him originally were silent.

"Welcome them, then," Piet said. "Raise yer bloody voices and call them in. Girls like that."

They set up a cry, compounded of grief and welcome, and waved their arms, a strange ululating that brought the sisters of M'dorah across the blood-soaked field to their midst.

They buried their own men in one common grave, the men of Kalas' army in another. The king and Iluna had separate graves. Above the king's they set a marker with his name and a crown carved by Sandor, who had some skill. He carved a marker for Iluna's as well, the goddess sign copied from the ring Petra was wearing.

The sisters of M'dorah were good nurses, binding up the wounds of those for whom binding would make a difference, the men who could still ride. The others that Piet determined could stand to travel, he insisted be sent back to New Steading. He had the men build makeshift sleds from the tree limbs, cushioned by blanket strips. These the horses could pull. Three of the older women, who were not warriors anyway, volunteered to guide the horses down the road and report on what had happened.

"The babes go, too," Jenna said. "If this is indeed an ending, then one of the things that ends here is our bringing children into any fray."

"But it has always been done," Maltia protested.

All around her the women nodded vigorously. "Always," they murmured.

"It says in the *Book* that: *A foolish loyalty can be the greater danger.* This I was reminded of by the one who anointed me. Surely you would not disagree?"

There were many looks passed between the women and not all of them, Jenna was sure, signaled an easy agreement.

"One can be as foolishly loyal to past customs as to people," Petra said.

"Yes." Jenna's voice was firm. "And this custom ends here. Today. We will, I am sure, sing of it in the future." She handed little Scillia to the True Speaker. The child whimpered as she went from hand to hand. "But I shall return and take this child for my own."

"She belongs to us, Anna," Maltia said. "She belongs to M'dorah."

"M'dorah is no more," Jenna reminded her gently. "When I took her from Iluna's care, my hands were still red from the blood of Iluna's killer. She is mine, little Scillia. I will love her well."

"I will keep her until ye return," Maltia said. "And

then ye can tell me, without the wind of battle in thy mouth, how well it is ye love her."

Jenna nodded.

The other two babies were handed to the sisters, with many whispers of farewell. Then the women embraced, not once but many times. Strapping the children onto their backs, Maltia and the other two women took up the horses' reins and started to guide the line of roped horses and their sleds down the road to New Steading.

"Mount up!" Piet called when they were nearly out of sight.

"We do not know how to ride," a woman cried out.

"You will learn on the way," Jenna promised cheerily, "even as I did."

"Horses!" a rosy-cheeked young woman said, and spat. "They be an abomination."

"But a necessary and quick one," Petra said. "If the Anna can learn to ride, anyone can." She smiled.

After several missteps and one disastrous hard fall suffered by an older woman with a chunky face and a determined mouth, the sisters were finally mounted.

"Which way now?" Jenna asked Piet.

"Farther north. They rode off that way and, I suspect, to Kalas' holdings. With prisoners—especially the young prince—they will not be staying in the old king's palace. Too many of his supporters live there yet. Besides, Kalas always had the biggest dungeons."

Jenna digested that information, then asked, "And they will not return here to end what they so foully began?"

Piet smiled sourly. "They believe it already ended. And so it seemed to me, girl. The Bear slew the king. They carried off Prince Longbow and another double dozen of our fighters. They trust the Bear to finish the rest and that he will follow."

"Do you truly believe that?" Jenna asked.

"I bet my life upon it," said Piet.

"You just have," Jenna answered. "And mine as

well." She turned and signaled them all to follow and
they rode, three abreast, toward the north.

THE TALE:

There was once a nest of seven mice who lived be-
hind the kitchen wall. They had been warned by their
Mam before she disappeared that when they were old
enough to go out of the nest, they had to go with great
care and all together, not one at a time.

"For if you go one after one," she said, "the great cat
who lives by the stove will eat you up. It will catch you if
It can."

Now the little mice listened to her, but that was all
she said. And so how could they be afraid of an It they
had never seen? One by one, when they were old enough
they crept out of the hole. And one by one they disap-
peared into It's mouth. Until at last there was only the
smallest mouse left, named Little Bit.

Little Bit's turn came on a bright spring day. But he
had heard the sound of It's teeth and claws outside the
hole. And though Little Bit was small, he was cunning.
He peeked out of the hole and sure enough there was the
monstrous It, snoring by the stove, with one eye open.

"This needs a plan," he told himself. So he searched
throughout the hole and all along the inside of the
boards, until he came up with enough materials to com-
plete his plan. He worked for many days, well into the
evening, for plans take patience and time. But at last he
was done. He looked at his handiwork: an army of
twenty mice made from sticks and gray cotton, with rai-
sins for eyes and string for tails. He tied them one to an-
other and the last he tied to his own tail with a special
knot.

"All home free!" he cried as loud as he could, to alert the cat. "Come on, boys!" Then he ran out of the hole hauling those toy mice behind him, lumpity, bumpity, over the floor.

Well, It was up in a single jump, certain of the fine meal ahead. And It picked off the mice from the back end first: one, two, three . . . but they were all stuck together. Their tails tangled in It's claws. It howled in anger and stuffed two in It's mouth. Phew! Phwat! Psssaw!

Little Bit ran free, as the knot slipped loose from his tail. When he got to the kitchen door, he stopped for a moment, singing out:

> "I am just a Little Bit,
> But I made a fool of It.
> Greedy guts and greedy paws
> Makes a tangle out of claws."

Then he ran out into the spring meadow to look for his Mam.

THE MYTH:

At last Great Alta shook her hair and a gift fell out of it onto the land below. The gift was a Babe in whose right hand was a star of purest silver. Her left hand was hid behind her.

"The star is yours, though you were not born with it. And in your left hand is a star of gold. Whichever you choose shall shine brightest of all. The star will be both your guide and your grief. It will be your light and your loss. It will be your close companion."

The child tossed the silver star into the night sky. It

glittered there and shone down on the roads throughout all the land.

At this the child smiled and brought her left hand to the front. She opened it. There was no star there.

Then Great Alta smiled. She braided up her hair, both the dark side and the light, and pinned it on her head as a crown. A golden star gleamed in the center.

"You have chosen and it is so," quoth Great Alta. "Blessed be."

BOOK FIVE

THE DARK TOWER

THE MYTH:

Then Great Alta set a pillar of darkness on the one end of the plain. On the other she set a pillar of fire. In between ran a path as thin as the edge of a knife and as sharp.

"She who can walk the path and she who can capture both towers is the one I shall love best of all," quoth Great Alta. "But woe to the woman whose foot is heavy on the path or whose heart is light at the tower, for she shall fail and her failure will bring doom to the land forever."

THE LEGEND:

There is an odd plain not far from Newmarket that grows neither grass nor trees. All that is there are dozens of high rocks, great towers of stone, some hundreds of feet in the air. The tallest of all stand almost two hundred feet high, one on the north side and one on the south.

The rock on the north side of the plain looks as if it had been blasted with fire. The rock on the south has the mark of the sea.

Atop the Fire Rock are strange remains: wood ash and bone buttons and the carved handle of a knife with a circle and a half cross incised in it. Atop the Sea Rock there is nothing at all.

The folk of Newmarket say that once two sisters lived on those two towers of stone, a black-haired one on Fire Rock, a white-haired one on Sea Rock. They had not spoken in fifty years. Their argument had been lost to memory, but their anger was still fresh.

One day a child came riding across the plain on a great gray horse. The child was beautiful, his hair a dazzling yellow, his face Great Alta's own.

Both sisters looked down from their rocks and desired the child. They climbed down and each tried to cozen him.

"I will give you gold," said the dark sister.

"I will give you jewels," said the light.

"I will give you a crown," said the one.

"I will give you a collar," said the other.

The child shook his head sadly. "If you had offered love," he said, "gladly would I have stayed though you gave me naught but stone to eat and naught but rock for a pillow."

The anger that the sisters had so honed for one another bubbled hot once again, and the desire that each had conceived for the child added to it. The dark sister took the child by the right hand, the light sister by the left. They pulled first one way and then the other until the child was pulled entirely in two. Then they scrambled up each to her own lonely rock, cradling the half child in her arms, singing lullabies to the dead babe, until they died of grief themselves.

Their tears and the child's blood watered the top of the tower of rocks causing a lovely flower to grow. Partling, the Newmarket folk call the flower, and Blood-o-babe. It brings ease to the pain of childbirth when boiled in a tisane.

THE STORY:

Kalas' army, having no need to disguise its trail, was easy to follow.

"North and north and north again," Jenna pointed out.

"To the castle," Piet added.

"And the dungeon," Jenna whispered grimly. "Surely it is not as bad as you say."

"Worse, girl. It is called Kalas' Hole and them that calls it so, mean no mere hole in the ground."

Piet made sure their approach was little noted by the few villages along the way. This was accomplished by breaking the riders into smaller groups, though the women of M'dorah refused to ride alongside any men. Marek, Sandor, and Gileas rode carefully ahead, reporting back every few hours. Though Jenna was frustrated by their slow progress, she agreed fully with Piet when he remarked, "Speed brings notice."

They supplied themselves in the woods without any great trouble, even with so large a group. The women of M'dorah were wily hunters and it being late into the spring, there were ferns, mushrooms, and good berries aplenty. For half the trip a small river paralleled the road and their skin bags were kept topped off with fresh water. Even when the stream turned and meandered on a more easterly route, they were never far from some small pond or stream. Fish were plentiful.

One man became sick from a purple berry, and seven of the remaining New Steading boys deserted one night. Two of the M'dorans developed horrible sores on their inner thighs from riding. The man recovered, though for a day he wished he might die. The boys were gone for good, but no others joined them. The two women could ride no longer and were left at a lonely farmhouse in the care of an old woman who welcomed them rather stiffly but nevertheless promised to treat them well.

That left barely one hundred riders, though they were well supplied with swords and knives, bows and shields.

Jenna had never been so far north and was amazed at the change in the woods. Used to the fellowship of larch, elm, and oak, she recognized fewer and fewer trees but the hardy pine which left scattered beds of sweet-smelling ground cover. When they camped the first time, Jenna remarked to Petra, "If there were not such need to go on, I could almost enjoy this."

"You *do* enjoy this," Petra said, leaning on one elbow. "You enjoy it for all that you know blood waits at the trail's end."

Jenna thought about Petra's words as they rode the next day. She wondered if Petra was right, and if so, what that meant about her own nature. How could she enjoy a journey whose ending would undoubtedly be blood-soaked? How could she admire a countryside that was the burial ground for so many good women and men? How could she let the scented pine needles rain through her fingers when the man she loved above all others lay in a foul-smelling dungeon? How could she even notice the difference in meadow and wood when they were potential battlefields? Her mind boiled like a soup pot with the questions. But the road held no answers for her and Duty's steady rolling stride only brought her closer to the bloody ending of which Petra warned.

The journey would take seven days.

"Four," Piet explained, "if care were not needed."

"Three," Jenna added, "if you and I went alone. And did not sleep."

"It would be good, girl, to cut that time. But then we'd be cutting our chances as well. Kalas' castle is nigh impregnable. All rock and stone with but one big gate and three portcullises, inner iron gates. Well guarded, too. They built it right into the cliffside so the back cannot be attacked. Then they made another cliff for the front."

"There is one thing good," Jenna said.

"And that be?"

"The M'dorans are rock climbers."

"I am thinking that, too." There was approval in his voice for the first time.

"They could be the other mice pulled along behind me . . ." Jenna mused aloud.

"For the cat to snatch up first." Piet chuckled. When Jenna looked surprised, he said, "That is an old family tale of mine. My mam told it to my little sister and me and she told it to her sons."

"Her sons . . ." He had thrown in the revelation so casually, Jenna could scarcely credit it. Finally she blurted out, "Are you . . . the king's uncle?"

He laughed. "The king's uncle? What be . . . oh, no, girl. They be Garuns and I be wholly of the Dales. No mixed blood in me at all. But my little sister and Carum's Mam, were childhood friends." He rubbed his finger roughly against his beard. "Met those boys when Carum was five years old. Prettiest little child ye ever did see. The darling of the court. And smart as a . . ."

"Not Carum's uncle then." She felt, somehow, disappointed.

"I was just back from the Continent. Horrid place. Full of foreigners," Piet said, throwing his head back in a laugh.

"So you knew them all?" Jenna asked. "Even saintly Jorum?"

"Jor—saintly? Who gave ye that idea? He was as sly as they come. Always in trouble. Always running up stairs to put the blame on someone else. And Carum always willing to take it. If there be a saint in that family . . . but not their uncle, no. For all they were good kings, they dinna think much of the folk of the Dales. Garuns first—and the Dales to make the sacrifice. That were the way. Though they were good to me and mine. And Carum, being half Dale, he was good altogether."

"Would . . ." Jenna suddenly interrupted. "Would it be wrong to pull the others along behind, to sacrifice them that I might get to the castle and get Carum out?"

"That is no sacrifice, girl. That is a ruse." He stroked his beard again and looked at her strangely. "Young Carum *is* king now. We must all do our part to set him free and some will likely die. That is the bloody way of war."

They rode on.

The days were as warm as ever, but as they rode north the evenings turned chilly, and the nights were positively cold. Northern weather made no obeisance to spring. The men were forced to share blankets with other men, the women with women.

The first time Jenna and Petra lay side by side, Jenna's blanket on the ground beneath them, Petra's on top, Jenna could not sleep. She stared at the sky for a long time counting the stars and Petra's smooth, even breaths. She got to a thousand before making up her mind.

At last she peeled back her side of the blanket and slipped out, careful not to disturb Petra. Signaling the men on watch, she walked to the edge of the woods, some fifty feet from the sleepers. Someone was there before her; she recognized one of the M'dorans, a young woman whose name she had never actually heard or, if heard, did not recall.

"You could not sleep either?"

The young woman grunted her response, then, as if the questions released something, began to talk in a whispery voice, alternately braiding and unbraiding one of a dozen thin plaits in her hair.

"Sleep? How could I sleep? I grieve. Iluna was my friend. My *closest* friend, closer even than my dark sister. And now she is gone. Gone. Gone where I cannot follow."

Jenna nodded, having neither an answer nor an easy sentiment to offer. She knew that sometimes simply talking out a grief made it easier to bear.

"I do not understand," the girl continued. "One minute we were all so . . . so . . ." She hesitated, looking for the right word, her hands still busy with yet another braid. "Happy—unhappy. Those words had no meaning on our rock. We were . . ." She gave a sharp tug on the braid as she found the word she was looking for. "*Content.* We were content. And then ye came, a prophecy most of us had never heard of and some of us could not believe in. Word become flesh." She turned slightly, her face all in shadow. It was as if a mask spoke.

"I thought . . ." Jenna began. "I thought you all recited the prophecy together and that was what convinced you."

"Words!" the girl said, voice shaking. "That is all it was: words. But Iluna was real. She was flesh and blood. Flesh of my flesh, blood of my blood. We swore to love one another always. We even cut our fingers and mixed our lives in blood when we were children. See." She turned and held out her hand to Jenna.

Jenna took her hand and held it up, as if she could read the girl's history there, but it was only a hand. Like her own. Nothing more.

"Words are for the old women. Iluna and I, we planned to leave M'dorah together. To see what else the world held. And when we were satisfied it held nothing, then we planned to return. But together. Together. And now she is . . . she is . . ." She began to snuffle, running the hand she had held up to Jenna across her mouth and nose, as if to stifle the sound.

Jenna nodded. "I understand. You will want the child after."

"The child?"

"Scillia."

"Oh no. I had told Iluna the child was not to come. It was our one argument, the only one we had ever had. No, White One, ye can keep the babe. I only want"—the snuffling began again—"Iluna." The name was a sob in her mouth.

Jenna put her arms around the girl, letting her cry. But she could not still her own thoughts. What if Carum said the same thing when she told him of the child. Would he cry out, "I want only you"? Would she still take the little one-armed babe if he denied it? She bit her lip hard to remind herself that her entire rehearsal of that conversation depended upon finding Carum alive. Taking the girl by the shoulders, she shook her.

"Enough! Iluna would not have you cry for her. She would have you remember with courage."

Pulling away from Jenna's grip, the girl nodded. She scrunged her shirttail over her face, drying her eyes and blowing her nose loudly. Then she walked away as if embarrassed that Jenna had comforted her at all.

For a moment Jenna considered following her. Then she shrugged and turned back to the encampment. Jareth, who happened to be on watch, stared at her, his hand covering his throat.

"Just battle jitters I expect," Jenna said, brushing a stray hair back from her face. She sighed. "Oh, Jareth, I am so tired of this. I want to be home. I want . . ." She looked at him. "I want to be able to talk to you. You were such a comfort before."

He stared at her for another moment, then took his hand from his neck. It was bare.

"Jareth—the collar—where?"

He mimed a sword cut, an upward blow. She suddenly remembered the sound of a gasp behind her when she had buried the knife between the Bear's eyes.

"Then you can talk now? You have been able to talk these past days?"

He shook his head vigorously, pointing strangely at his mouth.

"Gone?" she whispered. "The collar off and your voice still gone? Was it all a lie, then? Like the cradle and the hall? Is Catrona dead, Carum captured, and all those buried back there in the field for a lie?" She reached out to touch his arm, heard a noise behind her, and turned. Marek and Sandor stood close together.

"He can talk but he *will not,* Anna," Sandor said carefully, using her own dialect. "He *dare* not talk else he shatter the fellowship."

"What fellowship," Jenna asked, her voice heavy with sarcasm. "Women who will not speak to men and

men who laugh at women. A Dale warrior who rightly
blames me for the death of his beloved, and three boys
who believe a scared, incompetent girl is some sort of
goddess?"

"You be leaving out Petra," Sandor said softly, slipping back into his own speech.

"A rhyming priestess," Jenna said, "who surely
could not kill without getting sick on it."

"We be all that," admitted Marek. "Do you be feeling better saying it?"

"No," Jenna said miserably.

"Well, we be a fellowship nonetheless," Sandor said.

"That we be," Marek added, smiling.

"But what if it is lies," Jenna whispered. "If it is *all*
lies?"

"He still be not talking, Anna, because he *believes*,"
Marek said.

"And I," added Sandor. "Not until the king be
crowned and the king's right hand be winning the war."

"*You* be his right hand," Marek said.

"And Carum king. I be glad of that," Sandor finished.

"Oh, you brave, loyal boys," Jenna whispered, suddenly remembering Alta's fire that went ever before. "So
much braver and so much more loyal than I."

They put their arms about her then, all four thinking
about what had already been and what must surely come.
Jenna, Sandor, and Marek whispered memories back and
forth as if telling themselves a wonderful tale, but they
did it quietly, so as not to disturb the sleepers around
them. And when at last they pulled away from one another, their faces hot and tight with unshed tears, they
were each silhouetted against the night sky. To Jenna the
three boys looked as though they had been crowned with
stars.

She went back to the blanket which Petra had now
firmly wrapped around herself. Unwilling to wake her for

a share, Jenna lay down on the cold ground beside her and willed herself into a dreamless sleep.

THE SONG:

Well Before the Battle, Sister

Well before the battle, sister,
When the sky is crowned with stars,
And the world is clean of wounded,
And the ground is free of scars.

Well before the battle, sister,
When content with what we know,
We will sing the lovely ballads
From the long and long ago.

THE STORY:

By the time they reached the outskirts of Kalas' Northern Holdings, on a path which Piet insisted was marked by blood, though there was nothing to show it—not bones nor broken armor nor mounds of buried dead—the moon was coming into full again. That doubled the number of women at night, making even Piet uncomfortable. The men came up with both feeble and outrageous suggestions as to where the women had come from.

"Out of the woods," Gileas said to the New Steading boys. "They be trailing us all along."

"Mayhap they live here around," one boy said.

The others thought that a foolish idea, and told him so loudly.

"Nay," Piet said. "They be friends of our girls. Cousins, most like. See how much they resemble one another." It was the explanation they settled on in the end.

But it meant that at night, at least, the enlarged band was hard to disguise. Since Piet knew the land well, having served one year in the North, he kept them in the forest as deep as could be managed with horses. Under the heavy cover of trees, their numbers were once again halved. If the men wondered about it, they did so silently.

They left the horses crowded together in a small dell and went by foot the last mile toward Kalas' castle, single file and without talking. At the woods' edge, Piet signaled them to halt and they fanned out along the edge, being careful to each stay behind a tree.

Under the eye of a leperous moon, Kalas' castle was a great black vulture throwing a vast predatory shadow over the plain. It had two stone wings, the crenellated walls like feathers of rock. A single tower stretched up, the bird's naked neck. And in the single window, like a staring eye, a light gleamed. It was the only visible light in the place.

"There," Piet said, pointing. "The girls will climb straight up that rock face while I take the men to the gate there." His hand moved slightly. "We will make a great clamour and a rattling of swords. If they lower the gate to get at us, some will go through it. If it stays up, we will climb up it ourselves."

Jenna nodded.

"Two lines of mice are better than one against *this* great cat," Piet added.

"And the dungeon?"

"There is no way but from inside. That is why you go up the tower." His pointing finger shifted two palms worth to the left, where the rock seemed to grow right out of the ground forming an impenetrable wall.

"Kalas' tower!" Jenna whispered.

"How will you get up that, Jenna?" Petra asked.

Where the rock ended, the tall brick cylinder rose straight up into the air. Not a vulture's neck, Jenna thought, but a spear jabbing at the sky.

"Slowly," Jenna said. "And with a great deal of difficulty. But I will get up it all the same."

"If anyone can, you can," Petra said in her ear. "The prophecy knows it. Alta will see to it."

Jenna looked steadily at the tower. It was at least a hundred feet high. Privately, she prayed that Alta had a very long arm. "When I get to Kalas' room," she said steadily, "I will put my knife to his throat and make him take me personally to the dungeon to set the king free. If there is blood this night, it will be Kalas'." She spoke with the firm enunciation she had learned from listening to Gorum, but her heart beat erratically as she spoke. She was not nearly as certain as she appeared.

"We will have the surprise this time," Piet said grimly. "They think us all dead."

"We be having the right on our side as well," Marek added.

"Ah, lad, on the Continent they say: *The mice may have the right but the cat has the claws.* Whenever did right guarantee a victory but in a tale?" He stared ahead at the castle. "Do not be counting on the right. King Gorum did, and we buried him. I dinna want to bury you, too."

"Nor we you, Piet," said Jenna.

They waited until a shred of cloud covered the moon, then the women raced forward to the near wall, the men veering off toward the only gate.

Jenna set off on her own, avoiding Petra's attempt to catch her eye. If she thought about Petra or about all those who might be killed in the attempt on Kalas' castle, she knew she would become paralyzed, unable to climb. She forced herself to think only of the rocks ahead.

When she got to the precipitous stone, its sheer size overwhelmed her. At its base, she could see nothing above and nothing to either side but more and more stone, an endless wall of it. In the dark she could discern no handholds at all. Then suddenly the moon came out of its covering of cloud, and Skada was beside her pointing out the route.

"There!" she said. "And there."

"An odd sort of greeting," Jenna complained, tucking her braid down the back of her shirt.

"We have no time for pleasantries," Skada said, fixing her own hair. "And you are already breathing hard even before the climb."

"If I could appear and disappear under the light as you do," Jenna said testily, "I would not need to breathe at all." But nonetheless it was a good reminder that she had forgotten the first rule Mother Alta had taught her so long ago, that of proper breathing. She forced herself to think about the careful spider breaths for climbing. As she did so, she heard Skada's breathing synchronizing with her own.

Slow hand by slow hand, feet slotted into the shallow ridges, they began to climb. Every few moments they waited together, breathed together, gathered strength, then moved on up. The soft leather of their boots was scraped, their skin leggings had a hole in the right knee. Still they climbed.

The moon suddenly disappeared behind another cloud and Skada was gone, but Jenna, so intent on the rock under her hand, foot, and face, never noticed.

A minute later the moon came out again and Skada reappeared, clinging as Jenna did to the stone.

"You breathe hard, sister," Skada said.

"In my ear, sister," Jenna replied. "You are doing this to annoy. I wish to Alta you would stop." But she slowed her breathing down again and found the climbing easier.

The wall, shadow-scarred and crumbling, fooled both hand and eye. What seemed a chink was often solid. What appeared solid, a handful of dust. The mistakes cost them precious minutes, took them equally by surprise. Jenna wondered whether the others had reached their goals, the women scaling the far side of the castle, the men at the gate. But when she thought about them, her right hand slipped and she found herself desperately grabbing for rocks that kept falling to pieces beneath her. One shard cut deeply into her palm. She cursed, and heard an answering curse from Skada. With great concentration, she found another handhold and Skada's sigh was a welcome sound.

Above them—way above—was the lighted window. Jenna knew that they had to be there before dawn because she needed Skada, both for the sword she could wield and the comfort she might give. She said so aloud.

"Thank you for the thought," Skada whispered, "but keep on climbing."

For a moment, Jenna stopped, put her right palm to her mouth, and licked the small, bloody shred. Skada did the same, almost seeming to mock her. Neither of them smiled. Then Jenna set her hand back on the rock and began the climb once more.

Inches were gained at the cost of minutes. The wall did not so much fight them as resist them; their own bodies became their worst enemies. There is only so much stretch in the ligaments, so much give to muscles, so much strength in even the strongest arm and thigh. But at last Jenna's hand felt along the top of the stone wall.

"Tower base," she whispered. But the moon was once again behind a cloud and there was no longer anyone to whisper to.

"Alta's Hairs!" Jenna muttered, using a curse she rarely allowed herself. She pulled with both arms, heaving herself over the top. Even the skins were little protection against the wall. She could feel the roughness of the stone through the hides.

Rolling to her knees, she found herself staring at a large pair of boots.

"Look up slowly," came a voice. "I would like to see the surprise on your face before I strike you down. Look up, dead man."

From her knees, Jenna looked up slowly, never stopping her prayer for a sliver of moonlight. When she finally stared at the guard, his face was suddenly lit by a full and shining moon.

Jenna smiled at him.

"By Cres, you are no man," he said, relaxing for a fraction of a second and starting to smile back.

Jenna looked down coyly, a maneuver she had seen on the face of one of the serving girls in New Steading, and held out her hand.

Automatically the soldier reached down.

"Now!" Jenna cried.

Startled, he stepped back. But he was even more startled when, from behind him and below his knees, he was struck by another kneeling form. He tumbled over and was dead before the blade came sliding out of his heart.

Jenna hoisted the man's body on her shoulder and heaved it over the wall. She did not wait to hear it land. When she turned to speak to Skada, Skada looked stunned.

"What is it?" Jenna asked.

"I . . . I have never actually killed a man before," Skada whispered. "The knife went in and out and he was dead."

"But we killed the Hound," Jenna pointed out. "And the Bear. And cut off the Bull's hand which led to his death."

"No, Jenna, *you* did that."

"You are my dark sister. You feel what I feel. You know what I know."

"It . . . is . . . not . . . quite . . . the . . . same," Skada said, pulling each word across her tongue with great difficulty.

"No," Jenna said at last. "You are right. I do not feel about this unnamed guard what I felt about the others. My hand does not remember his death in quite the same way."

They touched hands for a moment. "We had better resume the climb up that tower. This is just the first stop. If there are other guards . . ."

Skada nodded.

"And once daylight comes, you are of no practical use. If I die . . ."

Skada smiled grimly. "You do not have to remind me. Every dark sister knows the rules of living and of light. I live as you live, die as you die. Only get up that wall. I cannot start without you."

Jenna stared up at the tower wall. The bricks were newer than the stone along the great wall they had just climbed, but the ravages of the northern winds had pulped part of the facade. Bits of the brick would crumble underhand.

As they began the new ascent, whispers volleyed between them, though nothing so loud they would awaken any guards. Occasionally, they cursed. The curses served as a cup of borrowed courage might, strengthening their resolve and reminding them that anger would serve when purpose faltered.

Jenna reached the tower window first, but only fractionally. Below one torn fingernail blood seeped. The cut on her palm ached. Her legs were beginning to tremble with the effort of climbing. There was a spot between her shoulders that was knotted with pain. She ignored them all, concentrating all her effort on the windowsill and the light filtering over it. Under her tunic, muscles bunched as, with a final pull, she hoisted herself up to the sill onto her stomach. The sill was broad and her legs kicked Skada's head. All she felt was relief to be off of the wall and irritation with Skada.

"Out of the way."

"It is your legs that are at fault," Skada answered huffily. "My head only moves in a limited direction."

Pushing herself up, Jenna tumbled them both off the sill. She caught hold of a lantern to stop the fall and dashed them both against the floor. The lantern landed first and went out; the fall seemed to take forever.

Voices scrabbled around Jenna in the dark.

"I have him," someone cried and Jenna felt her arms seized. She was pushed to her knees, the sword belt slashed from her waist. Struggling did no good; it only forced her arms up higher behind her till she was sure they would break. She relaxed into the hold, waiting.

"Light the torches, fools," came a command. The voice was soft, but no less powerful for its softness.

A torch was lit, stuttering to life. It was held over Jenna's head. An odd scrambling sound from the corner made the voice from the darkness add: "There's a second one, double fools. And idiots, all. Bring the torch over there."

Two men, one with the torch and one with a drawn sword, ran over to the corner but the strong light disspelled all shadows. Only along the far wall, where no one but Jenna looked, were a bent leg, a quick turn of head.

"There is no one, Lord Kalas."

"Just a trick of light," Jenna said smoothly. "Would I have been captured so easily if I had had a companion? I come alone. I am always alone. It is . . ." She hesitated thinking of the right word to cozen him. "It is my one conceit."

The men brought the torch back and held it close to Jenna's face.

"It is the White One, my lord Kalas," the man with the torch said. "If we have her as well as the prince, the rebellion is all but over. They say . . ."

"They say . . . they say altogether too much," Kalas said. "Let me look at her. Why, she is scarcely out of childhood." He laughed. "I had thought her a grown woman. She is but a long-legged, white-haired colt."

Meanwhile Jenna looked at him, past the glare of the torchlight. She had heard many things about him from Carum and Piet, and none of them good. But could this faded coxcomb, with the dyed red hair and the dyed red beard that only emphasized the pouching under his eyes, be the infamous Lord Kalas of the Northern Holdings? How could he be that wily toad they all so hated and feared?

"I'm not interested in what the others say, but you may be fascinated by what that late, lamented, sniveling princeling Carum—who calls himself Longbow for no discernible reason—says about you."

Jenna controlled her tongue, thinking quickly that Kalas had put Carum's name in both the past and the present. But the guard had not. Was Carum dead? It was not possible. She would have *known*, she would have felt something if he had died. *Late. Lamented.* Perhaps Kalas was referring to the title of prince and not the man himself. Garunians liked to play with words. She allowed herself to smile up at her captor, showing him nothing of what she felt.

"And shall I tell *you* what the very late and not at all lamented Bear had to say about you, you dyed rooster?"

"Ah," Kalas whispered, "not a child then. A woman with a woman's wiles. I should have known you even had you changed *your* hair color. Longbow's White Goddess. He said your mouth opened as quickly as your legs, like most women of the Dales."

"Carum would never . . ." She closed her mouth, feeling like a child, indeed, to have fallen for such a trick.

"A man on a rack says many things, my dear."

"Few of them true," Jenna added.

Kalas leaned over and put his hand lightly on her head, as if to stroke her. Instead he pulled the braid out of her shirt and yanked.

"Girls playing at women have a certain kind of

charm. Women playing at girls another. But women playing at warriors bore me." He pulled a smile over his dis-
colored teeth, yellowed with piji. "And you, for such a
pretty girl, do it badly. Your prince is in the dungeon, not
my chamber, so all your climbing has been for
naught . . ." He tapped her right knee with the flat of his
blade. "Except to strengthen those comely legs."

"By Alta's Hairs . . ." Jenna began, hoping that by
swearing she might better disguise her feelings.

"Alta's hairs are gray and much too short to keep
her warm," the smooth, mocking voice replied. "And that
is what we have you by—Alta's short hairs!" He laughed
at his own crudity. "But if you insist on playing a man's
game, we will treat you like a man, and instead of warming my bed—which you would doubtless do with little
grace though youth does have certain advantages, even
Dalian youth—you will freeze with the others in my dungeon."

Jenna bit her lip, trying to appear frightened, when
actually the dungeon was the very place she wanted to be.
Though she wanted to be there with both her sword and
her dagger.

"Ah, I see you have heard of it. What is it they call
it?" He yanked her braid again, this time wrapping it
three times around his fist and bringing his face close to
hers. For a moment she was afraid he was going to kiss
her. His breath was sickly sweet with the odor of piji. The
thought of that mouth on hers made her ill.

"They call it . . . Kalas' Hole," she whispered.

"Enjoy it," he said, pulling his face away. "Others
have." He turned from her so quickly, his lizard-skin cape
sang like a whip around his ankles. Then he was gone.

The guards pushed Jenna down the stairs, descending
it quickly. *Much more quickly,* she mused, *than the la-
borious climb up that wall.*

Her hands were so tightly bound behind her, she had
lost the feeling in her fingers by the second level. The one

consolation was that the man with the torch went ahead, and so the shadows of their moving bodies were ranged behind them. If he had been at the end of the line, there would have been a second bound woman on the stairs, with a dark braid down her back, leggings with a hole in the knee, and a head that ached.

Jenna promised herself that she would do nothing to make any of the guards look back to where Skada was following; neither by a remark nor by a movement would she betray her.

The stairs twisted round and round through the tower. When they began a straight descent, Jenna knew the tower had ended and the main part of the castle had begun. At each level, the air grew cooler and mustier. There were great wooden doors on either side, with a single barred window. As they passed, she could see pale patches at the windows, but it was only after the third that she realized they were faces. After that she lifted her head, turning toward the doors, so that whoever was inside might see and recognize her. She would not be buried in secret.

At the stairs' end was a final heavy wooden door barring the way. It took three keys to unbolt the door and when it was finally opened, Jenna was pushed in without further ceremony and the door locked behind. Not a word had been spoken the entire trip down the stairs.

The dungeon certainly deserved its name. Lord Kalas' Hole was dark, dank, wet, and smelled like the hind end of a diarrhetic ox. Even without ever having been behind one, Jenna knew the smell.

To keep herself from gagging, Jenna turned back and shouted at the departing guards, "May you be hanged in Alta's hair. May She thread your guts through Her braids and use your skull . . ."

"I have never heard you curse before," came a voice made almost unfamiliar with fatigue. "But you could at least try something original."

"Carum!" Jenna whispered, spinning around and

trying to find him in the dark. "That we were put in the same cell."

"Oh, this is the special one, lady," came another voice from the dark. "The worst."

It was not wholly black. Some faint light trailed in through the barred window in the door. After a bit she could distinguish some shadows, though she was not sure which was Carum and which the other captives. Of Skada there was no sign, but with just that splinter of light, Jenna hardly expected to see her. And she did not wish her dark sister the pain in her wrists.

She felt fingers touch her shoulder, move down to her bound hands, and begin to work at her bonds.

"Actually," Carum whispered in her ear, "I think you have it wrong. I looked it up once. The curse is really: *May you be hanged by Alta's heirs,* meaning the sons and daughters she bore. Not the long braids you copy. It was in a book at Bertram's Rest. Still, I love your hair. You must never cut it. I mean to shake it free again in the light."

He was having trouble with the ropes around her wrists and she stood absolutely still to let him work on them, though her legs suddenly trembled. He smelled nothing like the Carum she knew, but she doubted she smelled very good either.

Finally he got the knots undone and silently rubbed her aching wrists. "There. What good is my right hand tied?"

"What good am I at all," Jenna asked wearily, "if I am caught? At least I know you are alive. I had hoped to stick my knife in Kalas' mouth and pick his piji teeth."

"Did you see him?" Carum's voice was suddenly cautious.

"See him? The toad caught me. As easily as a child catches an eft."

"Did he . . ." He stopped, drew in a breath, and let it out saying ". . . touch you?" His arms encircled her protectively.

Very gently she turned in his arms. "He said since I was playing a man's game, he would treat me like a man."

"Bless your Alta for that," Carum said.

"Could his bed be worse than this dungeon?" Jenna asked lightly.

Carum did not answer, but someone in the dark did. "Far worse, lady, for the girls of the Dales. He worships the Garunian women. They, alone, are exempt from his foul attentions."

She whistled a long, low sound through dry lips.

Carum whispered again, this time so softly no one but Jenna could hear. "Are you by yourself?"

"I am here in the dark," she answered as softly.

"I don't mean Skada. I know she is gone without the light. But the others? They aren't all . . ."

"Dead? Gone? No. Though your brother . . . oh, Carum, you are the king now. I am sorry." She turned so that the light lit her face just a little that he might see that she was truly sorry.

"It's as I expected," he whispered. "As Kalas hinted. And Jenna, I'm sorry, but it's as prophecy wrote. You are to be the king's bride, and I would let no one else wed you. I'm not surprised."

"You will not be king if we are in a dungeon. And by my sword, which I have unfortunately lost and my dirk which . . ." She felt in her boot knowing it was gone, too. "And by my temper, which is fast going, *I can't think in the dark.*"

"You can't think with your hands tied," Carum said, raising his voice to match hers. "But you do very well in the dark."

For a moment she was furious with him, turning their lovemaking into a joke. But when she heard the slight rattle of laughter around them, like cold water over bone-dry stones, she realized it was the first laugh these men had had in days. It stumbled inexpertly out of their mouths, but it *was* a laugh. She knew instinctively that

men in dangerous situations needed laughter to combat
that feeling of helplessness that would, in the end, con-
spire to defeat them. She put her pride behind her and
added a line to his. "Longbow, you do fairly well yourself
in the dark." Then she spoke rapidly, more thinking out
loud than a question to him, "But why so black? Why is
there no light at all?"

A slight shift of sound and a shadow moved. One of
the men stood up. "Lord Kalas' jest, Anna. He is a true
Garun. He says one's enemies are best kept in the dark."

Her wrists still hurt where the ropes had cut into
them, and she rotated them to work out the ache. "When
do they feed us? And do they do that in the dark as
well?"

"Once a day," Carum said. "In the morning, I think,
though day and night have little meaning here."

"I came in the night," Jenna said, adding as casually
as she could, "and there was a fine moon."

Nodding, Carum whispered, "Skada?"

She did not answer him directly. "But do they bring
light then?"

"They bring a single torch, Anna," came a voice by
her shoulder.

Another added, "They set it in the wall, over there,
by the door."

"For all the good it does. It shows us how degraded
we have become in three short days." Carum laughed a
short angry bark. "Or two days. Or ten. Is it not ironic
what a little bit of dirt and dark and dank and a delicate
diet can do to beggar a man?"

"Carum, this does not sound like you," Jenna whispered, furious.

"This doesn't look like me either, Jenna," he answered. "Oh Jen . . ." His voice caught suddenly. "I've
made a royal hash of it." He laughed shortly at his own
bad joke. "And I wouldn't have you see me this way."

"I have seen you many ways, Carum Longbow,"
Jenna said. "And not all of them handsome. Do you re-

member the boy running from the Ox, scared and curious at the same time? Or the boy dressed in girl's skirts and scarf at the Hame? Or the drowned ratling in the River Halle?"

"As I recall it, *you* were the ratling and I the rescuer," Carum said, his voice almost back to normal. Then it dropped again. "How could I have let Gorum talk me into . . ."

One of the other men put his hand on Jenna's arm. "They put something in the food, Anna. A sprinkling of some witch's berry. It takes a man's will away. Yet we must eat. Each of us has his moments of such despair. Do not tax him with his answers. We are all like that—high with expectation one moment, low and despairing the next. You will feel the corrosion of it soon enough. We are our own worst torturers."

Jenna turned back and placed her hand against Carum's cheek. "It will be better by and by. I promise."

"Women's promises . . ." he began before his voice bled away, like an old wound reopened.

"What do you mean?"

"It be an old bit of wit from the Continent, lady," a new voice said. "Best leave it."

"No—tell me," Jenna said.

"No, Anna."

"Carum, what do you mean?"

His old voice was suddenly returned. "It is something Kalas is fond of saying: *Women's promises are water over stone—wet, willing, and soon gone.*"

"Water over stone . . ." Jenna mused. "I had that advice once, long ago. Be water over stone. It meant something quite different."

"Don't tax me with it, Jen," Carum pleaded.

"I keep *my* promises, Carum, and well you know it. All I need is that light."

Carum was about to speak when one of the other men broke in. "It will do you no good, Anna. It does none of us any good. They hold the light up to the hole in the door and then they make us lie down on the floor, one atop another."

"One atop another?" Jenna asked.

"It is a cruel and humbling act," Carum said. "They do it in the dungeons of the Continent. An invention of Castle Michel Rouge, where most of the instruments of torture come from as well. Kalas has cousins there." He hesitated, finally admitting, "As do I."

"They count us aloud, lady, afore they open the door. After each lock they count us."

"Better and better," Jenna said mysteriously.

"If you have a plan, tell me." Carum's voice was strong and full again.

"Tell us," a dozen men's voices agreed.

Jenna smiled into the dark, but with her back to the single sliver of light in the door, none of them could see. "Just be sure," she said to them, "that I lie on top of the pile."

The men gave forced, muttered laughs, but Carum added—as if he understood—"It would not do to have the Anna, the White Goddess, lie beneath."

Jenna laughed with them, extending the joke. "Though there have been times when I have fancied *that* place as well . . ." She was glad they could not see her face, hot with furious blushes. If Carum continued *this* jest, she swore to herself she would kill him before Kalas ever got the chance. But sensing her desperate embarrassment, he let it go. The men were as buoyant as they were likely to be. Jenna walked over to the door. Holding up her hand into the splinter of light, she watched as Skada's hand appeared faintly against the far wall. Jenna waved and was delighted to see Skada's hand return it.

"Will you be ready?" she called to the wall.

Thinking she was addressing them, the men cried out, "We will, Anna."

"For whatever you require," Carum added.

But Jenna had eyes only for the hand on the wall. It

made a circle between thumb and finger, the goddess' own sign. For the first time Jenna felt reason to hope.

Forcing herself to sleep on the cold stones, Jenna gave her body time to recover from the long climb. She curled next to Carum, breathing slowly, matching her breath to his. When she slept at last, her dreams were full of wells, caves, and other dark, wet holes.

The clanging of a sword against the iron bars of the window woke them all.

"Light count," came the call. "Roll up and over."

The prisoners dragged themselves to the wall and attempted a rough pyramid, not daring to complain. Last to sit up, Jenna watched as the sturdiest six, including Carum, lay down on the floor. The next heaviest climbed on top, and then the next until a final skeletal two—obviously long interred for other crimes against Kalas—scaled up to the perch, distributing their weight as carefully as possible. It was easier to see all this because of the additional light from the torch shining through the window in the door.

The sound of the guard's voice counting began. "One, two, three . . ."

"Wait!" It was a new voice, well in command. Not Kalas' voice. Jenna was disappointed but not surprised. After all, why should Kalas himself oversee a dungeon full of prisoners?

The voice had a soft purr to it. "You misbegotten miscalculators," came its smooth mockery. "Don't deny us the best. His highness, King Kalas, spoke movingly of the lady. Is there not room on top for her?"

"There is room," Jenna said, her voice soft so that the speaker had to come closer to the door to hear her. She could only see a shadow, a smallish shadow, almost boy-sized.

"Always room," came the purring voice, "because a pyramid is altogether a pleasing figure."

Jenna guessed. "The Cat!"

He laughed. "Smart women are annoying. But I understand I have nothing to fear from you. You have already killed one cat. And I have lives to spare, is that not so?"

His men chuckled.

"Climb up, my lady. Ascend your throne."

"Why should I?"

"Ask the men upon whose backs you will make your climb," the Cat said in his purring voice.

"We tried denying him his pleasure in the pyramid," Carum said, "and they simply refused to feed us at all until we lay one atop another."

Jenna nodded and kicked off her boots. Then she set her right foot carefully on someone's buttocks and began the climb. When she reached the top, she lay down gingerly, trying to distribute her weight evenly.

"Will they bring the light now?" Jenna whispered to one of the men under her.

"Yes," he whispered back. "Look, here it comes."

Two men—one with a torch—entered the room. The Cat, disdaining to draw his own weapon, entered after them. He was a small, wiry man who looked pleased with himself, like a puss over a saucer of cream.

The light-bearer stood at the head of the pile of bodies counting them aloud once again. The second went to a corner, sheathed his sword, and dropped a bag that had been draped over his shoulders onto the floor. He emptied its contents on the stone. Jenna made out a pile of hard breads and wrinkled her nose. Then she looked up at the wall nearest the door where shadows thrown by the flickering torch moved about.

"Now!" she shouted, flinging herself from the pile.

She calculated her roll to take her into the shoulder of the guard at the pyramid's peak. His torch flew into the air, illuminating another hurtling body that seemed to spring right out of the far wall. Skada rammed into the Cat, just as he unsheathed his sword.

Jenna reached for the guard's weapon as Skada

grabbed for the Cat's, then completed identical rolls in a single fluid motion and stood up.

At the moment of their impact, Carum and the other captives collapsed the pyramid. The strongest leaped to their feet, surrounding the guard near the bread and stripping him of his sword and a knife in his boot. Holding the torch aloft, Carum laughed.

"At least one of those lives ends here, my Cat."

"Perhaps," the Cat said, smiling. "But indulge me for a moment and let me ask the lady why at yesterday's count, there were twenty prisoners in this cell. Yet today, though there should have been twenty-one, a perfect pyramid, there was one extra. Where did the extra come from?"

Skada laughed behind him. "From a darker hole than you will ever know, Cat."

Jenna hissed through her teeth and Skada was immediately silent. But the Cat smiled.

"Could it be . . ." he said, his eyes crinkling, "could it be that the stories about you witches raising black demons out of mirrors is true? Mages lie, but images . . ."

Skada made a mocking bow. "Truth has many eyes. You must believe what you yourself see."

Jenna bowed as well. When she stood straight again, the Cat had a finger to his lips, obviously thinking.

"I see sisters who may have had the same mother but who had different fathers." He took the finger away. "It is well known that the mountain women take pleasure with many men."

"Some," Skada said, "take no pleasure with any men."

The Cat laughed, and at the same moment leaned forward dashing the torch from Carum's hand. It fell to the stone floor, started to gutter, and almost went out. Without the light, Skada was gone and the Cat's sword which had been in her hand clattered to the floor. He bent quickly and picked it up.

"Like my Lord Kalas," he said into the dark, "I chew

piji. It stains the teeth but gives one wonderful night sight." His sword rang against Jenna's.

"Dark or light," cried Jenna, "I will fight you. Stand back, Carum. Keep the others out of the way. And *do not move!*"

The Cat was not as strong as the Bear, being a small man, and so he could not overcome Jenna with sheer strength. But he was a clever swordsman, quick on his feet, and cunning. Twice his sword stroked open a small wound, once on her right cheek, once on her left arm. But he counted too much on his night sight, thinking it an advantage. What he did not know was that Jenna, like the other Hame warriors, had learned swordplay and wandplay in both dark and lightened rooms. Though she could not see as well as he in the blackness, she had been taught to trust her ears as well as her eyes. She could distinguish the movement of a thrust that was signaled by the change in the air; she could read every hesitation of breath. She could smell the Cat's slight scent of fear under the piji, the change in the odor of his sweat when he realized that he did not have the upperhand after all.

She slowed her own breathing to give her the steady strength she needed and with one last twist of her wrist managed to catch up his blade on hers and send it clattering away into the corner.

"Light!" Jenna called.

Carum picked up the torch and held it overhead. Once off the cold stone it managed to flutter back into smoky life.

The Cat stood with both hands held out, almost playful in his surrender, though no one was fooled by his stance. Jenna's blade remained in his belly. Behind him, Skada had her sword at his back.

"If you move," Skada whispered to him, "I will spit you like a sheep over a roasting pit. And I will turn that spit very, very slowly."

He shrugged, but with exaggerated care.

"You have rightly guessed that Jenna and I are sisters," Skada continued. "And that we are not at all alike. *I* do not yet have your blood on my blade, though it is she who has sworn your death."

Jenna turned to Carum. "Keep the torch high, my king. And stand at the head of the line as we go. Skada and I will take the rear."

They left the Cat and his two men locked in the dungeon without any light at all, and made their way up the stairs. Carum held the torch in his left hand, one of the guard's swords in his right. After him came his men. At the rear was Jenna, the wound on her cheek and arm wiped clean of the fresh blood and already starting to close, though both still stung. And, when the light was right, Skada trotted along behind.

At each new door they fumbled the locks open with keys they had taken from the Cat's belt. Carum greeted each released prisoner in turn, both those who had ridden with him and those who had been in Kalas' Hole for other crimes.

All in all, they opened eight dungeon doors and gathered almost a hundred men, most still in fighting condition, though they had only three swords and nine torches for weapons. There was not even a chair or a table that might be broken into cudgels.

"My lord, Carum," a thin voice cried.

Jenna strained to make out the speaker in the flickering torchlight. Carum spotted him first and, handing the torch to someone, gave his hand to the speaker. The man was as thin as his voice, and knobby; his hands were too big for their wrists, his nose oversized on a bony face.

"What is it?" Carum asked.

"I know this castle well, sir. I have served here all my life, first as serving lad, then as cook's boy, now as cook."

Someone laughed. "Don't they say: *Measure a cook by his belly?* This one is all bones."

The man shook his head. "I have been in the dungeon four or five weeks now. It thins a man."

"Maybe less," someone cried. "If he cannot remember."

"He's a spy," another called.

Carum held up his hand for silence. "Let him speak."

"If I do not remember rightly," the cook said, "it is because time has no dominion here. Day is night. Night is day."

"That be true enough," a man with a blond beard said.

"To your point," Carum urged.

"I know every passage in this castle, every hall and every stair."

Coming forward, and heedless of Skada following her, Jenna put her hand on the cook's arm. It trembled slightly beneath her touch. Skada took his other arm. His trembling increased.

"Then tell us where this passage leads to."

"Out of the Hole, lady."

"He *is* a spy," came a voice.

"He must give us more," came another.

"And what does the door open into," Jenna persisted. She suspected he was the kind of man who could not say anything straightaway but must have it pulled from him.

"An arras, lady."

"What does *that* mean?" asked someone.

"A curtain, he means. An arras is a curtain," explained Carum.

"He *is* a spy. Spit him!"

Jenna tightened her hold on the cook's arm. "These men are getting restless and Longbow and I will not be able to control them if you do not speak plainly."

"No, listen to me," the cook said hastily. "This passage leads to an open door in the wall of Kalas' Great Hall and it is hung over, covered over, by an arras."

The muttering men hushed.

"That is better," Jenna said, relaxing her grip.

"Much better," Skada said from the other side.

But the cook, once started, seemed unable to stop. "It is a heavy arras," he said. "One of the finest in the castle. A tapestry dedicated to Lord Cres. He is feasting with his heroes and they are . . ."

"Throwing bones over their shoulders to the dogs of war," Skada whispered to Jenna.

The cook did not hear and continued in his thin voice, ". . . hangs over the door. But often King Kalas . . ."

The men began to mutter again at that, an angry sound, like bees. Carum silenced them with a cut of his hand.

". . . I mean, Lord Kalas when he dines has the arras pulled back to listen to the cries from the Hole. He calls it *seasoning* for his meals."

Carum's lips closed tight together but he made no comment other than a nod.

"Lord Kalas had been away much lately, but he returned precipitously a few days ago. After a message from one of his chiefs."

"The Bear!" one man said, turning to stare at Jenna.

"Na, how could *he* know all that?" asked another.

"They tell it to me, the guards," the cook said quickly. "To crow over it. My pain their pleasure; their gossip my only meat."

"I don't like it, sir. 'Tis too easy," one of the men cautioned Carum. Several others agreed.

"But it makes good sense," Jenna mused.

"Who guards this arras, this tapestry?" Carum asked in a harsh whisper. "How many? What arms?"

"It is an *open* door, my lord. Kalas' boast is *No one escapes from the Hole whole.* Sometimes he shows the gaping door to the ladies, just to frighten them a little bit."

"What ladies?" Jenna asked, hardly breathing.

"The ones he captures. The ones he beds. Young ladies, some of them. Scarce more than girls."

Jenna shivered, thinking of Alna and Selinda, thinking of Jareth's Mai, thinking of the children from Nill's
Hame.

"Do you mean *no one* guards it?"

"I mean it opens directly into the Great Hall which is
always full of an army of men, especially when Kalas is
home."

The men mumbled their opinions, volleying them
back and forth. Crowding tightly together, they discussed
their options.

"It's no good then."

"We're doomed."

"Better dead at once than dying slowly down there."

"Wait," Skada said. Now that the torches were close
together, she held her shape. "Listen. There is something
you do not know."

Jenna nodded. "There are one hundred armed
women on the walls outside who may have already made
it to the top."

"And fifty armed men battling through the gate."

The cook laughed mirthlessly. "There are three portcullises between the gate and the keep. They will not get
in."

"Whether they get in or not," Skada said, "they will
be a distraction."

"They are the mice," Jenna cried to Carum.

"And we already have the Cat!" he rejoined.

"Listen," Skada said, "we have few weapons but the
torches."

"Do you mean to burn him out?" asked someone.

"Trust me," Skada said. "Set all you can on fire. If it
is day and the women have gotten in, they fight—better—near a fire."

"Better a hot woman than a cold dinner," someone
called.

Laughing, they started up the stairs again, but became quiet at the next turning for it was clear the exit out
of the Hole lay just ahead.

Jenna and Skada signaled them on, and they crept silently up the rest of the cold stone steps, amazingly quiet, Jenna thought, for so many men.

Since only Carum, Jenna, and one other man were armed with stolen swords, they went ahead. Skada, with her shadow weapon, followed close behind. When they reached the last step, Carum poked the sword slowly at the heavy curtain, looking for a way out. Finally Jenna knelt down; she tried to lift the arras. It was a heavy weave and weighted along the bottom. She gestured with her head for help. Two of the unarmed men stepped forward to lift the curtain up, and Jenna and Skada crawled through, sliding their swords before them.

It was bright daylight on the other side of the tapestry and Jenna blinked frantically, trying to adjust her eyes to the sudden light. She turned to speak to Skada but Skada was gone. Jenna felt a terribly loneness, as if she had been forsaken, though she knew it was but a trick of the sun. Skada would be back again in the evening. If they were still alive by evening.

Then she realized that the room was unnaturally quiet for the central room of a castle. Slowly she looked around. No one was there.

"Empty," she whispered at last to the slightly raised tapestry.

The curtain inched its way higher until there was a doorway held between hands. The rest of the prisoners boiled through, blinking awkwardly in the light and staring about in confusion. If they had expected anything, it was not this. The Great Hall was totally deserted.

"I don't understand . . ." Carum began.

"I do," Jenna said. "Listen!"

They all heard it then, the faint tumble of voices coming from outside where an uneven battle was being waged.

"We must help them," someone cried.

"First set fire to this hall," Jenna said. "You—the curtains there. And you—the arras on the other wall."

"And break up those chairs. At least we will have clubs to fight with," Carum called.

The tapestries smoldered slowly at first, refusing to take up the flame, till at last one section flared suddenly, and within minutes that Cres and his heroes were completely consumed by the fire. The men armed themselves with chair legs and the table bracings and several caught up cushions from the chairs to use as shields. The rest of the furniture they piled in the middle of the hall and set on fire. As the central flames rose higher, Skada danced next to Jenna for a second.

"I will follow whenever I can," she said.

"I know," Jenna whispered, then waved to the empty air as she followed Carum and the men out of the door and down a wide hallway.

Racing along the door-lined hall, they followed the cook's shouted directions, heedless now of any noise. They came upon two guards who turned to face them but were quickly and efficiently disarmed and bound by Carum and three of the men wielding clubs. The guards' swords were taken up by two of the men, and a dagger in a boot was found as well.

"I will take that," said the cook, pointing at the dagger. "And I'll dice the next one into small, bite-sized pieces." He giggled.

"Just get us outside," Carum cried, "and you can carve up who you will."

The cook led them to a wide stone stairs flanked by a pair of magnificent banisters polished to a high gleam. At the bottom of the staircase, ranged across it to block them, were some twenty castle guards armed with swords and fully shielded.

"What now?" Jenna asked. "We have but five swords and a knife."

"Let them come up to us," Carum said. "They'll have a harder time of it, unbalanced on the stairs, though what I would give for a bow now. Still, we have more men. And clubs."

As if guessing Carum's strategy, the guards remained below, unmoving. Long minutes went by.

At last Jenna said, "We cannot just wait."

"If we go down there one at a time, they'll take us one by one. If we try and rush them with the weapons we have, it will be a slaughter."

"Then we must fool them with a line of false mice."

"Too late. They've seen us and counted our weapons. Time is on their side," Carum said.

"Cook," Jenna said suddenly, turning. "What of those doors we passed in the hallway. Any escape there?"

"They are closets, lady. With extra dishes and linens and . . ."

"Ha!" Jenna said, turning back to Carum. "We will have our mice! You"—she touched one of the men on the shoulder—"take my sword. And you—take Carum's." When they hesitated, she shoved her sword at one, took Carum's and handed it to another man. "And you three"—she pointed to some of the weaker-looking men—"come with us."

Carum chose a raw-boned, blond-bearded man to be in charge while he was gone, then ran to catch up with Jenna. "Where are we going?"

"To make us a line of mice."

Kicking open the first door, she stripped the shelves of priceless wool and linen weavings, of banners and toweling.

"Take it all," she told them.

. The second closet yielded goblets and platters and, best of all, carving knives.

A third closet would not open even to their frantic kicking, and they left it, hurrying back to the stairs with their treasures. The guards were still waiting below with the studied calm of hunting cats, but the men at the top of the stairs had not been as patient. A few were several steps down and pacing. One had already tried to get through the line by himself, his bloody body testimony to the foolishness of such an act.

"He was not one of us, my lord, but a prisoner of Kalas' from before. He had not our training," the blond-bearded man said.

"Still we must count him as ours," Carum said softly. "He died on Kalas' blades."

"Here is what I would have us do," Jenna said, showing them how to tie together the line of banners and linen, threading into place the cups and platters and bowls.

"A woman's wiles," complained one man.

"A mouse's," Carum said, smiling grimly. "Listen to her."

Below the soldiers were curious at first, but at a shouted command from their captain, stilled again, waiting with swords raised.

It took precious minutes to complete the *little mice,* as Jenna called the strange assortment of cobbled-to-gether tableware. She traded the men carving knives for cudgels, adding the pieces of wood to her strange tapestry. Then she gave the final orders in a whisper, telling the men of their places.

"The signal," she explained, "is *For Longbow!*"

She stationed herself at the top of one banister, one end of the tied banners slipknotted around her waist. Carum stood at the other. He had a similar line bound around. They each held a sword. Behind them, not yet taut across, was the quick weave and behind it, the waiting men, knives, torches, and three swords at the ready.

"For Longbow!" Jenna shouted suddenly, and at the signal she and Carum both leaped onto the banisters as if onto horses. They pulled the line taut between them, a strange curtain of heavy implements, and slid straight down. Screaming their defiance, the men came trampling down the stairs right after. The bemused guards watched their advance.

The mouse-line hit the guards neck high, tangling

them long enough for Jenna and Carum to slip the knots from their waists. By the time the guards had gotten free of the weaving, Carum's men were on them, too close for the swords. The carving knives, sharp enough for tough venison, found little resistance in the soft meat of a man's neck. It was over in minutes, and only one of Carum's crew had been injured from tripping in the lines himself and cutting his shin on a piece of broken glass.

Quickly they stripped the guards of their weapons and shields and then hurried, under the cook's nervous direction, toward the main doors. A heavy piece of wood deadbolted the door, but they managed to push it aside. When they flung open the doors, the scene outside in the courtyard was bedlam.

Outmanned but fighting steadily and well were the women of M'dorah, light sisters only, battling under the glaring eye of the afternoon sun. There was no sign of Piet and his men.

"They are still behind the gates," Jenna cried.

"Or caught in the trap between the portcullises," Carum added. "We must raise those gates."

"I will, my lord," cried the blond-bearded man. "I'll take several with me." He hurried out, careful to sidestep a number of the fighting guards. Jenna watched as he made his way across the courtyard and knew they could count on his success, for he was single-minded in his march, and the men around him saved him from many a blow.

"And where is Kalas?" Carum cried. "Where is that toad? I do not see him."

Jenna realized that she had not seen him, either.

"He is where toads always are, my lord, hiding in a hole," the cook said. He smiled and Jenna saw that his teeth were as yellow as Kalas' had been. As yellow as the Cat's. She wondered that a cook could afford such an addiction.

"In his dungeon?" Carum asked.

"In his bolt-hole," the cook said. "He will wait there till he is sure of his victory."

"Are *you* sure?" Jenna asked, staring in fascination at the man's teeth.

He nodded and, mistaking her attention, picked at his teeth with the knife.

"And you know where that hole is?" Carum asked.

"I do, sir, I do. Surely I do. And haven't I many times taken him his meals there?"

"The tower!" Jenna said suddenly.

The cook nodded his bony head. "The tower."

"Take me," Carum said. "I have a score to settle with him."

"Take us both," said Jenna. "We have lost more than one family each."

They trailed after him back up the stairs, along the hallway, and into the Great Hall again. The fires they had started there had sputtered out, and one wall of the tapestry was but partially burned. There was still heavy smoke in the air, as if the floor had been draped with gray bunting. Putting their arms across their faces to shield themselves from the smoke, Jenna and Carum followed the cook to a door in the wall next to the gaping opening down to the dungeon.

"Here," the cook said, pulling open the door and pointing up the twisting stairs.

"You go before," Carum said. "I trust you more in front of me than behind."

"He has done nothing wrong, Carum," Jenna said, though she was uneasy as well.

"Like my men, I feel things have been too easy so far," Carum said. "And as they said at Nill's Hame: *The day on which one starts is not* . . ."

". . . *the day to begin one's preparations.* You are right," Jenna said. "*Better to be safe than buried,* we said at our Hame. He will go in front."

The cook mounted the stairs before them. The passage wound up and up, unrelieved by any landings or windows, and was the darker since they had just come from the light. They went up by feel alone, putting their

feet where the stone was worn smooth by many tread-
ings.

"If we had a torch now," Carum whispered.

"Skada would appreciate that," Jenna whispered
back. "And we could certainly use the extra sword."

As they rounded the final twist, a sliver of light announced an open door. Jenna pushed aside the cook and
put her eye to the crack. She could see nothing but a
wedge of light on a polished wood floor, but she could
hear Kalas' voice speaking in an oily, cozening fashion.
Having heard it only for a few minutes the night before,
she could still not forget it. It was at once powerful and
weak, full of dark promises and hinting at even darker
secrets.

"Come, my dear," Kalas was saying, "it will not be
so bad as all that. Once done and it need never be done
again. At least with me."

Jenna breathed slowly. So he was alone—with only a
girl as company.

There was a silence, and then a young woman's
voice, wheezy and achingly familiar.

"Leave me be," she said, catching her breath.
"Please."

"Alna!" Jenna's mouth shaped the name though she
did not speak it aloud. Surely that was her Hame mate's
voice. Alna, who had been on her mission year to Calla's
Ford, had been stolen away. But it had been weeks—no,
years in actual time—since she had heard Alna. She could
not be sure without seeing her. Still, she could feel heat
rising to her cheeks, could feel her stomach roil, as if her
body already believed what her mind hesitated to accept.
Turning to Carum, she whispered, "Kalas is alone in
there with a girl. I can handle this. Best you see to the
others."

"No. I will not leave you."

"The sword is my weapon, not yours. This is my
fight. That is my Hame mate in there."

"It is my fight, too. Kalas murdered my family."

"I will not match blood with you. But if you stay and your men below go marching off to Lord Cres because you did not lead them . . . ."

He kissed her cheek, turned, and left, so light on his feet she did not hear his footsteps go. When she turned back it was to see the cook tapping lightly on the door.

"No!" the woman inside screamed, then coughed violently.

Jenna pushed the cook hard on the small of the back, and he fell against the door, springing it open.

"It is a trap!" the woman cried, but she was too late.

Jenna was already inside. Before her was Alna, hands bound behind her, lying on a great canopied bed. To her right Kalas squatted toadlike on a carved chair. Ranged before him were seven large men. *Very large men,* Jenna thought. Seven to her one, with little room to maneuver as the door swung shut behind her. The stranger's sword in her hand was lighter than she was used to, the pommel sitting awkwardly in her hand.

She knew she had to stall. Stall—and silence the cook who had betrayed them. She took a half step to the side and kicked the fallen man in the head, hard enough to quiet him for an hour or two, not hard enough to kill him. But her eyes never left Kalas and his men.

"Jenna!" Alna managed to get out, "it *is* you. I could not be sure it was not another lie."

"Alna!" She could not spare her old friend another glance, not even out of the corner of her eye, though she had known her at once. Alna was older and thinner than when they had parted on the first day of their mission year. And that, Jenna thought wryly, was the day she had believed that her life was at its worst, when she had been separated from her best friends and sent off to a strangers' Hame alone.

"Alone again, White Jenna," Kalas said slowly, as if he had been able to read her mind. "What an odd habit you are developing. Always arriving uninvited into my little tower room."

"Perhaps not entirely uninvited," Jenna said. "I think you sent the invitation by way of this skinny bit of . . ." She kicked again at the cook, this time deliberately bruising his ribs. He did not stir.

"Ah, you have uncovered my little deception," Kalas said, smiling. "But not—alas—soon enough."

"Tell me," Jenna said, "was he at least a good cook?"

"A terrible cook, but he had his *other* uses."

"What I do not really understand," Jenna said, "is why you let us get away, why you did not just kill us in the Hole."

"Such an uninteresting death, don't you think?" Kalas asked. "And I have made such a study of death, it would not do to just kill people outright. Besides"—and he laughed, showing again his horribly yellow teeth and running his fingers through his thinning red hair, which exposed darker roots—"I did not believe that even you, Prince Longbow's White Goddess, would really dare the castle on her own. I needed you as bait for the redoubtable King Pike, who is even now at my door."

Jenna's eyes opened wide, but she let nothing else betray the fact that she was startled. So Kalas did not know that Carum was king; did not know that Gorum was dead. She would keep that little piece of information to herself.

He smiled again, reminding Jenna of her Mother Alta when she had a particularly devastating bit of news to impart. "I did *not* expect you to escape, not with my Cat watching carefully at the Hole. What a fascinating little mouse you are. But I have clipped the Cat's claws for him. He will not make that mistake again."

Jenna nodded. *Keep him talking,* she reminded herself. "But how did you know we had gotten out?"

"Oh, little girl, I know everything. This castle is mined with passages and set about with traps. You cannot go from one level to another without my knowing. *Everything.*"

"Then we could not have gotten out without you letting us go?"

"Not in a hundred years," Kalas said. "Not in a hundred hundred years."

She had her back to the tower's one window, could feel the sun warming her. She could always leap out as a last resort, but she knew—having climbed it so painfully the night before—that it would be a long and fatal fall to the wall below. And that would leave Alna to the mercy of Kalas still, and the rest without their Anna.

There would be no help from Skada either. The sun was only half down the sky, so Kalas had no torches lit. Carum was gone below, sent away by her, past recalling. And Jenna knew she was out of polite conversation.

"Get her!" Kalas said to his guards, no change in the pitch of his voice.

They moved in a well-trained wedge toward her and she stepped quickly to the other side of the bed, putting it between the men and herself. When they split and three came after her, she leaped onto the bed, straddling Alna, and beating them back with some quick, though awkward sword work. Then with a quick slash of her weapon, she severed the hanging curtains from the canopy's crossbar, tangling the men below in its heavy brocaded folds.

As they fought to free themselves, their companions came to their aid, giving Jenna just a moment. It was all she needed. She flung the sword point first into the breast of one of the guards. He did not have the Bear's quick hands and the sword pierced him straight through, skewering the arm of a man beneath him who cried out in agony.

Jenna bounced once on the bed and grabbed the cross bracing of the canopy, swinging herself feetfirst nearly out of the door.

"After her!" Kalas cried.

But before the remaining guards could untangle themselves, Carum and two of the M'dorans burst through the open door, swords in hand. Behind them came a fourth woman, carrying both a sword and a torch. She flung the torch onto the bed.

The linens caught fire at once and Alna, moving faster than Jenna would have guessed, rolled off the bed on the window side, scrambling over the guards, where she cowered against the far wall.

As the cloth flared to life, Jenna moved around the bed to stand between Kalas and the flames. She was weaponless while he still had a thin rapier in his one hand. The other hand rested on a heavy tapestry behind his chair.

"My sword, Jenna!" cried Carum, ready to fling it to her.

She shook her head, smiling. There was nothing sweet in that smile. "I need no sword, *my king.*" She spoke the final two words with deliberateness, to be sure Kalas understood, then added, "Do you not remember that tribe in the East you told me about so long ago."

With one sharp movement, Kalas drew back the tapestry disclosing an open door. But Jenna put her hand in back of her neck, pulling her white braid forward, stretching it between her hands, like a rope. Behind her was the blazing bed sending crazed shadows against the wall. One of those shadows, framed in the doorway behind Kalas, was a womanshape holding a black braid stretched taut between her clenched hands.

Jenna reached up, exposing her breast to Kalas' blade, and leaned forward. He smiled triumphantly until he felt the braid from behind slip over his head and catch him, suddenly, around the neck. He dropped the blade and tried to rip the noose from his throat but Skada and Jenna had, simultaneously, pulled their braids tight, twisting and twisting it.

Kalas' face turned a strange, dark color as he struggled against the garroting plait. At the end his hands dropped to his sides and his feet beat a final tattoo against the wooden floor.

"Alaisters!" Carum said suddenly. "Alaisters was the name of the tribe. They were . . ."

". . . never weaponless because of their hair," Skada said, unknotting the noose from Kalas' neck.

"Promise me you will never cut your braid," Carum said.

They both nodded, but neither one of them smiled.

THE BALLAD:

The Ballad of Langbrow

When Langbrow first was made the king,
Proclaimed by all his men,
He took to him a goodly wife
Whose name was Winsome Jen.
He took to him a goodly wife,
Her name it was Sweet Ann,
And light her hair, and long her limb,
And Langbrow was her man,
And Langbrow was her man.

When Langbrow first was made the king,
Proclaimed by all his peers,
He opened up the prison gates
That had been closed for years.
He opened up the prison gates
With just one little key
And all the men condemned within
Straightways were all set free,
Straightways were all set free.

When Langbrow first was made the king,
He killed the callous crew
That tortured many a fine woman
And slaughtered not a few.
That tortured many a fine woman
And brought them many a shame

Till Langbrow came to rescue them
Returning their good name,
Returning their good name.

When Langbrow first was made the king,
The country did rejoice
And sang the praises of the king
With cup and wine and voice.
We sang the praises of the king
And of his winsome Jen
And of the men who followed him,
And also the wo-men,
And also the wo-men!

THE STORY:

Carum carried Kalas' body down the stairs and into the courtyard where he threw it onto the stones. Jenna stood by his right side, her hands clasped together, watching.

As soon as Kalas' body hit the ground, a strange hush fell upon the crowd. The soldiers, most of whom had been hired from the Continent, flung down their weapons. Those who were Garunian bred knelt, offering up their swords.

Carum ignored their fealty, speaking instead as if it had always been his, saying, "I am the one and true king, for my brother Gorum is dead. And here"—he pointed to the corpse at his feet—"here is the one who would have severed us. Even Lord Cres will not have him, for only heroes feast at the dark lord's side."

The kneeling men stood, sheathing their weapons. Behind them, rising slowly over the crenellated castle walls, came the moon. Jenna saw it and smiled.

Carum took the leather thong from around his neck, holding up the crested ring that they all might see. "Here is the sign of the Bull and it belongs where I vowed it belonged—on the body of its dead master."

The ring bounced on Kalas' chest and tumbled onto the ground beside him. Watching silently, the crowd waited for Carum's next words.

Instead, Carum took up Jenna's left hand and set his mouth solemnly on her palm. Then he looked up again at the waiting men and women before speaking. As if weighing his words carefully, he said at last, "By my side is the one who was promised us, the White One of prophecy. Born of three mothers, born to lead us out of the ending of one era and into the beginning of the other, she is both light and . . ."

At that very moment, as though he had timed his speech exactly, the great full moon cleared the walls entirely, moving above the crenellations. Shimmering like water and starlight, Skada came into being next to Jenna, her black hair and dark eyes marking Carum's text.

There was a sharp intake of breath from the watching men who did not even notice that the same was happening to all the women by their sides. Only Carum, staring down at them, and Piet, who stood near his king, saw that for every M'doran woman there were now two.

Carum held his hand up again and there was a complete hush.

"She is both light and dark, and shall rule by my side. She has made the hound, the bull, the cat, and the bear bow low. She has herself killed Kalas, and with that brought to an end his hideous reign." For a moment after, the courtyard seemed to echo with his words.

Then Petra mounted two steps to stand in front of Carum and Jenna. She bowed her head to him briefly, solemnly, before turning more toward Jenna and raising her hands above her head, fingers extended, palms flat.

"Holy, holy, holiest of sisters," she intoned.

The men chorused back, "Holy, holy, holiest of sisters."

Petra turned and signed to Sandor and Marek to stand by her, and they climbed to her side.

"And Alta said this one shall crown the king," Petra cried.

"The first Herald!" shouted one of the women.

Reaching into his shirt, Marek took out the circlet of sweetbriar which was, by some miracle, uncrushed, and placed it carefully on Carum's head.

A great cheer went up from the crowd.

Petra raised her hand for quiet, and there was complete silence again.

"And Alta said this one shall guide the king's right hand."

Sandor slipped the wristlet of wild rose off his own arm and slid it onto Jenna's. It hung loosely around her wrist.

An even wilder cheer, this one led by Piet, rose from the men and women.

Petra spoke into the noise and they quieted at once. "And Alta said that one shall be True Speaker for all, yet say nothing until the king be crowned, lest he sever the fellowship. Can you speak the truth to us now, True Speaker?"

Jareth pushed forward from the crowd, holding up the piece of green rag that had been his collar, calling in a strange croaking voice: "The king shall live long and longer yet the queen. They shall be for us whenever there is need."

"Long live the king!" Piet shouted.

The crowd gave back its answer: "Long live the king!"

"And his queen, Jenna," a woman with a wheezy voice cried.

"Long live the queen!" the crowd answered.

Petra turned her head slightly and winked at Skada who winked back. Then, as if singing an ancient chant, to the tune of the most sacred Altan prophecy's plainsong, Petra let her voice ring out over the crowd:

> *"Then Longbow shall be king,*
> *And Jenna shall be queen,*
> *So long as moons they reign,*
> *So long as groves be green.*
> *Holy. Holy. Holy."*

"And what will *that* one turn into?" Jenna whispered.

"Some ballad sung in taverns and accompanied by a plecta and nose flute," Skada answered. "Called *When Langbrow was Made the King* or *How the Warrior Jenna Broke Heads* or some such."

"But," Carum added, grinning, "it will be lovingly sung."

THE HISTORY:

To the Directors, Dalian Historical Society
Sirs:
  Although I have been a member in good standing for twenty-seven years, a past president, and two-term general secretary, I find it impossible to remain a member any longer now that the Society has seen fit to give its highest award to that charlatan Dr. "Magic" Magon.
  By so honoring Dr. Magon, you have given credence to his theories about the dark and light sisters, and his left-wing ravings about the circle of the Grenna as well as the cultural superiority of the indigenous populations of the Dales.
  History must needs be even-handed and there is nothing surer than that legend, myth, balladry,

*and folktale are cultural lies that tell us the truth
only on an incredible slant. To believe them
without adjusting the glass, as Dr. Magon does,
makes for warped history and a warped historian.*

*That this Society is now crediting such
history and honoring such a historian forces me to
tender my resignation until such a time as history
itself shall prove me the prophet and Magon the
liar.*

Yours,

THE AFTERWARD:

Carum Longbow ruled the Dales for a full fifty years, till his hair was as white as Jenna's and age had bent him.

Jenna was not always by his side, for she called the throne "a troubling seat" and she was ever uneasy with ceremony. Often she took long journeys into the countryside, accompanied by her one-armed daughter Scillia or one of her two sons.

At these times she sometimes traveled back to the southern parts of the Dales, passing by the Old Hanging Man and Alta's Breast, to visit with old friends. Selden Hame, where the last of the remaining women of Alta lived, was always a home to her.

At Selden there were no priestesses anymore; the last—Jenna's original Mother Alta—had died twenty years earlier. The M'dorans who had settled at Selden Hame had chosen a singleton without a dark sister as their True Speaker. Her name was Marget, still known to Jenna as Pynt, and she helped all the women in the Hame learn new ways, though that is another story altogether.

When Jenna was at court, her closest friends were

Petra and Jareth, who married after a long mourning period for Jareth's Mai. Petra proved a gentle stepmother for Jareth's five girls, the eldest of whom was called Jen.

But Jenna did not stay at either court or Hame very long. She always found herself searching the woods and fields, the small vales and great valleys, for something. She could not have named it, though Skada—if asked—would have said she was searching for another great adventure. And perhaps Skada, who knew her best of all, was right.

However, her daughter swore that Jenna was looking for a simpler time, her sons, Jem and Corrie, for a finer one. Carum made no guesses at all, but welcomed her back from each trip with open arms and no questions asked except one: *Are the people happy and well?*

And they were happy and well. Carum made certain that all his people—Dale and Garun alike—were well fed, well housed, and safe from marauding strangers. With Piet as the head of the army, the Dale shores were patrolled and the peace kept. Marek stayed on to become one of Carum's advisors, but Sandor returned home, taking over his father's ferry and writing the story of his youthful adventures in a small spidery script for his own sons.

It was fifty years and a week since the coronation that Jenna came back from one of her sojourns in the hills. She had been uneasy the whole time, though she could not have said why. The journey had been undertaken alone, with nothing in her pack but a skin of spring wine and a loaf of bread. The hunting had been plentiful; she had not wanted for food. It was midway through the moon time, and Skada had not appeared, except for one evening when Jenna had put her blanket right next to the fire. They had quarreled briefly, for no reason, Skada as uneasy as Jenna, so that Jenna had not been cast down when the fire burned out and Skada was gone.

Jenna cut the journey short, heading back to the castle, for it was in her mind that perhaps Carum had need of her. Often they knew one another's thoughts before a word was said, even as she did with Skada, though with Carum it came from living with him so many untroubled years.

She rode up the long, winding road on her white horse, one of Duty's great granddaughters, with the smoothest canter and the sweetest mouth of any horse she had owned. As she went forward, the great gates opened and a rider came galloping toward her. She knew immediately it was Scillia by the missing arm.

They greeted one another from afar, Scillia calling, "Quickly, mother, it is father. He is sick and the doctors fear for his life. I was coming to trail you."

Jenna nodded, her uneasiness gone. She knew now the author of her unhappiness. They raced back into the castle together.

Carum was propped up in bed surrounded by both sons, the doctors, and even Petra, as gray-faced as Jenna felt. Jenna sent them all away. She sat on the bed by Carum's side and did not speak until his eyelids had fluttered open.

"You have come back in time," he whispered.

"I am always in time."

"Ich crie thee merci."

"I will give it, my love." She held his hands in hers. "I will take you to the grove. Alta said I might bring one back. And we will live there, young again, until the end of time."

"I cannot leave the kingdom," Carum said.

"Nonsense. Our sons and our daughter have been helping you run it these past twenty years. You have trained them well in castle ways."

"And you in the forest."

"So . . ."

He smiled, that old slow smile. The scar beneath the one eye, caught up in the wrinkles of laugh lines, disappeared. "So . . . I never *quite* believed in the grove."

"Believe it," she whispered. She kissed his hands and then leaned over and kissed his brow as well, before standing. "It will be a short journey, Longbow, and you will go in comfort."

A carriage with a bed carted Carum to the King's Way where the forest still lay unbroken on either side.

"We are almost there, my love," Jenna whispered to him when they had stopped. "Now we come to the difficult part. You must leave your comfortable bed and ride on the sledge."

"As long as you are near, my Jen," he said, his voice hardly audible with the wild caroling of birds around them.

She dismissed the men and women who had accompanied them, then turned to Scillia.

"You must make sure that they all return to the castle. No one"—she stopped, then repeated—"*no one* must remain behind."

"Do you know what you are doing, Mother?" Scillia asked.

Jenna reached out and smoothed a lock of Scillia's hair that had come unbound in the ride. "Oh, I do. And so do you and Jem and Corrie. You belong to now and your children to the future. It is another turning."

"Riddles! You know I hate that kind of talk."

"Ah, Scillia, I learned long ago that riddles hold their own truth. And the truth is that your father and I were the beginning, but . . ."

"Will I ever see you again?"

"When you look in the mirror, child. When you speak to your own daughters and sons. Kiss me now. I will be with you when you need me most."

They embraced, and Scillia turned away, before her mother could see her tears, gathering the others to her. Jenna watched until they were out of sight, then tied up her braids atop her head like a crown. Picking up the ends of the sledge on which Carum was bound, she pulled it off the roadway and across the grassy field.

*   *   *

The Grenna met her halfway through the meadow. She could not tell if they were the same ones she had met before. They *looked* the same: ageless, with the translucent green glaze of skin over fine bones. They made a circle with Jenna, Carum, and the sledge in the center, but they did not offer to help pull. Carum watched them fascinated, often half sitting up until the motion exhausted him.

Three times the circle stopped that Jenna might make Carum more comfortable and give him a drink of water. For a while he tried to get them to talk, but they were silent. When the odd procession got to the woods, where even the shadows were green, one of the Grenna said, "Here." That was the entire conversation. At the Grenna's voice, Carum slipped into a kind of fitful sleep.

A new moon rose overhead, but Jenna had only intermittent glimpses of it through the lacings of the trees, and it was not until they came to the clearing that ended on the cliffside that Skada appeared. The moment she was visible, the Grenna faded back into the trees. But Skada only smiled wryly, and bent to take one pole of the sledge. It moved more easily then and they brought it quickly to the front of the black cave entrance framed by oaken doors.

Jenna touched one of the carvings, Skada another.

"Apple," Jenna whispered. "Bird."

"Stone, flower, tree," Skada countered. "Jenna, you must choose."

"I know," Jenna said. "I have thought of nothing else since this journey began."

"Alta said you can bring *one* other into the grove, Jenna. One."

"And there are no shadows within." Jenna paused. "I do not know how this will end."

Carum moaned, then opened his eyes. "Are the Grenna gone, Jen? Are we there?"

"Almost there," Skada answered him.

"Good, you are here, too, Skada. For we are all three, or we are none," Carum whispered.

"Candle by the bed or not, I know you loved me well, my king," Skada said.

"I loved you best for your true tongue," Carum answered.

"You have been listening!" Jenna's voice was suddenly accusing.

"A king's privilege." He tried to shift a bit on the sledge, and moaned again. "The trip was long. But I would not have missed it. Jenna, you do not have to choose between us. I am dead already. Let the stories tell what they will. Our children will rule wisely and well." He closed his eyes again. "And whatever we do here matters not. It's the stories told about it that will last."

Jenna smiled. "I know that, my love. But still we must do what the heart reminds us. Sister? Are you ready?" She held out her arms.

Skada smiled, her arms out as well. "Ready, sister."

THE LEGEND:

There are two tales told about White Jenna and how she returned to Alta's cave. One is told by women and one is told by men.

The men's story speaks of a sledge on the cliffside, where, years ago when the Wilhelm Valley was mined for gold, it was discovered before an entrance to a cave. The sledge held the long bones of a man bound to it with bindings of leather and gold. Still, the men say, on moonlit nights two women can be seen running naked through the glades, women compounded of starlight and water. They run through the glades, past the rocky cliff, step over the long bones, and disappear into the cave just at dawn.

But the women tell a different tale. They say that White Jenna carried her lover, King Longbow, in her arms through the cave to the grove where Alta greeted them. And there they were made young again, and hale. They wait there, with their bright companions, feasting and drinking, until the world shall need them again.

THE MYTH:

Then Great Alta took down her hair, both the golden side and the black, and lifted the dark and light sisters out of the abyss of the world, saying, "You have come at last to the end of this turning. Whether you go forward or whether you go back, whether you go left or you go right, whether you go up or you go down, the end is the beginning. For each story is a circle, and each life a story. The end is the beginning and only I am the true end and only I can begin the circle again.

Here Ends Book 2:
White Jenna

THE WISDOMS OF
THE DALES

The heart is not a knee that can bend.
Telling a tale is better than living it.
Fish are not the best authority on water.
When a dead tree falls, it carries with it a live one.
Wood may remain twenty years in the water but it is still
    not a fish.
If your mouth turns into a knife, it will cut off your lips.
Miracles come to the unsuspecting.
Spilled water is better than a broken jar.
There is no medicine to cure hatred.
Does the rabbit keep up with the cat?
Words are merely interrupted breath.
The sun moves slowly but it crosses the land.
You must set the trap before the rat passes, not after.
Better the cat under your heel than at your throat.

No tracks, no trouble.

Three are better than one where trouble is concerned.

Spring berries are for dye and dying.

*Downy head and thorny spine/On the roots you safely
    dine.*

Hunger is the best seasoning.

A foolish loyalty can be the greater danger.

Wicked tongues make wicked wives.

Laugh longer, live longer.

Sleep is the great unraveler of knots.

Not to know is bad, but not to wish to know is worse.

*The day on which one starts out is surely not the time to
    begin one's preparations.*

Do not measure a shroud before there is a corpse.

In the wrong, in the Rest.

Better in the Rest than in the battle.

They stumble who run ahead of their wits.

Sisters can be blind.

Sleep is death's younger sister.

The heart can be a cruel master.

A cat who boasts once is a cat who boasts once too often.

No blame, no shame.

*It is a fool who longs for endings, a wise woman who
    longs for beginnings.*

*It is best to eat when the food is before you than go
    hungry when the food is behind you.*

*In a flock of black birds, t'would be harder to miss one
    than find one.*

The gift horse is the swifter.

A crow is not a cat nor does it bear kits.

*The swordsman dies by the sword, the hangman by the
    rope, and the king by his crown.*

An hour can spare a life.

*A man's eye is bigger than his belly and smaller than his
    brain.*

*In war one takes quickly and saves regrets for the
    morning.*

*Stand in the way of a cart and you will have wheelmarks
    across your face.*

If a man calls you master, trust him for a day; if he calls
  you friend, trust him for a year; if he calls you brother,
  trust him for all ways.
Perfection is the end of growing.
First up, first fed.
First up, finest fed.
Experience is rarely a gentle master.
Stories feed the mind when the belly is not full.
Kill once, mourn ever. (Kill twice, mourn never.)
If you have no meat, eat bread.
Belief is an old dog in a new collar.
In the council of kings, the heart has little to say.
To kill is not to cure.
A stroke may save a limb.
You cannot cross the river without getting your feet wet.
A warrior has no conscience until after the war is done.
In a fight, anything is a sword.
Forever is no distance at all.
A dream is worth a little sleep.
Every end is a beginning.
No one stands highest when all stand together.
If you rise too early, the dew will soak your skin.
One is not a multitude.
The grape brings slow death.
The mice may have the right but the cat has the claws.
Women's promises are water over stone—wet, willing,
  and soon gone.
Measure a cook by his belly.
Better to be safe than buried.

THE MUSIC OF
THE DALES

The Ballad of Langbrow

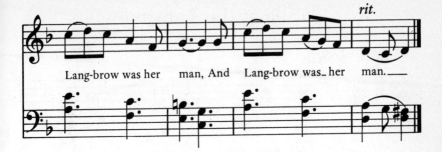

Lang-brow was her man, And Lang-brow was her man.

2. When Langbrow first was made the king,
   Proclaimed by all his peers,
   He opened up the prison gates
   That had been closed for years.
   He opened up the prison gates
   With just one little key
   And all the men condemned within
   Straightways were all set free,
   Straightways were all set free.

3. When Langbrow first was made the king,
   He killed the callous crew
   That tortured many a fine woman
   And slaughtered not a few.
   That tortured many a fine woman
   And brought them many a shame
   Till Langbrow came to rescue them
   Returning their good name,
   Returning their good name.

4. When Langbrow first was made the king,
   The country did rejoice
   And sang the praises of the king
   With cup and wine and voice.
   We sang the praises of the king
   And of his Whitsom Jen
   And of the men who followed him,
   And also the wom-en,
   And also the wom-en!

Anna at the Turning

2. Sweet in the springtide, sour in fall,
   Winter casts snow, a white velvet caul.
   Passage in summer is swiftest of all
      And Anna at each turning.

3. Look to the meadows and look to the hills,
   Look to the rocks where the swift river spills,
   Look to the farmland the farmer still tills
      For Anna is returning.

4. They laid her down upon the hill,
   Rosemary, bayberry, thistle and thorn,
   And took her babe against her will
   On the day the child was born.

5. They left her on the cold hillside,
   Rosemary, bayberry, thistle and thorn,
   Convinced that her new babe had died
   On the day the child was born.

6. She wept red tears, and she wept gray,
   Rosemary, bayberry, thistle and thorn,
   Till she had wept her life away,
   On the day her child was born.

7. The sailor's heart it broke in two,
   Rosemary, bayberry, thistle and thorn,
   The sisters all their act did rue
   From the day the child was born.

8. And from their graves grew rose and briar,
   Rosemary, bayberry, thistle and thorn,
   Twined till they could grow no higher,
   From the day the child was born.

Ballad of the Twelve Sisters

Hauntingly

There were twelve sis-ters by a lake,

Rose-ma-ry, bay-ber-ry, this-tle and thorn, A hand-some sail-or

one— did take, And that day a child was born.—

2. A handsome sailor one did wed,
    Rosemary, bayberry, thistle and thorn,
   The other sisters wished her dead
      On the day the child was born.

3. "Oh, sister, give me your right hand,"
    Rosemary, bayberry, thistle and thorn,
   Eleven to the one demand
      On the day the child was born.

The Long Riding

With a rocking motion

1. In-to the val-ley, come rid-ing, come rid-ing, In-to the mead-ow and
2. In-to the vil-lage, come rid-ing, come rid-ing, In-to the hames where the

in - to the dell, In-to the moon-light where shad-ows are glid-ing,)
sweet wom-en dwell, In-to the rests where the men are a-bid-ing,)

In-to the for-est where en - e - mies hid-ing, Rid-ing, rid-ing,

Three come a-rid-ing In-to the mouth of hell.___

The Trees in the Forest

Sister's Lullay

King Kalas and his Sons

Boisterously

King Ka-las had four sons, And four sons had he,

And they ram-bled a-round In the north-ern coun-trie.

And they ram-bled a-round With-out ev-er a care.

The Hound and the Bull And the Cat and the Bear.

2. The Hound was a hunter,
The Hound was a spy,
The Hound could shoot down
Any bird on the fly.
The Hound was out hunting
When brought down was he
Alone as he rambled
The northern countrie.

3. King Kalas had three sons,
And three sons had he,
And they rambled around
In the northern countrie.
And they rambled around
Without ever a care.
And they were the Bull
And the Cat and the Bear.

4. The Bull was a gorer,
The Bull was a knight,
And never a man who would
Run from a fight.
The Bull was out fighting
When brought down was he
Alone as he rambled
The northern countrie.

5. King Kalas had two sons,
And two sons had he,
And they rambled around
In the northern countrie.
And they rambled around
Without ever a care.
And the names they were called
Were the Cat and the Bear.

6. The Cat was a shadow,
The Cat was a snare,
Sometimes you knew not
When the Cat was right there.
The Cat was out hiding
When brought down was he
Alone as he rambled
The northern countrie.

7. King Kalas had one son,
And one son had he,
And he rambled around
In the northern countrie.
And he rambled around
Without ever a care,
And the name he went under
Was Kalas' Bear.

8. The Bear was a bully,
The Bear was a brag,
His mouth was brimmed over
With bluster and swag.
The Bear was out boasting
When brought down was he
Alone as he rambled
The northern countrie.

9. King Kalas had no sons,
And no sons had he,
To ramble around
In the northern countrie.
Though late in the evening
The ghosts are seen there
Of the Hound and the Bull
And the Cat and the Bear.

Death of the Cat

With great emotion

The trees were grow-ing high And the wind was in the west

When a hun-ter aimed his ar-row In - to the Cat's broad chest.

And she di - ed, she di - ed A - gainst her lov-er's breast

And we laid her in the earth So long and nar-row.

2. It was early, so early
   In the graying of the morn,
   When we sang of the days
   Before the Cat was born.
   And how from her mother
   She was so swiftly torn,
   As we laid her in the earth
   So long and narrow.

3. Come all ye young fighting men
   And listen unto me.
   Do not place your affections
   Upon a girl so free.
   For she'll take the mortal wound
   Another meant for thee,
   And you'll lay her in the earth
   So long and narrow.

The Heart and the Crown

2. Her horse was pure white
   And his horse was gray.
   She wanted to go
   But he asked her to stay.
   She gave him her heart
   And he gave her his crown,
   But they never, no never
   Went down derry down derry down.

3. Her eyes were pure black
   And his eyes were so blue.
   She wanted him strong
   And he wanted her true.
   She gave him her heart
   And he gave her his crown
   But they. never, no never
   Went down derry down derry down.

4. Come all ye fair maidens,
   And listen to me,
   If you want your young man
   To be strong and free
   Just give him your heart
   And he'll give you his crown
   Just as long as you never
   Go down derry down derry down.

Well Before the Battle, Sister

Emotionally

Well be-fore the bat-tle, sis-ter,— When the sky is crowned with stars,

And the world is clean of wound-ed,— And the ground is free of scars.

Well be-fore the bat-tle, sis-ter,— When con-tent with what we know,

We will sing the love-ly bal-lads. From the long and long a - go.